FROM CLAUDIA TO DAVID

FROM CLAUDIA
TO DAVID

By

ROSE FRANKEN

THE BOOK CLUB
121 CHARING CROSS ROAD
LONDON, W.C.2

MADE AND PRINTED IN GREAT BRITAIN BY
MORRISON AND GIBB LIMITED, LONDON AND EDINBURGH

ONE

IT WASN'T AS EASY as it sounded, to pick up bag and baggage and move a family, one—two—three. Even Bertha admitted that it might be a little too much, what with the baby teething, and winter outfits to buy for Bobby and Matthew, who had either outgrown or worn out every stitch they owned. "The best thing to do," she advised Claudia, "is to leave the children in New York with me, and you and Mr. David go on ahead, and we will follow later."

Claudia wasn't crazy about putting so much responsibility on Bertha's shoulders, but Bertha seemed to thrive on responsibility and hard work. Besides she was right, it would be idiotic for them all to land in a strange little village in the middle of the mountains without so much as a roof over their heads. This way, she and David could stay at the boarding-house that Dr. Morrisson had recommended until they found a place of their own to live in.

Claudia did all the finding, of course, and it wasn't any great shakes of a house—just a shabby little cottage on the outskirts of the town, with no charm but a low rent, and a good-sized sleeping porch for David, which was the main consideration.

What with one thing and another, October was half over before they were ready for the children. Julia was wonderful and offered to drive them up. "However," Claudia told David, "if we had one drop of the milk of human kindness, we wouldn't let her, she doesn't know what she's in for. Among other things, Matthew gets car-sick on long trips."

David looked affronted. "No son of mine gets car-sick," he said.

"I'm sorry, but your middle one does," said Claudia, "and Julia's not going to care for it at all."

"Let him sit with the chauffeur," said David, with an air of "throw him out of the window."

"The chauffeur will be so grateful," said Claudia. "And anyway, that's the only place Bluff can ride. Unless," it occurred to her brightly, "we could ship him on ahead by freight."

David looked even more affronted. "Coop a Great Dane up in a baggage-car? I wouldn't dream of it."

"But Bluff will be lots happier cooped up in a nice baggage-car," Claudia argued. "Just count it out on your fingers how many there'll be—Bobby and Matthew and the baby and Bertha and the cat and the chauffeur and tons of luggage. In fact Julia might prefer the baggage-car herself."

"She undoubtedly would," said David. "Why don't we call the whole business off, and let them all stay on in the apartment with John and Candy? There's ample room, and Candy can't do any more than beg to have them."

"I know, but it would be an imposition. At least Julia's your sister-in-law, but Candy isn't even a relative."

"All the more reason," said David.

"I see what you mean," said Claudia, "but even so, it wouldn't be fair, Candy and John are still on their honeymoon. And another thing, they're neither of them mature enough. I wouldn't have an easy minute."

"John's mature enough to be my partner and run the firm while I'm away," David returned, with a double edge to his voice which Claudia chose to ignore.

"That's different," she said. "Nothing can go wrong with architecture except a blue-print."

"And that's plenty."

"But it's not measles or chicken pox or scarlet fever. You simply can't foist the responsibility of your children on anyone else, no matter who."

"Exactly," said David, hitting neatly below the belt. "I had no right to let you leave them in the first place, you should have stayed right in New York where you belong."

" Fat chance," said Claudia lightly. Nevertheless, she could have kicked herself for upsetting the apple cart at this late day. Small vertical lines had settled at either side of David's mouth, which told her that he wasn't fooling. He had never been wholly in favour of dragging the family along—or herself either—and now, when everything was arranged and settled, she had to go and try to be funny about Julia.

The original plan had been for Candy to drive Bertha and the children up, which would have been another matter; Candy was young and her car was old, and the whole expedition would have added up to fun. As luck would have it, though, Candy discovered at the last minute that she was almost pregnant, and although she was ashamed to run to the doctor right off the bat again, she said she had a feeling that this time it had really happened.

" I'm simply heartbroken not to come," she wrote them in her square round handwriting, " I miss you both so frightfully, it would have been heavenly to see you, but John's mother scared him about joggling, so he's acting like a husband and won't let me take the chance. He said he'd love to drive the children up himself, but as long as Julia's offered, he thought it might worry David if he left the office alone, what with things so active now, thank goodness. Everybody seems to be starting in to build all at once."

" A fine time," said David, when he came to that part of the letter, " to be laid up on your back."

Again she pretended not to notice the bitterness in his voice. " I don't call a few months taking it easy being laid up on your back."

" From where I sit, it looks like it's going to be a hell of a lot more than a few months."

" Then you've been sitting in the wrong place," she retorted, with as much assurance as she could muster. " I'd be depressed too, if we'd had to stay in that dreary boarding-house much longer."

As if she weren't depressed, and frightened as well, at taking matters in her own hands like this. It had seemed so simple and so right to keep the family together when she'd talked it over with Dr. Morrisson in New York. Dr. Morrisson had agreed that a patient's happiness was more important than anything else, but up here, everybody said that outside doctors didn't know what it was all about, up here there was an entirely different point of view. Time enough for happiness after you were cured, and there were some who maintained, with sepulchral optimism, that you were never cured of T.B. In any event, the business of getting well came first, and that meant day after day, lying out on the porch, keeping a check on temperature and pulse, and stuffing down incredible quantities of milk and eggs.

"There's something obscene about it, poor devils," David had commented in the beginning, and Claudia had felt the same way. Yet gradually, she had lost a little of her aloofness, and the slow poison of fear and vigilance must have set in without her knowing it. She realised it only now that the children were on their way to join them, and they were about to pick up the threads of normal living.

Once, in the early days of their marriage, David had taken her to the circus, and on a twilight evening, a good ten years later, she suddenly remembered the comedy routine of an endless procession of clowns and goats all streaming out of a small, rickety automobile. Julia's limousine was anything but small and rickety, but just the same there was something reminiscent in the way it came to a stop on the road in front of the house, with Julia emerging painfully to the ground, followed by a general exodus of animals and humans.

"We started at a quarter to seven this morning," she greeted Claudia with elliptical brevity.

Claudia downed the impulse to giggle. "You poor things," she sympathised. "Bertha looks dead, too."

" No, I am not dead," Bertha denied with a valiant smile. " Bluff, don't push me like that ! " she broke off in startled protest. " You will make me drop my baby ! How is everything, Mrs. Naughton, how is Mr. Naughton ? "

" He's fine. How are the children ? Better hold the dog on the leash, Bertha, and I'll take the baby——"

Her arms were hungry for Michael, but she couldn't help thinking that he was anything but attractive, with his cap sliding down over one eye, and the whole solid bundle of him unpleasantly moist. Bertha, however, seemed to be waiting to hear that he was the most beautiful baby in the world, so Claudia exclaimed with enthusiasm that he'd got as heavy as lead, which was the best she could say for him at the moment.

" I've got heavy too ! " Matthew shouted, as he tumbled out. " I gained a pound and I grew an inch ! "

" I can see that you did, you're simply huge ! " Claudia agreed. " I'll kiss you as soon as I put the baby down inside. . . . Hello, Bobby, I'll get around to kissing you too ! "

" That's all right," said Bobby, companionably.

He looked wonderful, she thought, better than the other two put together. She'd forgotten how grown up he was in the long pants she'd bought him after camp last summer. Boys went into long pants so much younger, these days. David said he'd worn knickers until he was fourteen.

" I don't see Dad around," said Bobby. " Where is he ? "

" He's on the porch, we'll go right up to him."

The chauffeur was ahead of them, bent double under a mound of unpackable items. " Just dump everything in the first room you come to," she took pity on him.

" Hold on a minute, and I'll help you ! "

She stopped short. There was David, hurrying down the rough path that led from the house. She might have known he wouldn't stay put, he'd want to be right in the middle of the excitement, and making more of it, which he certainly was. She felt like slapping him, he knew better than to let Bluff jump at him like that. " Please," she whispered importunately.

" Mamma, mind your own business," he told her with a friendly whack across her rear.

" Same old David," Julia smiled, without significance.

" He looks good," Bertha exulted. " Better even than I thought he would."

" There's nothing wrong with me that a little normal work won't fix," said David. He picked up the baby's scales, which had, heaven only knew how, been sandwiched into the luggage compartment. " David, don't ! " Claudia implored.

He took pity on her. " It's not heavy, foolish. It's only bulky."

" I'll carry it," Bobby offered. " Let me have it, Dad."

Claudia could have hugged him, but David waved him away. " You'd better walk Bluff before we take him indoors."

" He won't," said Bobby, from past experience.

" Try anyway," Bertha urged. " Maybe he might. And Matthew, you can carry the cat-box but don't drop it."

" Why should I drop it ? " Matthew requested coldly.

They moved off, up the path. Bertha paused to observe the small brown cottage, lop-sided with porch. " It's beautiful," she stated, almost too firmly.

" Bertha, you lie," said Claudia. " But I love you for it. Anyway, houses are scarce, and I was lucky to get it." She refrained from adding that it had come vacant only because the previous occupant had died, but as he was quite an old man, who'd been sicker from his blood-pressure than from his lungs, she felt a great deal more comfortable about living in the house than if he had been around David's age.

" Isn't it a little isolated ? " Julia asked doubtfully.

" Yes, it's real country," said Claudia, trying to sound pleased about it. She led the way into the box-like parlour, fortunately sparse with nasty furniture. Julia couldn't think of another thing to say and still be tactful, but Bertha said quickly, " It's clean, it's very, very clean."

" It had better be," said Claudia, " I've had every inch of it scrubbed like mad."

" This place smells funny," Matthew announced abruptly.

" It's a nice smell," Bertha corrected. " It shows how clean everything is. Let Shakespeare out of his box."

" I am. He doesn't want to get out. I don't like that smell."

Claudia didn't like it either. It was too much like Dr. Geiger's linoleum waiting-room in the village. " It'll wear off," she promised. She sat down and drew Matthew to her, and gave him his belated kiss, which he accepted with indifference. She ruffled his hair to make him look less peaked. " Was he car-sick ? " she asked Bertha in an undertone.

" Ach, a little," said Bertha largely, as if a little didn't go a long way.

" I was a lot," Matthew stood up for himself.

" Well don't let your father hear you brag about it," Claudia advised, glad that David had tarried outside with Bobby. " I feel sorry for your poor Aunt Julia." She glanced at Julia, who, under the brutal glare of the electric light, looked even paler than Matthew.

" I think I'll wash up," she said delicately. " Don't bother to come with me, I'll find it."

" You can't go too far wrong ! " Claudia called after her. She waited until Julia was out of ear-shot. " Bertha, how am I going to put her up overnight ? We only have two tiny bedrooms besides ours, and this sofa isn't fit to sleep on."

" We can find a way to manage," said Bertha.

" It's a nice philosophy," said Claudia, " but on the other hand, you can't get blood out of a turnip, and this house is a turnip, Bertha, you might as well face it."

" Turnips are good for a change once in a while," Bertha remarked judicially. She laid the baby in a neat package across her knees, and untied his cap and let him go on sucking his thumb. Claudia obligingly didn't see him either, but they both felt Matthew's outspoken stare. " Go like a nice boy and help Watson with some of the bundles," Bertha suggested hastily.

" His name isn't Watson, it's Watkins," he informed her.

" Watkins, then."

He eyed her in chilly disapproval. " You shouldn't call him Watson if his name is Watkins."

" Bertha already apologised," said Claudia. " Now run along."

" I want to stay here. Michael's sucking his thumb."

" Ach, no ! " Bertha decried. " Then he must be hungry. Maybe you could find me the box with his bottles in, it is on the ledge of the car, underneath the window."

Matthew lingered, certain that something was being put over on him. " I hate turnips ! " he threw out in a burst of delayed passion.

" Matthew," said Claudia, " March."

It wasn't a march exactly, but it got him out of the room. Claudia looked after him. " Bobby was never that irritating, was he ? "

" Yes, surely," said Bertha. " It's the age."

" Bobby seems so grown-up all at once. I was really glad to see him. I mean, glad as if he were a person."

" I know how you mean," said Bertha. " He is getting to be a pleasure and not so much a worry. It is good for both of them that you wrote there is a nice school here."

" Yes, but I found out since then that they have to walk about a half-mile to the bus."

Bertha shrugged. " A half-mile is nothing in this wonderful air, it is healthy."

" I'm an idiot," Claudia sighed, " to believe everything you say, but you make me feel a lot better. Only wait. I haven't told you the worst yet about the house."

" The house is all right," said Bertha loyally.

" You haven't seen your kitchen."

" I peeked already, and it is so big I couldn't believe my eyes."

"Don't let that fool you. It's big because there isn't any dining-room, so it has to do for both."

"That is fine," Bertha beamed. "I like it that we eat in the kitchen, it is friendly, and it saves steps. Is that the worst now that you have to tell me?"

"No," said Claudia, "it isn't. There's only a coal stove to cook on."

Bertha continued to look entranced. "A coal stove gives the best cooking, anybody will tell you that."

"If it works," Claudia amended in a small voice. "I wasn't able to get it to work, and I didn't want to bother David about it."

Bertha tried not to show that her equilibrium was finally shaken. "But surely it cooks enough to cook a light supper for the children on? They are hungry."

"It will cook nothing," Claudia affirmed. "It just smokes. I bought a two-burner electric stove to use until I can get it fixed."

Relief sighed through Bertha's lips. "For a minute you had me a little worried," she admitted.

"I bought a few new cooking utensils, too."

Bertha looked upset again. "I hope not a frying-pan by all means. I brought our big black one along, and the little black one also."

"I had a feeling you would," said Claudia, "so I bought no frying-pans. I bought an inexpensive crib for the baby, though, and a couple of cotton mattresses for the boys. I was squeamish about using the ones that were here."

"Very smart," Bertha approved. She studied Claudia with an anxious frown. "You have been worrying too much and working too hard. I think you have lost a little weight maybe."

"I probably did. Anyway," she added happily, "there wasn't a soul in the boarding-house who didn't think I was the sick one."

"That is nothing to be so pleased about," said Bertha severely.

Matthew returned with a box of bottles a few minutes later and another chip on his shoulder. " Where's the snow ? " he demanded.

" Hold your horses," Claudia told him. " It's only October."

" But Bertha says it snows in the mountains even in the summer-time."

" Only some mountains," Bertha qualified.

" There aren't any mountains here anyhow." Matthew included them both in a sweeping accusation which made Claudia bridle.

" There certainly are," she snapped back at him. " There's a mountain staring you in the face right outside the window."

He hurried to the window and pressed his nose against the pane. " Where ? "

" There. You'll see it better in the morning. But you can see the outline against the sky, going way up in the air."

" Is that a mountain ? "

" That's a mountain."

" What kind ? "

" An Adirondack. One of the best."

He wasn't impressed. He picked a new flaw. " This isn't like the farm," he said.

" Stop scowling," said Bertha. " You will spoil your forehead, and anyway how can it be like the farm, the farm is far away in Connecticut."

" But you said it would be more fun than the farm."

" It will be," Claudia held out, " when the snow comes."

" Are there any cows or chickens ? "

" No. Just us."

" And Bluff and Shakespeare, isn't that enough ? " Bertha chided. " And your Daddy ? "

" A farm has cows and chickens," he insisted doggedly.

" Never mind, you are tired and hungry," Bertha gave up.

" I'm not tired," he said, very loudly, to prove it. " What are we going to have for supper ? "

" Nothing," said Claudia, " that can't be cooked on a two-burner electric stove."

He couldn't make up his mind whether that was good or bad. He shifted his weight thoughtfully from one foot to the other. Claudia waited, with a degree of apprehension for what was coming next.

" I have to go," he said finally.

" You'll have to wait," said Claudia succinctly. " Aunt Julia went."

" Isn't there two bathrooms ? "

" No, there isn't two bathrooms."

" We had two bathrooms on the farm."

" Three," said Claudia, as long as he wanted to split hairs, " and a half. Do you want your money back ? "

To be fair about it, one bathroom wasn't going to be any joke ; she'd been aware of it when she'd taken the house. On the other hand, there were thousands and thousands of people who didn't have any bathrooms at all, and they got along perfectly well. One bathroom, of course, would mean even more organisation than none, and maybe they'd all be the better for it, especially Matthew, who was a great dawdler. As a matter of fact, Julia seemed to be a dawdler, too. Claudia wondered what was keeping her, and went to see.

She found Julia trying to find a place to put her mammoth suede bag while she powdered her nose. The bag was almost as big as the bathroom. Claudia sat down on the sharp curve of the old-fashioned tub. " Here, I'll hold it for you," she offered.

She was glad of a little time alone with Julia. Although they had never had very much in common they had struck up quite an intimacy when Julia had suddenly gone in for spiritualism the winter before. David would have divorced Claudia if she ever took up fortune-telling or anything of that sort, but Julia frequently relayed messages from the Beyond, which was like having the name without the game.

Julia, who had a distinct flare for the stock market and

politics, was the last person one would have expected to run to a medium, especially since old established Boston families seemed to live on for ever, and she had never lost anyone she was particularly close to. However, it was all part and parcel of the gradual change that had come over her ever since she had had most of her important organs removed in one fell swoop some years back. There had been a time when her busy, active life had given Claudia a sense of the deepest inferiority, for Julia used to think nothing of sandwiching an important committee meeting between a fitting with her tailor and a luncheon with her broker, and end up with a cocktail party and an evening at the opera into the bargain. Then, all at once, she retired from the social whirl, and Claudia began to inherit quantities of hand-made underwear, and large stacks of expensive blouses and gloves " I'm simplifying my life," Julia had explained, making the word sound as if she'd spoken it with a capital S.

The simplification of her physical being was but a short step to Julia's preoccupation with her soul, and before she knew it she was up to her knees—and higher—in the Other World, and it was one more lucky break for Claudia that the first person Julia contacted was Claudia's mother.

Julia had had only a passing acquaintance with Mrs. Brown in real life, but nevertheless they struck up a great friendship the minute they met through the trumpet. Ordinarily, Julia was stand-offish with people she didn't know well, but there was apparently a wonderful quality of hail-fellow-well-met all through the spirit realm. Indeed, Julia had told Claudia in tremulous confidence that she sometimes talked to the child she had never had. She actually believed it, and Claudia had suddenly glimpsed the intolerable loneliness that could reside within the human heart. Even David hadn't made fun of Julia after that. " I don't like the smell of this," he'd remarked soberly. He blamed it partly on Julia's glands, and partly on Hartley's glands, but mostly he blamed it on the loose thinking that was rampant in the world. Still, he didn't offer any explanation as to how some of the messages hit pretty close to the truth, such as the medium's Indian control saying that David was going away to a land of ice and snow . . . and here he was.

"Also explain to me," Claudia had persisted, "how any-one could know that Bobby was Mamma's favourite? Yet he's the only one of the children she ever talks about."

"Pooh," said David, or words to that effect.

Claudia wasn't strong-minded enough to say "Pooh." Now, as she sat on the tub holding Julia's pocket-book, she was dying to ask, "Have you any messages for me," but it was a service she wasn't paying for, so she just waited on pins and needles while Julia powdered her nose, and carefully covered the bluish corners of her mouth with scarlet lip-stick. "I look like something that's been dragged through a keyhole," she mentioned gloomily.

"You practically have," said Claudia. "Nine hours of close confinement with Matthew is almost the same as."

"I was tired before I started," said Julia. She snapped her compact closed and with deliberation dusted a trace of powder from her dark cloth suit. Claudia held her breath. Unmistakably Julia was searching for the proper opening.

"Look, child," she said at last, "it may be none of my business, but I can't help feeling that this is all a great mistake."

Claudia's throat went dry. Every message that had been relayed so far, had been couched in the most lyrical terms of understanding and encouragement. What was Julia going to tell her? What dire prophecy had come through from the omniscient departed? She hadn't realised until now that these vicarious communications had been a source of actual comfort and strength. Perhaps David was right—this sort of thing wasn't good, and it was high time that she stopped tuning in on Julia's sittings. "Why has it been a mistake?" she asked as calmly as she could.

Julia evaded a direct reply.

"Darling, don't you honestly think it might be better

for David to be where he could have the proper care and quiet in some pleasant little boarding-house ? "

" We just left a pleasant little boarding-house, and it was anything but pleasant."

" Other people stand it."

" David could stand it, too, but why should he, as long as we can all be together ? It seems such a waste of living to be apart if we don't have to."

" Claudia, darling, listen to me," said Julia gently, " I do know, believe me I know, how much you want to keep the family from being broken up, and Hartley and I both hoped that it would work out, but frankly, darling, I wonder if it really can."

It was easy to see that Julia was disturbed, because she kept saying " Darling," a term she reserved only for unfriendly social intercourse. " It isn't fair to yourself," she ended up. " It's going to be a terrific strain on you."

Claudia felt a surge of relief that Julia's concern was not primarily for David. " Oh, I'm all right," she returned, almost gaily. " I don't mind anything as long as we don't have to be separated."

" Aren't you making too much of a bugaboo of a little separation ? It wouldn't kill you, you know, you'd all live through it."

It wasn't a point that she could argue with Julia, who felt that periodic separations were a good thing for even the happiest marriage. " It wouldn't kill us, but we wouldn't like it," she said.

" But are you going to like housekeeping under these difficult conditions ? It's really a most elemental little place, if you don't mind my saying so."

" I don't mind. And I think calling it ' elemental ' is being very polite. But it was the best I could find, every-thing considered."

Julia frowned. " I can't understand it, the Trents rented a charming house here last winter."

" It was probably much bigger; larger places are

comparatively easy to get, especially in the village. . . .
The Trents. They sound familiar."

"Lydia Trent is a cousin of Phil Dexter's. I think you
met them at my house for dinner one night."

"Oh, yes, wait a minute, doesn't Mrs. Trent look a little
like the profiles that people draw on telephone pads?"

David would have got the idea immediately, but Julia's
eyes went perfectly blank. "Telephone pads?" she echoed.

"Round forehead and high pompadour and ears showing," Claudia explained with effort. "I mean it's the only
kind of face I can draw and it's usually when I'm telephoning."

"Oh," said Julia, and added, "Lydia's supposed to be
quite a beauty, in a Grecian sort of way."

Actually, Claudia wasn't interested in anything about
Lydia Trent except her health. "I didn't know the poor
thing was ill," she said.

"Lydia isn't. It's Byard, her husband."

Claudia wanted desperately to find out if Byard was well
again, but she didn't have the courage to ask. "Then they
housekept, too," she said instead.

"Under different circumstances, though," Julia pointed
out. "Firstly, Byard had had sanatorium treatment for
six months before Lydia joined him up here. Secondly,
they have no children, and thirdly, they had the good sense
to take a cottage that had every comfort and convenience.
Quite a bit larger than this, I grant you, but a big place
is often easier to keep in order than a small cramped one."

Claudia thought of Julia's immaculate five-storey house
just for herself and Hartley, with four servants to keep it
running. In spite of all Julia knew about stocks and bonds,
she had very little sense about money. Couldn't she see
that the initial rent of a place like the Trents', plus the
heating and general upkeep, would go through David's
savings in no time? "We can't swing anything larger,"
Claudia explained. "David doesn't want to draw more
from the business than he absolutely has to. He says even
healthy architects never get rich."

"David doesn't have to give a thought to finances. Hartley's told him that time and again."

"I know, but David loathes the idea of borrowing."

"It's ridiculous," said Julia, "to feel that way about his own brother. And I don't have to say that Hartley wouldn't want it to be a debt, he wouldn't hear of David paying it back."

"You've both been wonderful to us," Claudia acknowledged gratefully, "but we don't need anything, really. We've enough put aside to see us through until David's back on his feet again—that is, if we're careful."

"Wouldn't it have been quite a saving then," said Julia, getting back to where she started, "not to have gone to the expense of a house at all? Candy told me she'd have kept the children gladly."

"I don't think so, by the time we counted everything in. Besides, John and Candy might want to sell the apartment, and they couldn't if the children were there."

Julia's mind took a switch. "Sell that beautiful apartment? But why? Almost every room overlooks the river, what more do they want?"

"They want less," said Claudia. "The apartment was perfect while Elizabeth was alive, but it's much too much for a young married couple. John couldn't possibly afford the maintenance on what he draws."

"But Candy certainly can afford it. She must have come into quite a fortune at her mother's death."

"John won't touch it. He's got David's kind of pride."

"Dear me," said Julia, "I can't see why money's so damned important."

"Candy can't either," said Claudia. "I guess it's because you both have it."

Julia got one of her blank looks again, and Claudia hastily reverted to the more pressing issue of David's health and well-being. "Julia," she said bluntly, "if there's anything on your mind, I wish you'd come straight out with it. I mean, did you get any message saying it would be better for David if I hadn't taken this house?

If he were up here alone, or if he had six months in a sanatorium like Byard Trent?"

"You silly girl," said Julia, "of course not. I was simply voicing a personal reaction. I began by saying that it was none of my business, and I'm sorry if I've upset you."

Claudia was torn between relief and disappointment. "It looks like mamma's lost interest in us," she said, half facetiously. "Haven't you even talked to her since we've been away? No message of any kind?"

"No message of any kind," Julia repeated slowly. "You see," she added in a low tight voice, "I haven't been to a sitting in almost two months."

"You haven't?" Claudia exclaimed, feeling cheated. "But you've always gone twice a week, like a religion——"

"I've stopped going," said Julia.

"Oh," said Claudia. She could hardly believe that Julia had given up those precious sessions which had filled the emptiness of her busy life. She wanted to say that she was sorry, deeply sorry, for whatever had happened to bring that unmasked moment of despair to Julia's eyes, but it was kinder to say nothing. She averted her eyes from her sister-in-law's thin, naked face. "How's Hartley been?" she asked lamely.

"Only fair. This thing about David hit him awfully hard."

"It must have. He's more like a father than a brother to David. And being just the two of them for so long makes it doubly hard, I suppose."

"It came so suddenly, David's never had a day's real illness in his life," Julia went on, as if she were telling Claudia something she didn't know. "Hartley can't seem to accept it; he keeps blaming himself for being so blind to what was going on."

Claudia shook her head. "There was nothing you could put your finger on."

"But you'd been worried about him for a long time," Julia reminded her. "I remember your telling me once that you didn't like the way he looked behind his ears."

"That doesn't mean anything, I always worry," said Claudia. Her thoughts shuddered away from the strange presentiment that had stalked her for months, and yet she hadn't been able to get David to a doctor until the awful nightmare of that afternoon on John's boat.

"John still blames himself too," Julia tuned in unexpectedly. "He told us he should never have let David lift those heavy anchors."

"He mustn't feel that way," Claudia said over a closing throat. "How was he to know? We'd gone sailing every week-end the whole time the children were at camp, and it was wonderful for David. If it hadn't happened when he lifted the anchors, he might have gone on indefinitely thinking it was the malaria he caught during the war that made him feel a little low at times. Dr. Morrisson—and Dr. Geiger—both said that a hæmorrhage is often a blessing in disguise."

"What else does Dr. Geiger say about David's condition?"

"He isn't the talking kind. He just says David's an incipient case, and the prognosis is favourable if he behaves himself."

"That's what you wrote us. But you didn't mention whether they were trying any of the modern methods."

"No, Dr. Geiger doesn't think it's indicated at this point. He hopes David will respond to the old traditional rest treatment."

Julia patted Claudia's shoulder. "You forget everything I said, darling. I'm glad he approves of you and the children being here, that makes me feel entirely different about it."

Claudia was silent, numb with conflict. "Not completely, he doesn't," she admitted with honesty. "But he said to give it a chance, and the next X-rays would tell the story."

"How long before the next X-rays?"

"About three months. We'll be able to get a general idea of David's improvement long before that, though. He goes for a check-up every two weeks. And of course Dr. Geiger would come to the house if David should ever run a temperature, or if he has another——" Suddenly, she couldn't bring the word to her lips again. She was ashamed of her cowardice, ashamed that this whole talk with Julia had left her shaken and uncertain of having done the right thing. Matthew's shrill voice in the hall did not add to her conviction.

" Mother ! " he shouted importunately. " Where are you ? What are you doing so long ? "

She flung open the door. " If you don't want to be shipped back to New York, you'll have to learn not to yell ! " she adjured him angrily.

" I am not yelling."

" You are. Suppose Dad had been asleep ? "

" But he's not, he's still outside with Bobby and Bluff."

" Well, run and join them. I'm talking to Aunt Julia."

" I have to go first."

" All right, come in." She gave him an impatient yank. " And heaven help you if you don't."

He looked at her, aggrieved. " I don't like you," he quavered, with his lower lip thrust forward.

She bent to kiss him in quick contrition. " I don't blame you, Matthew, I'm not sure I like me either," she said.

The living-room was empty when they returned to it, except for Shakespeare, still huddled in his travelling basket, regarding them with half-closed eyes and outraged dignity. " How long will that foolish cat stay there ? " Julia asked curiously.

" Until his feelings stop hurting."

Julia said, " Matthew ought to take a leaf out of his book," which was the nearest she came to complaining about the various ins and outs of the trip. She glanced at her watch. " Dear me, it's almost six, I have to be pushing off."

" But aren't you going to stay overnight ? " Claudia protested, being completely two-faced.

" I'd adore to," Julia returned, with another two-faces,

"but I promised the Trents to spend the night with them."

"I didn't realise that they were still here, after a whole year," said Claudia, with a wave of discouragement sweeping over her.

"Oh, they're not here now, or they'd have looked you up. They bought a place near Lake Placid. Byard says he never wants to set foot in New York again. He loves this life."

"I can't imagine not wanting to go back. Not that I'm in love with New York, but it's just the idea."

"You'd be surprised," said Julia, "how many people get to feel like Byard does."

"I can tell you that David's one person who won't," said Claudia. "He counts each day like crazy."

Julia walked to the window. "Well, let's hope he learns to like it."

David being David, Claudia wasn't sure whether she hoped he would or not.

"I wonder where Watkins is, he's not in the car," Julia continued.

Ultimately, they found him in the kitchen, wrestling with dampers that had rusted into stubborn immutability. Without his chauffeur's cap, and with his hair perspiring, he looked about half his salary, and Julia probably didn't like it any more than Watkins did. Bertha liked it, though.

"Watson is good and strong," she announced blandly, "I am sure he can fix my stove better than a stove-man."

Claudia managed not to catch Julia's eye.

TWO

SHE FELT A SENSE of desolation when Julia finally drove off. Julia, lifted high on the wings of illusion, had been able to lift her too, but Julia, without faith, had succeeded only in pulling her down. " So-long, Mamma," she thought with wry humour. It had been rather wonderful, even if it hadn't been true, to have had those comforting little messages from her mother. " What a weak-minded fool you turned out to be in your old age," she upbraided herself in disgust, " when are you going to learn to stand on your own two feet ? "

She knew herself well enough to know that it wasn't going to be easy. She had always had someone to lean on. When her mother died, there had been David to take her place, but now she mustn't lean on David. She mustn't lean too heavily on Bertha, either. Bertha was not young any more. Bertha had lost both child and husband, and her strength was hard won. It was not right to borrow of that strength.

She was aware that she was still waving to Julia, although the car was almost out of sight. Darkness had fallen, but it wasn't dark enough to see the stars. Far down the road, lights from the nearest house twinkled through the bare branches of the trees. Perhaps Julia was right about being in the centre of town, even if it did cost a little more. Out here, it was lonely, and frightening.

" What are you doing standing in the cold by yourself ? " She almost jumped out of her skin. " You scared the wits out of me ! "

" Guilty conscience."

" It could be, at that. Where on earth did you and Bobby disappear to ? I called and called."

" We took a little walk," said David, " and then we sat on a rock until Bluff made up his mind."

25

"Julia couldn't wait any longer. She said to tell you good-bye, and good luck and all the rest of it."

He had the decency to look abashed. "I thought she was going to stay overnight, or I'd have hung around."

"She didn't. She was too tired to stay."

"She looked pretty done-in. I suppose you got your usual earful?"

She recognised, in the crudeness of his phrasing, a sheepish desire to hear what Julia had had to say. It was strange that there was such fascination, even for so-called normal people, in the workings of the supernatural.

"Julia doesn't go any more," she said.

David's eyebrow climbed his forehead. "That was quicker than I expected. What happened, did she find out that her great medium was a fake?"

"I don't know. But she did look badly, didn't she? I don't imagine it was all due to the trip, either."

Bobby said, "It took much longer, Watkins told me, than it should have. We had to stop such a lot on account of Matthew, and he wouldn't hurry. I had to keep running in after him."

"That young man is going to change his habits, and fast," David decided on the spot.

"Could there be something wrong with him?" Claudia wondered anxiously.

"He doesn't really do anything," Bobby assured her. "It's just when he thinks about it he thinks he has to, and he always thinks about it because he knows it makes us mad."

"That," said David, "is the perfect diagnosis. Where is he? I don't see him around."

"I left him in the bathroom," said Claudia faintly.

David literally smacked his lips. He went in the house and left her alone with Bobby. She put her arm around his shoulders. He was quite tall now, almost as tall as she was.

"How do you think Dad acts?" she whispered.

"Fine," he whispered back. "I think he's glad to have Bluff, I think he missed him."

" He missed you too," said Claudia. " Are you glad to be here ? "

" Men don't say how much they miss people," Bobby replied obliquely.

She smiled into the darkness. " You still haven't said whether you like it here ? " she pursued, remembering Matthew's many complaints.

" Sure," said Bobby simply, and added, " It's like the farm."

" Even without any cows or chickens it's like the farm ? "

He nodded slowly, puzzled because, in a way, it wasn't like the farm at all. " Look ! " he cried out suddenly in excitement, " it's snowing a little ! "

It was true. All at once, it had begun to snow. " The snow's for Matthew," Claudia said.

Bertha had supper ready in no time—hot cereal and poached eggs, and a jar of caviar that Candy had sent along for David. " I hate that stuff," said Matthew, eyeing it with disfavour.

" Splendid," said David, with a slight carry-over of whatever had transpired between them on the subject of dawdling. He buttered a biscuit for Claudia. " Onion ? "

" Certainly onion," she said. " Only you take it, you put too much caviar on."

" Would you like me to hold your nose ? "

She took it, avoiding rough-house.

He buttered another biscuit for Bertha, and one for himself, and then Bobby decided to try some, but without onion. He said he liked it, but he didn't. " Give yourself another year or two," said David.

" Not that we intend to live on caviar," Claudia amended. " It's just for celebrations."

" Why is this a celebration ? " Matthew asked.

" Why do you think ? " said David.

" Because we're eating in the kitchen. I like to eat in the kitchen."

" That's good," said Claudia. " Maybe we can always manage to eat in here, if you really enjoy it, darling."

" That's right, go on and spoil him," said David severely, and broke down with a grin.

" This is what I meant," thought Claudia, with her spirit soaring. " It's wonderful."

Later, it wasn't so wonderful, though There was a great scramble for towels and toothbrushes, and Matthew trod where angels wouldn't dare, and made another bottle-neck in the bathroom, and the baby cried and held his breath, which Claudia couldn't get over getting nervous about.

" It's a back tooth," Bertha explained apologetically. " I'd better walk him."

" No, I will," said Claudia. " You have enough to do."

David caught her at it. " This is a fine business," he disapproved and meant it. " Put him down."

" He'll cry."

" Let him cry."

" I don't want him to disturb you."

" Rats. He won't disturb me."

" Please get undressed and go to bed," she begged him. " You've had a big day."

" Very big," he agreed bitterly. " I lifted one end of a scale that weighed all of ten pounds."

" I didn't mean that."

" What the devil did you mean, then ? "

She bit her lips to keep from lashing out at him. " Oh don't be so damn sensitive, other people have been sick too and don't make such a thing of it ! " For an instant she was afraid that she really had said it. " I'm sorry," she murmured.

" Sorry for what ? "

" Nothing."

" You're tired," he accused her. " You're trying to do the work of six people. What do you think you are, a horse ? "

She put the baby down in his crib. He began to cry, and beat the air with his fists. " Shut up ! " David shouted.

The baby stared at him with puckering lips, his private world hidden behind opaque blue eyes. He whimpered off, and then stuck his thumb in his mouth and began to suck loudly and with arrogance. Claudia caught David's outstretched hand. " Oh let him, it won't ruin his character just this once," she implored. " Don't try to train him tonight, *please* ! "

" Tomorrow," David planned with relish, " he and I will have a talk together."

It was time enough to worry about tomorrow, when tomorrow came. She steered him out into the hall, unfortunately into the very jaws of the boys' room directly opposite. " Just look at that pig-pen," he said. " I thought you said they learned to be tidy at camp last summer."

" Now listen, be reasonable, nothing's unpacked yet," she placated him. " Tomorrow it will all be as neat as a pin." (Tomorrow is getting to be more of a day every minute, she thought.)

" Where'd they go to ? "

" Washing."

" Did you warn them about keeping their towels separate ? "

" Of course."

" Did you tell Bertha about the dishes ? "

" Yes."

" How much longer are they going to be in there ? If Matthew's reading, so help me, I'll break his neck."

" Calm down, he hasn't got anything to read," said Claudia.

To make sure, though, she stuck her head in at the door, meeting Matthew's icy disapproval. " You ought to knock," he reproved her.

" You'd better hop," she returned. " if you know what's good for you."

" And how," Bobby observed with pleasure. He was slicking his hair back at the basin, until the water dribbled down his forehead.

2

" You'll rot your roots," Claudia reminded him wearily, from the limbo of some mistaken information. His hand froze in mid-air. What good was it going to do to train his hair back if he didn't have any hair to train? He tried to peer at the top of his head to see if the rotting process had already set in. Claudia took pity on him. " Maybe it doesn't hurt it," she relented. " But don't wet it so wet anyway."

" He always does," Matthew put in virtuously. " Sometimes his pillow is all wet, too."

Bobby's temper snapped. " You shut up ! " he cried furiously.

" And where do you get language like that ? " David enquired from the threshold, leaving himself wide open.

" You just told the baby to shut up," Matthew remarked.

" You," said David with dignity, " are a very fresh boy."

" I think you're very fresh, too," Matthew returned quite amiably.

David turned on his heel and left the room, barely in time to save his face. Claudia followed him. They walked down the hall, swallowing noisily. " Are they crying ? " Claudia heard Matthew ask in alarm.

" Don't be such a dope," said Bobby paternally. " They're only laughing."

It was the first time they'd really laughed since they'd left New York. Bertha looked up from a parcel of winter underwear she was unpacking in the living-room. " It is good," she said, " to be all together again. It is like old times."

It wasn't exactly like old times. She didn't realise that they weren't sleeping together, and she had turned down both the beds in their room. If David got the impact of it, he gave no sign. " Is it too much to hope," he said, slipping off his coat, " that the menagerie's out of the bathroom ? "

" You actually act as if we were crowded for space."

" Nonsense. What gave you that peculiar notion ? "

" Seriously, though, it's a matter of adjustment. If you

had one tenth as much room as this on a boat, you'd say it was marvellous."

"You have something there. I suppose you think we'll never go on a boat again ? "

"I think no such thing."

"Well, you'd better not. Where's Bluff sleeping ? "

"In the hall. So kindly don't talk to him when you pass, or he'll get bigger and better ideas for himself."

While he was in the bathroom she turned down the bed on the porch. It was still snowing, very lightly. In the boarding-house, they said you were supposed to sleep out even in a blizzard, so again it was a matter of adjustment, because a mere sprinkle of flakes was enough to put her into conflict. She rolled the bed as far out of the reach of weather as she could, and moved the night table with all its grim paraphernalia close beside it—thermometer and cheese-cloth, and the little brown paste-board box that flicked open at the touch of a finger. He hardly ever had to use it, which was something to be thankful for, although Mr. Berwell, who was Mrs. Jenkins' oldest and sickest boarder, said that there were two schools of thought on the subject.

One thing, however, that nobody ever quibbled about, was a normal temperature. It was unquestionably good to have. She took the thermometer out of its case to check on the eight o'clock reading, since she wouldn't put it past him to have lied about it. But he hadn't. There it was— a hairbreadth over ninety-eight-seven. If only tomorrow would show no ill effects of today. They'd said, at the boarding-house, that you couldn't get away with murder, you always paid for it the morning after. What with lifting the scales and taking a walk with Bobby, David had got away with quite some murder this afternoon, and suddenly the little glass stick became a gigantic club over their happiness. She put it back in its case, and hurried indoors, chilled with something more than the cold night air.

He noticed at once that she was shivering. "What were you doing outside, without anything on ? "

" Opening your bed."

" My bed's open. Bertha did it."

She raised her brows, in imitation of himself. " Really ?
That's interesting."

He came toward her. " Look, it's snowing out," he said
plaintively. " You wouldn't put a poor man out in the
snow ? "

It was hard not to let the clear, enticing smell of shaving-
lotion and toothpaste invite her senses. " Oh, I wouldn't,
wouldn't I ? You'd be surprised."

His lower lip thrust out, like Matthew's. " I didn't sleep
out at Mrs. Jenkins'."

" Naturally you didn't, we couldn't get a room with a
porch. Which was another reason I wanted to get our
own house."

" You wanted to get your own house because you're a
greedy, omnivorous female. You want your men around
you."

" David, you're not really sorry, are you ? "

In answer, he pulled her down beside him on one of the
beds and pressed her nose with the tip of his finger in lieu
of a kiss. " Bobby's got to be quite a fellow, hasn't he ? "
he said with one of her own *non sequiturs*.

She realised, perhaps for the first time, the particular
relationship of a father to his eldest son. " Your middle
and youngest aren't so bad either," she reminded him.

" Bobby was never like that little brat."

He meant Matthew, but there was enough affection in
his voice to make it all right. " He was, though, it's just
that we don't remember," she said.

" He has a perpetual grudge. Where does he get it
from ? "

" You. Now stop trying to woo me into a conversation
about the children, it's time you were asleep." She gave
him a great shove off the bed. " Out you go, and no more
talk. You're more trouble than the three of them put
together."

" You'll be sorry." He dragged himself off, sulking

broadly because she didn't love him any more. When he
was outside, he beat a tattoo on the pane and made faces
at her through the window. She knew that he was clown-
ing to cover up. Tears burned hot against her eyeballs.
How wonderful it would have been for them to be together
this first night that they were all a family again. It
was right that it should be. But she was afraid. It was
not David's fear, he had no fear, or if he did, his love
surmounted it. She wished that she could rise to meet
his courage. " Darling, wait—" she besought him silently.
" Be patient."

A moment later, she heard the creaking of his bed. She
put the light out so that it would not disturb him, and
undressed in the dark.

The sheets gave back an icy rebuff. Her limbs moved
frugally, searching for a warmth that wasn't there. It had
been like that during the war, but their hearts had been
joined in the common hurt of mankind, and the vastness
of their separation had lent stature to their loneliness. Now
they were separated only by a small square of glass, yet
they were as far apart as if a continent lay between them.
Emptiness ached within her, and bitterness visited her soul,
for this that had happened to them spelled only a personal
indignity, a frustration of their physical beings. She was
beginning to understand why David had always felt that
there was a kind of moral ugliness in ill-health. That was
why he was fighting it, every inch of the way. She wondered
if she ought to help him fight it, or must he learn to accept
incapacity before he could overcome it ? Perhaps that was
the good, underlying reason for boarding-houses and
sanatoriums, and the discipline of learning how to use one's
body with discretion.

The baby suddenly whimpered. She held her breath.
There, Bertha had hushed him, quickly, frantically. She
lay, tense and waiting, lest he cry again and waken David.
The months ahead shredded into a thousand tiny problems.
She was no longer certain of anything, least of all that she
had done the right thing either to David, or the children,

in bringing them all together in this cramped little house. She wept, out of sheer weariness and confusion. It took all her strength not to go to David on the porch.

At last she fell asleep, but with one ear listening for the baby and the other out for David. He coughed once, but it didn't mean anything, he stopped before she got to the window. She could see the dim outline of his body beneath the covers, humped away from her, with the blanket caught up around his neck. Bobby slept that way too. It was funny how much alike they were.

She stood, for a long while, watching the way his shoulder moved up and down in slow, even breathing. Then she noticed, before she turned away, that the snow was falling more thickly, and that it was drifting across the foot-board. It was enough to keep her awake for the rest of the night, worrying about it.

By morning, there was quite a high mound on the bed. It was marvellous snow, dry and powdery, so that when she brushed it off, the quilt was scarcely damp beneath. "Thank goodness," she said, feeling David anxiously all over.

"Get away!" he cried. "You tickle!"

It would have taken New York weeks to work itself up into such a snowfall. Even at the farm a first snow was never anything more than a timid overture to winter, a delicate white icing that hardly frosted the trees before it was off with the sun. By the time real snow came, the edge of excitement was apt to be gone, as if it had cried wolf once too often.

Matthew, of course, was enchanted with the dazzling white world that had come into being while he was asleep, and didn't doubt for a moment that the heavens had performed the miracle for his especial benefit. He hurried up to get out into it, leaving the bathroom free for Bertha to bathe the baby before David was ready to shave. "It's a good system," Claudia decided. "We ought to manage this way every morning."

Eight o'clock found them all eating breakfast in the pleasantly steamy kitchen just as if nothing had happened to threaten the happiness and security of their lives. Looking at David across the table, it broke her heart to think that he had to be banished again to the porch until lunch time. It might have been easier for him, this first morning, if it hadn't snowed. " Why can't Daddy go out and shovel with us ? " Matthew demanded shrilly. " He always used to at the farm."

" Don't talk so much," Bobby adjured him. " Pass the sugar, you dope."

" Bobby," David remarked with a kind of smile. " You are a gentleman, if not a scholar."

" What's a scholar ? " Matthew queried. " Can I have some more sugar on my oatmeal too ? "

" ' May I ' " Claudia corrected automatically.

" Now you see Mother is a scholar," David pointed out.

" If not a gentleman," she added.

" That's where you're wrong," said David. " I consider you to be quite a gentleman."

His eyes were suddenly blue instead of blue-grey, which was a key-note to the way he really felt, no matter what his lips said, or how he acted. She blew him a kiss. " Thank you, darling, that's the nicest thing a man could say to a woman."

Matthew scooped a second spoonful of sugar. " It's a crazy thing to say," he remarked laconically. " How can a lady be a gentleman." No one seemed to be paying any attention to him, so he dug in for another spoonful. David caught him in the act.

" Matthew, put that sugar back ! " he commanded sternly.

" Matthew isn't even a lady," Bobby injected. " He's just a thief."

The word shocked Claudia's ears. " Bobby, that's a terrible thing to say about your brother, even in fooling."

"I wasn't fooling," he said, as he slipped Bluff a piece of bacon beneath the table.

" Be careful, Bobby, your halo's slipping," David commented.

It certainly needed team-work to bring up children properly, but Claudia wished that David would tune out from the small issues that kept cropping up. " Do you think these little discussions hurt him ? " she asked Bertha when they were clearing the breakfast dishes together.

" I don't think so," said Bertha. " Maybe it is good for him to have a little something to handle."

" But Dr. Geiger doesn't want him to. He told me the only way he can get well is to make himself into a piece of protoplasm for the next six months."

" What is that ? "

" Mush."

Bertha looked doubtful. " Never. Not Mr. David. And yet I was very surprised how nicely he went right out on the porch."

" I only hope," said Claudia, " that it isn't the case of a new broom sweeping clean."

She moved cautiously to the window to check up on him.

The porch ran the entire width of the cottage, open at the living-room end, but glassed-in outside the bedroom. From the projection of the kitchen, she could, by peering sideways, catch a glimpse of him in the long steamer-chair, a lonely solitary figure against the background of the snow-topped mountains. If he had stayed on at the boarding-house, she reflected with misgiving, loneliness might not have been added to his burden. His would have been one of a long row of chairs, there would have been others to share the experience of illness. So many things that hadn't seemed important to her during their brief stay with Mrs. Jenkins kept coming back in her mind with new significance. Like the time Mr. Barwell hadn't appeared at breakfast one morning, and everyone except herself and David had known immediately what it meant.

" Mr. Barwell shouldn't ought to have carried on like he did at supper last night," Mrs. Jenkins had held forth from her place at the head of the table. "A hæmorrhage case should know better than to joke and laugh the way he did."

Mrs. Jenkins always said, with becoming modesty, that she knew more than any doctor, because she had the practical experience of being with the patients day in and day out, whereas doctors only saw them periodically. "What your husband had ought to do," she'd advised Claudia in private, " is to go to the sanatorium here for six months, and if he can't get in, he ought to stay right here where he is and learn how to take care of himself the way he should. This idea of renting a house for yourselves, with three children and a dog and cat besides, is plain suicide at this stage."

"But Dr. Morrisson, the specialist in New York, said it was a good idea," Claudia defended.

"I know Dr. Morrisson," Mrs. Jenkins said. "He sends me people all the time. He's a great diagnostician, none better, but that's all he is."

"He told me that my husband was a very light case," Claudia edged in quickly.

Mrs. Jenkins edged her out again. "They're all light cases when they first come up," she said with a short laugh. "Some of them even go as far as to try to make you believe they came for eye-trouble, it's a standing joke." Personally, Mrs. Jenkins had continued, she had no patience with that kind of sensitiveness. What was there to be ashamed of? Look at Robert Louis Stevenson and Elizabeth Browning——

"And Oscar Wilde," Claudia had thrown in for good measure, before she remembered that that was something else again.

Mrs. Jenkins herself had less than half a lung left that was any good at all, and she was proud of it. At first, Claudia had thought that she was just putting on airs about her half-lung, for she was more than the picture of health, with red hair and redder cheeks, and an immense middle. Still, Mr. Barwell was the picture of health, too, so it was

impossible to go by looks. " The fact is," Mrs. Jenkins
had sized Claudia up on their first meeting, " you look
sicker than your husband. I bet you don't weigh a hundred
pounds."

" A hundred and eight, in Dr. Morrisson's office."

" Did he examine you ? "

" Yes. The children, too."

" What'd he do, fluoroscope ? "

" And listened. We're fine."

" Fluoroscoping's not as good as X-ray. It just goes to
prove that outside doctors don't know this field from a
practical angle. They're full of new theories about drugs
and surgery, and climate not mattering any more, but in
the long run, and for the majority of cases, it's the same old
routine that does the trick—good dry mountain air, and
plenty of milk and eggs and rest, flat on your back. Don't
tell *me*," she'd added darkly, " I've seen too many of them
come and go in my day."

Claudia had been afraid to ask what she meant by " come
and go." It sounded ominous, although maybe she merely
meant " coming and going " like herself and David. Mrs.
Jenkins didn't cater for transients, she liked her people to
be permanent. " Of course, I'm always glad whenever a
patient is well enough to go home," she'd made clear, " for
my sake as well as theirs. I've got a waiting-list from here
to the next street."

Claudia remembered Mrs. Jenkins saying that as she
stood at the window this morning, looking out at David.
A waiting-list for illness. It was hard to acknowledge that
they had become part of a strange new world, so separated
from reality, and at the same time so devastatingly real that
at times illness seemed the only reality. David didn't want
that to happen, any more than she did. It was the one
solid and sustaining reason that she was glad she had chosen
to carry with them their own small universe, uninterrupted
and complete. How it was going to work out was largely up
to David from this point on. She realised it suddenly with
apprehension and foreboding. Bertha was right, it was not

going to be easy for him to make himself into Dr. Geiger's lump of protoplasm.

" It does not help to worry about what will happen." Bertha's gentle admonition brought her back into the warm, and already familiar kitchen.

" What were you doing, reading my mind ? "

" Your mind was on your face. But you must give Mr. David credit for some sense. He knows he must take good care of himself if he wants to get well."

" Here come the children," Claudia broke in. " The less talk they hear of sickness, the better."

" You are right," said Bertha.

A moment later Matthew burst into the room, full up to the neck with muffler and wind-breaker. " I'm going out to make a snow-man ! " he announced. " I've got on my snow-boots and everything, good-bye ! "

" Come back here, not so quick ' good-bye ' ! " Bertha barely caught his coat-tails. " I think you have on Bobby's snow-boots by mistake."

" I have not."

" You have so." Bobby appeared on the threshold, smouldering with indignation. " No wonder they went on so easy, take them off and get your own ! "

" I won't," said Matthew.

Bobby advanced a slow step, the replica of David in the deliberation of his movement and his speech. " Do you want to give those boots to me, or would you like me to remove them by force ? "

Bertha hid a smile but Claudia watched her two sons with dispassionate interest. There was a strength in one and a weakness in the other that had nothing to do with the differences in their ages. Already Matthew was backing away. " All right for you," he mumbled, as he kicked off the snow-boots.

" You knew they were mine when you put them on, you little sneak," Bobby lashed out in contempt. " You just wanted to see if you could get away with it."

With his charm, he almost had, thought Claudia. It

was something to recognise, something to reckon with, but not now, not until David was more fit to meet the problem with her. For the present, it must suffice that the children were healthy and happy, and that the snow had come to take up their slack until she got around to enrolling them in school. Surreptitiously, her knuckles reached for the under-side of the kitchen table, and tapped out a hymn of gratitude. Bertha didn't know what it was about, but she played safe and followed suit. It never hurt to knock on wood, and certainly this was no time to tempt fate in any department whatsoever.

THREE

THE NEW BROOM in David swept reasonably clean until eleven o'clock. Then he appeared in the kitchen and announced with a little of Matthew's bravado, that he was going out to show the boys how to shovel snow.

Claudia poked at a pan of dish-towels that were boiling on the stove. She was boiling too, but she tried not to show it. " That would be very smart of you, I'm sure," she said evenly.

" It would. We need a path cleared, nobody can get up to the door."

" Nobody has to get up to the door. I did enough marketing for the rest of the week."

" And suppose somebody has to get out in an emergency ? "

She'd thought of that too, but she hadn't mentioned it since there was nothing that could be done about it until she found out who her neighbours were. Perhaps the farmer up the road might know someone, or take over the chore himself. The town shovel had cleared the main thoroughfares at daybreak, but the drifts were virgin high from the house down to the gate. Out at the kitchen entrance, Bobby and Matthew were making a valiant hash of it, and she was itching to take a shovel herself, and so was Bertha, but they knew it would be gall and wormwood for David to watch them. Even with the children shovelling, she had to be tactful not to hurt him. " You'd better leave them alone," she advised, as if there were really a choice for him to make. " They're having a wonderful time, and if you go out and join them, there'll be a general rough-house and they'll start throwing snowballs down each other's necks again."

" I'll clear the front door then."

He'd got her into a corner. Anger flared up in her.

" Oh, stop being a fool, David ! You're not a child, you know perfectly well that shovelling snow is the last thing in the world that you should do ! "

His nostrils got white, and his voice came, hard and bitter. " Very well then, why didn't you say so right out instead of beating about the bush ? "

It was poison for him to get excited and lose his temper, and yet she knew that what was going to be said between them needed to be said. It was time that they stopped trying to save each other's feelings and settled down to the seriousness of the job ahead of them. It was time that he forgot his precious pride. " You make me feel," she said slowly, " as if it's been a terrible mistake, my trying to keep us all together."

" It is if you keep nagging me. ' Don't do this ! Don't do that ! ' For God's sake, quit it, can't you ? "

Between the hammering of her heart and the trembling of her knees, she could scarcely hold herself erect. " That's exactly what I meant," she brought out with an immense clarity. " You'd probably be a great deal better off in the boarding-house, where you'd learn to take orders and obey them, like everyone else."

His eyes were no longer blue, they were a sick, cold grey. He turned on his heel and left the room without another word.

A few minutes later Bertha came back from giving the baby his vegetable. " What is the matter with Mr. David," she asked, " that he is sitting by himself in the parlour like company ? "

" He wanted to shovel snow," Claudia explained in a muffled voice. " He isn't as sensible as you thought he was."

Bertha carefully scraped the baby's dish of scraps for Shakespeare, who turned his nose up at them. " It will take a little time. Fritz was the same when he had to stop work and be careful of himself. It is hard for a strong man to be weak."

" And still be strong," said Claudia.

Bertha thought about it. " And still be strong," she repeated softly. " That is the thing . . . Shakespeare, make up your mind, don't do me any favours, all that nice butter . . ."

Claudia left them to argue it out, and found David still sitting on the hard sofa in the living-room. He was not even paying attention to Bluff, who was standing patiently beside him. " Bluff," she said, " if you hurry, I think Bertha might have some scraps for you."

In Bluff's language, the word " Bertha " stood for food. He put two and two together, and lost no time in heading for the kitchen. Claudia took his place at David's side. " Stop being maudlin," she adjured him crisply. " Let's go out on the porch, it'll do me good."

It was a long moment before he as much as moved a muscle. Then he pulled her toward him. " I guess we had to clear the air," he said.

" I guess we did."

" I wouldn't have shovelled very hard. It's just that I don't want to be scared of this damn thing."

" I know," she said. She turned away from the agony in his eyes. " Wait for me, I'll get my coat."

He had mastered the art of wrapping the blankets around him in his chair, and called her a cluck for getting herself tangled up in them. " Here, lie back, I'll do it for you."

She lay back. " This is wonderful," she sighed. " Such air."

" Don't get ecstatic. You're not the type."

" I could easily be, though, looking at those mountains with the snow on them."

" You can have them," he said shortly. But she could tell by the way he lay there, staring up at their lofty peaks, that he was slowly making friends with them. " Some day," it came to her, " I'm going to be jealous because they give him more than I can."

They didn't talk again, nor feel the need to talk. The need for many of the old expressions of their love was growing less. Even before his illness, she had noticed how often silence had come to take the place of chatter, and how a little understanding had offset spurts of physical exuberance. Candy and John were images of their old selves—hoodlums in love, quick to passion, quick to grief.

"What are you smiling at ? " David asked.

"How old is John ? "

"Twenty-six or seven. Why ? "

"And Candy's eighteen. No reason. I was just thinking."

"Thinking what ? That we were that age when we were married ? "

"Partly," she admitted. "But mostly I was thinking how glad I am that we've got those years behind us." She reached for his hand and carried it to her lips. "Except for one thing. Oh, darling, if only I could have been the one instead of you——"

"Hey, stop that——" he said huskily. But he didn't let her hand go. "I'd have wrung your neck," he said, "if you'd played me a dirty trick like that."

Their fingers, tightly linked, were messengers of all they felt. It seemed no time at all before Bertha called them in to lunch.

They were at dessert when Julia unexpectedly stopped by on her way back from the Trents. Her car couldn't make the grade up to the house. Claudia saw the gleam that came into Bertha's eyes. " No, Bertha ! " she expostulated. " You just can't do it ! "

"But Watson was very obliging about fixing the stove," Bertha argued.

"Not that obliging. I bet anything he gave notice the minute he drove away."

"Then if he is leaving anyway," Bertha returned with logic, "it is surely no harm to ask him to move a little snow. I will ask him nicely as a favour."

Claudia covered her ears, cheating somewhat so that she could hear. "Watson ! " Bertha carolled beguilingly from the porch. " Oh, Watson ! I would like to talk to you ! "

" Bertha's crazy," Matthew remarked in disdain. " She always keeps calling Watkins Watson when his name is Watkins."

" That's just to make Watson feel better," David explained. Claudia thanked her stars that he was enjoying the situation instead of resenting it. She walked to the window to see what was happening. Bertha had picked up the shovel, and was brandishing it in the direction of the parked limousine. " Watkins, would you be so kind, please ! "

" Watkins is now getting out of the car," Claudia reported to David, who was still at the table finishing his coffee, " but I don't know whether he's ' being so kind, please.' Anyway, Julia can't get anywhere in thin pumps so I'll put on Bobby's snow-boots and go down and sit with her while she's waiting."

She swam in Bobby's boots and wore Matthew's instead, which swelled his ego.

" I have a pretty big foot," he bragged.

" You mean I have a pretty small one," Claudia took him down smartly.

It was hard going. She sank deep with every step, and tasted how the children must feel, sloshing around in the soft drifts. " I'll buy them a sled on my first trip to town," she decided, and immediately had visions of them belly-wopping down the slopes and smashing headlong into trees. " Borrowing trouble is certainly your two middle names," she told herself impatiently, " why don't you try having a couple of nice thoughts for a change ? "

Already Watkins had begun to clear a path up the drive. He wasn't used to exercise, and in spite of the cold, he was sweating all over his face, which was the only part of him that Claudia could see. " I know you must hate this," she greeted him impulsively, " and you're an angel to help us out of a jam."

He wasn't used to being called an angel, but he seemed

to prefer it to being called Watson. " That's perfectly all right, ma'am, I'm glad to be of service in any way I can." (No matter if it kills me, he gasped silently.)

It was to Julia's everlasting credit that she was outwardly composed and smiling when Claudia reached her, but she was ready to break out in red spots all over her neck just the same. " Look, I'm sorry about using Watkins up like this," Claudia apologised. " You'll bless us if you have to go out and find another chauffeur."

" We'll see," said Julia enigmatically, and added that Bertha would have made an excellent general.

" She would. You should have seen her face light up when she saw the car," said Claudia. " Mine, too. I didn't expect you. Isn't it out of your way ? "

" A little. But I wanted to be able to tell Hartley that you were all nicely settled and everything was fine. Is it ? "

" Yes, really it is. I was a little depressed last night."

" I could see you were," Julia interrupted. " That's why I stopped by."

" It was awfully nice of you, but things began to smooth out today. I mean it."

" Well," said Julia, " I'm glad to hear it. At any rate the Trents have promised to keep an eye on you. I told them, when they drove down, that you're about a mile beyond the Sanatorium."

" On the old road," Claudia specified. " But they'll find us. How's Mr. Trent feeling ? "

" He thought he was getting a little cold, but he seemed quite well to me. Oh, and Lydia says to tell you the school here is supposed to be excellent. Very modern, and the children will have the best of care."

" That's what they told me at the boarding-house. They'll start on Monday, I hope."

" It ought to make the household considerably easier," Julia said, " if they're away most of the day."

" It will. Especially Matthew. He's at the age when he has to do something every minute."

" Yes, I noticed that," said Julia. " But Bobby's a lamb, I'm devoted to that youngster."

" I like him too," said Claudia softly. " He's David, all over again."

Julia dropped her glove on the floor of the car, and they both stooped for it and bumped their heads. Julia straightened her hat. " Now be sure to sing out," she said, " if there's anything you need. And keep us posted about David."

Claudia nodded. " I will, and I imagine I'll have some good news on the next check-up. I'm hoping against hope that Dr. Geiger will put him on fifteen minutes' exercise. I never knew fitfteen minutes of walking could be so important. I don't think I ever wanted anything so much in all my life." Her throat choked up; she could have kicked herself for getting emotional. " Don't forget to phone Candy and John, will you, when you get back to town ? Tell them we're fine, and that David just lives for news about the office. I wish he didn't, but he does."

" I'll phone them first thing in the morning," Julia made note.

" Oh, look," Claudia exclaimed, " what beautiful headway Watkins is making——"

" Yes, he has you pretty well cleared, so we'll be pushing on. Give David my love and kiss the children for me."

" But aren't you going to get out for a minute ? Have a cup of tea or something before you start back ? "

" I'd like to, but I'd better not. The driving's going to be very slow with this storm, and Hartley will be waiting up for me."

Claudia didn't coax her. It was already two o'clock, and two-to-four was the most important rest period of the day. David wasn't supposed to talk, or even read.

She said good-bye to Julia, and got into the house through the side door without David seeing her. Then she tip-toed to the bedroom window and looked out at him. There he was, bundled up in his chair, with a book in his hand, smoking his pipe. Anger fought with pity. How hard, how terribly hard it was, for him to give in and obey orders.

Candy telephoned that evening. She said she simply couldn't wait until Julia got back to find out how everything was.

"Everything's fine," said Claudia, " you can stop worrying about us. What about yourself ? "

Candy's young voice lilted up into the air. " I'm absolutely positive. How long before you feel life ? "

" Months. Is Dr. Rowland positive, too ? "

" I didn't pay any attention to him any more. I went to see him again this morning, and he said it was still too early to be certain. But as far as I'm concerned, it's official, and the baby will be here June eighth. That's John's mother's birthday and I'm in a mood to be generous."

" That is big of you. How do you feel ? "

" Wonderful ! Didn't you ? With all three ? "

" All four," said Claudia, with a pang of memory. " Do you think you and John will be able to drive up during Thanksgiving ? "

" Not Thanksgiving, I don't think. But surely Christmas. John's mother has a feeling that this is going to be the last Thanksgiving she's alive—she says she's just waiting around for her first grandchild, and then she'll pop quietly off."

" John's mother is going to live to be ninety," said Claudia firmly.

" Thanks," said Candy. " Anyway, Thanksgiving's out, darn it."

" Christmas will be even better," said Claudia. " You can stay longer, and David might be on half-an-hour exercise by then and he can spend more time with John."

" That's what John thought, too. . . . Save Michael's scales for me, and everything else."

" I should say so." Mentally, Claudia was clocking the seconds, frugally mindful that the traditional three minutes were almost up. " David's waiting to talk to John," she said.

Candy, however, was completely emancipated when it came to long-distance calls. "Don't be in such a hurry," she said, "I'm not through yet. I met an old beau of yours on the street yesterday and he gave me a message for you."

"I didn't have any old beaux. Who?"

"Philip Dexter."

"Philip Dexter? He wasn't an old beau, he just thought he was. For about five minutes."

Candy giggled. "Be that as it may, he wants to drop in and see you for another five minutes, sometime soon when he goes up to Placid to ski. He has cousins up there."

"Yes, I know. The Trents. It would really be nice if he'd come by on his way."

"The hell it would," said David.

"Hey, stop that!"

"What did you say?" Candy asked.

"Nothing," said Claudia. "David was getting funny. You'd better put John on——"

"What does an old beau mean?" Bobby queried. "Somebody who liked you?"

Claudia turned. "I thought you were in bed. No, somebody who just thought he liked you, usually," she explained.

"Didn't Mr. Dexter send me a big set of blocks once, when I had the measles?"

"Yes, I believe he did."

"Why?"

"He had a little boy just your age who died."

"What did he die of?"

"I don't remember. You sound like Matthew, so many questions. Run and take your bath."

He dropped his voice, with a look in David's direction. "I can't, until Matthew gets out."

"Oh, Lord. Again?"

"No, still."

"I'll see to that young man while Dad's phoning. Let Shakespeare in, I hear him at the back door."

She passed the baby's room and paused to listen to him laugh. Once in a while, Michael put on a great performance of laughter, and it was something to hear—deep, old-man chortles that came from the bottom of his belly, and shook his fat shoulders like twin bowls of jelly. Now he was laughing at Bertha, who was making a fool of herself, hopping up and down on one foot, and bellowing forth a loud " Go-Boom ! " every time she did it.

" A fine spectacle for a woman of your age," Claudia observed from the doorway. " I suppose you'd stand on your head if you thought he'd like it."

At the sound of his mother's voice, Michael's laughter shut off like a tap, leaving Bertha high and dry on one foot. He was finished with her. Without a trace of mirth on his round, hypocritical face, he heaved himself aloft by the bars of the crib, picked up his rattle, and threw it on the floor with business-like intention. Bertha picked it up, like an idiot, and returned it to him. Then she gave one more hop and one more go-boom, only to be rewarded by a sphinx-like stare. " Oh, dear," she said sadly. " I wanted him to keep on laughing until Mr. David came——"

" And you'd have fallen dead of heart-trouble—he's on the phone. Bertha, don't keep picking up that rattle, can't you see that child is making a monkey of you ? "

Bertha saw. She retrieved the rattle for the last time and put it on the bureau. " So," she said, " if that is the case, it is time to go to sleep."

Michael read the handwriting on the wall. He wrinkled his nose and showed the little new kernels of his teeth in a propitiating and wholly spurious smile, but Bertha was the business-like one this time, with not a go-boom in sight. Before he knew what was happening, he found himself on the flat of his back, pinned firmly beneath the covers by a deft strong twist of Bertha's competent hands. He burst out into a howl of indignation.

" He's all yours, Bertha," said Claudia pleasantly. " You asked for it."

Michael's wails followed her to the bathroom door. She

found it locked, and jiggled the knob in fury. " Matthew ! Open at once ! "

She heard him take his time about it. " I was only brushing my teeth," he announced grievedly.

" I don't care what you were doing, Daddy told you never, never, never to lock the door."

" He does it."

" You do not happen to be your father—and anyway, he doesn't."

" Well, Bertha does."

" That's a different thing."

" Why is it different ? "

" Because Bertha's a big girl. Which is beside the question. If you ever lock that door again, Matthew, you're going to get the biggest punishment of your life, and I mean it, I mean it absolutely, and I'm not joking."

He was intrigued by the reiteration. " What kind of a punishment ? " he enquired with interest.

She knew that anything she hit upon would fall short of his ideas. " Never mind what," she evaded. " Just take my word for it. It'll be more than you bargained for."

Then David appeared, like Shakespeare, out of nowhere, and because of the locality of the argument, he drew his own conclusions, and administered a sound paddling across Matthew's rear. " David, please ! " Claudia protested.

Matthew hadn't been certain up to this point whether the spanking was in fun, but if his mother saw fit to intercede on his behalf, he decided that it must be in earnest. " You hurt ! " he shouted in belated outrage.

" Good," said David.

" That was a mighty stupid thing to do," Claudia muttered under her breath.

" Don't be silly, I was careful," David assured her.

" You were not careful ! " Matthew whimpered. " Look how red I am and it stings ! "

" Oh, hush," Claudia shut him up heartlessly. " I'm talking to Daddy. David, I'm serious, you've got to develop a little discipline and not exert yourself like that."

" Yes, Mamma," he said meekly. " I'm sorry, Mamma. My hand slipped."

Matthew looked affronted. " You were fooling," he discovered, too late to save face or its equivalent.

" Next time I won't be," David warned him. " Put the cover back on the toothpaste, slob, or I'll make you eat it."

He was in high spirits. Talking to John had cheered him up, it had brought his old world close again and taken away that desolate sense of isolation. " Isn't the telephone a wonderful thing," Claudia exulted. " I'll never understand how it works, but it's wonderful. What did John have to say ? "

" He's landed a new contract. We'll have a lot of details to go over. I hope he can make it up here during Christmas week. That is, If I'm still here."

" Where do you expect to be ? Do tell."

He seemed surprised. " Home, of course. Christmas is almost two months off, and we've already been here for a month. Dr. Morrisson said about three months in all, so count it out for yourself."

She knew that he was fooling himself, but there was no harm in it, if it made him feel better. " I suppose you realise though," she took the opportunity of impressing upon him anew, " that rough-housing is no short-cut back to the office."

" Stop being an old fuss-box," he said. " Let's go to bed."

" Let's," said Claudia, wondering.

" Why do I have to get undressed before supper every night ! " Matthew threw after them.

" To take your bath, why do you think ? " Claudia threw back at him.

" But why can't I take my bath after supper. I always took my bath after supper at the farm."

Claudia retraced her steps with great purpose. " Now listen to me," she said, " we're going to get this settled once and for all. You took your bath after supper at the farm because you had your own bathroom. You have not got your own bathroom here, you only act as if you had. There is water and time for exactly one bath after supper and Bobby takes it."

Matthew scowled. "I wish I was back at the farm. Why did we have to go and sell it anyway?"

It was ironic to recall that the increasing demands of David's professional life had been one of the not inconsiderable factors in their decision. "Because Mrs. Riddle wanted to buy it," she said, which was the easiest explanation to give him.

His grudge shifted. "I hate Mrs. Riddle."

David wandered back into the scene. "I thought you liked it in the mountains."

Matthew refused to commit himself. Having to get undressed before supper rankled. "Why can't I take my bath in the morning before breakfast?" he persisted.

"A very good reason. Your father happens to take his bath before breakfast," David enlightened him in a tone to end all further discussion.

"Incidentally," Claudia inserted, *sotto voce*, "I hope dear father appreciates that the schedule has been worked out to give him the maximum of privacy and hot water. It's quite a system, unless you haven't noticed. The baby gets bathed after breakfast, and Bertha takes her bath late at night before she goes to bed."

"Where does the system let you in?"

"Oh, I don't bother about me," she returned cheerfully. "I catch as catch can." Privately, she thought it was a lucky thing that she wasn't the sort of woman who made a big production of bathing. A bath, in her secret estimation, was an over-rated and excessively boring procedure, and the faster she could pop in and out of a tub the better it suited her. To be perfectly frank, even if she had to skip a day—or in a pinch, two days—it didn't bother her at all, nor anyone else, fortunately. However, it was wiser not to air this sentiment in front of Matthew who would doubtless find in it an immediate solution to his own problem. "Now good night, dear, be a good boy," she dismissed him with a slightly too-loving smile.

"Good night," he said, and trailed them into the bedroom, where Bertha had turned down Claudia's bed, and laid her night-gown and robe across the foot-board. "Why don't you and Daddy sleep together any more?" he asked.

She searched for an answer that would not tempt his mind to further questions. "It's too cold for me to sleep on the porch," she got around it neatly. "Go let Bluff in."

"And let the cat out," David added, to give him more to do.

Reluctantly, Matthew departed. It took him a little while, and a large scratch across his wrist, to discover that Shakespeare had already been out, and didn't want to go out again. By the time he ambled back to the bedroom, he was preoccupied with more urgent matters. "I hate iodine. Could I have a tangerine?"

"You could," Claudia granted generously, "if we had any, but we haven't."

"Then can I play my radio?"

"No," said David.

"Why can't I?"

"Because," said Claudia.

"But I want to."

"Enough's enough," said David. "March."

"My hand hurts."

"It'll stop," said Claudia. She gave him an ungentle shove. "Not another word out of you. Now march!"

FOUR

SHE FELT SORRY for Matthew's teacher, but the house had a heavenly quiet from Monday on. "I miss him like a toothache," she told David, as she sat with him on the porch.

"I really do miss Bobby," David said. "He's getting to be a lot of company. This is the time I ought to be taking him out shooting and fishing and all the rest of it."

"You sound the image of a book." She changed the subject quickly. "Matthew has a great deal of character, you have to say that for him."

"It's not all good, either," David commented.

"He'll grow out of it," she defended. "I think he's going to amount to something some day."

"Provided he grows out of it enough. I think Bobby has the makings of a fine surgeon. I watched him when Shakespeare caught his paw in the door the other day. He could do anything with that cat."

"Yes, I noticed. And he'd have clawed Matthew to bits. You always wanted to be a doctor, didn't you?"

"It was a close toss-up."

"Lucky for me you chose architecture instead. A doctor's wife hasn't an easy life."

"I don't notice that you picked yourself a bed of roses, exactly."

"And what's so hard about a winter's vacation in the Adirondacks? I'll get fat as a pig, with all this air mixed in with Bertha's cooking."

"That," said David, "is something I would like to see."

"I bet you'll have gained a couple of pounds too, by the time you go to Dr. Geiger's," she said, wishing it more than she let on.

"I weigh plenty. I weigh exactly what I ought to for my age and height."

" That may be, but he wants you to gain about ten pounds, just for spare."

" That's very nice of him," said David. " But it happens to be my waist-line."

As if on cue, Bertha came out with a glass of milk.

" Now don't be difficult," Claudia forestalled him. " Drink it, and no back-talk."

He drank it, but not without a little back-talk on the side. " There's an egg in it," he said, eyeing it with distrust.

" An egg ? " Bertha repeated innocently.

" Yes, an egg. You heard me the first time."

" Well, supposing," Claudia made a clean breast of it. " An egg isn't poison."

Anyone would have thought it was, the way he carried on, going through the same shivers as Bobby with calves' liver. " This once," he laid down the law, " and never again. I'll feel stuffed all day."

" Then feel stuffed," Claudia begged him, " for my sake. I want Dr. Geiger to say, ' Young man, your improvement is nothing short of miraculous. I wish all my patients were in a position to have their families with them.' "

" The hell with Dr. Geiger," said David.

He said it, but underneath he must have been as nervous as she was about this first check-up, because for a full week before the examination, he showed definite signs of behaving himself. True, he drew the line at egg-nogs, but he rested punctiliously between two and four, and kept an accurate chart of his temperature three times a day, noting smugly that he was levelling off to a uniform swing between ninety-seven-six in the morning and ninety-eight-eight or nine in the evening. Once in a while, it was actually ninety-nine, but Claudia didn't make an issue of the extra fraction of a point. " I'll bet you ten to one," he proclaimed with such bravado that it was easy to see where Matthew got it from, " that I'll be out of this place by the first of the year."

She couldn't bring herself to destroy his hopes, although

she knew, from those few weeks in the boarding-house, that one swallow did not make a summer, any more than a single negative report meant a cure. And yet it was always in the back of her mind that a miracle could happen. Before they left New York, Nancy Riddle had told them about a young musician who returned to his job after two months, and the last Nancy had heard of him, he was working hard, and feeling fine. "It just goes to show," Nancy had contended, "that each person is different, no matter what the doctors say. Take me, for instance. I never ran more than a half a degree temperature the whole time I was away, and I was flat on my back for better than a year."

Claudia remembered feeling very cheered, and then suddenly very uncheered by the whole conversation. Looking back on it now, however, she was perfectly willing to make a deal half-way between the young musician's extraordinary come-back and Nancy's slow but sure recovery. It was still too soon to tell whether the young musician was heading for a flare-up, but Nancy never had a sick day during all the years they'd known her. Neither of them had dreamed that she'd ever been ill until she told them about it after she'd heard about David. It was hard to believe, with all her energy and bounce. She was always in and out of something or other. That was why she bought the farm, she didn't have enough acreage on her own place to run beef-cattle as well as Jerseys. Not that she knew a great deal about either, but she had lots of money and could afford to farm. Claudia liked to think of her, with her well-meant tactlessness and abounding health, striding across their old fields and scrambling over fences. No matter if she didn't know a good cow from a bad one, she was an example of someone who had got well, and stayed well. Nancy was a good person to bring up every so often just as an encouragement.

Oddly enough, they got a post card from her the very day of the appointment with Dr. Geiger. It was a plain penny post card, written in Nancy's middle-aged up-hill scrawl, and post-marked Texas. "Switching to Herefords," she wrote. "Just bought some handsome breeding stock. Hope you can see them before too long. Affec'ly, Nancy R."

"See ? " Claudia gloated.

"See what," said David sourly.

"Texas and everything."

"She's a jack-ass," said David. "Next thing she'll be switching to goats." Still, although he wouldn't admit it, the penny post card was a heartening omen, coming when it did, and Claudia noticed that he stuck it in his bureau drawer when he got dressed, instead of throwing it away.

It was the first time that he'd put on a starched white shirt since they'd taken the cottage—it was the first time that he'd set foot off the porch. "I feel like a human being again," he said, as he set his hat at a rakish angle.

"Oh, you look much better than a human being," Claudia assured him.

The taxi driver asked them if they wanted to take the short cut to town through the Sanatorium grounds, and they said they did. "I was a patient here twenty-three years ago," he offered between wheezes. "They didn't have no chapel, then, and no post office. It was nothing but a bunch of little cottages and a main house about half the size of the one they got now."

"It's certainly developed into a beautiful place," said David.

Her heart misgave her. "Are you sorry you didn't come here instead ? "

"No, I'm not sorry I didn't come here instead," he mimicked, squeezing her knee.

She squeezed back. "The cottages are awfully attractive," she acknowledged. "In a minute we'll pass the new work-shop. You could do some work there if you ever wanted to, they let outsiders come in."

"How do you know ? "

" Another taxi-cab driver told me, when I took the children to school to be enrolled. . . . David, look at that snow-covered mountain looming up behind the infirmary, isn't it breath - taking with those long purple shadows ? "

" Very handsome. But I like our mountain from the porch better."

" Don't go falling in love with a mountain, I couldn't compete." She meant it more than she cared to admit, and hurried on to talk about something else. " I wonder," she said, " why the grounds look so deserted, I don't see a soul."

" Two-to-four," said David.

" Of course. Now that I look, I can see the tops of people's heads on the porches." Her eye caught the solitary figure of a woman, going up the steps of the Administration Building. She sat forward, with a little cry of surprise.

" What's the matter ? " David asked.

" That woman—I thought I knew her, but I guess I couldn't have, we don't know anybody here." She turned back to peer out of the rear window, but the woman had vanished.

" Who'd you think it was ? "

" Nobody in particular. I mean, it all happened too fast, I only caught a glimpse of her back. She looked so familiar, though, like someone out of a dream that happened a long time ago."

" Don't tell me you're getting metaphysical like Julia."

" Julia's not metaphysical any longer, she's just sad. Besides, that woman was no spirit, she was wearing a beaver coat."

" Who do you know with a beaver coat ? " David joked.
" Me."

" Some day I'll buy you a mink. When I get that job in Iceland."

" Oh, thank you darling, thank you. What's the matter with me anyway, that I don't like furs or jewellery ? "

"Something pretty serious. You're lacking in all the usual female instincts."

"Except one or two," she amended demurely. "Are you complaining?"

"No, I'm not complaining," he said.

They were making small talk, and not very bright small talk, but suddenly she couldn't any longer. "Oh, darling," she whispered. "You don't know what you mean to me."

"Hey," he said, "your hands are like ice, stop being nervous."

"I'm not nervous," she lied. "I'm just excited. We'll phone John and Candy tonight. Hartley, too."

"What makes you think everybody's so interested?"

"They are. You know they are. We're lucky. It's wonderful to have even one person who cares what happens to you."

"It is," he conceded. He couldn't hide the fact that this first examination seemed suddenly the most important thing in their lives, as if their very happiness and future depended upon Dr. Geiger's findings. She forgot about the figure of the woman, although for the moment it had been tantalising not to be able to harness the impression into memory.

Half-way into town, they were held up by a long funeral procession. David gave a one-sided grin. "Lots of people die in New York, too," he said.

"More," Claudia rallied faintly.

They didn't talk again until they reached Dr. Geiger's square white house, set firmly on a tidy corner plot. There was a side door that said "Surgery." Claudia knew that for as long as she lived, she would never forget the black-and-whiteness of that sign.

The waiting-room was empty when they walked in. It was impersonal with new maple and blue linoleum—and almost pretty. The nurse said, "Just have a seat. Doctor hasn't come in yet from his afternoon calls."

They sat together on a stiff settee. "It's nice to think

that Dr. Geiger was a patient himself not long ago, and he doesn't have to rest from two to four any more," Claudia remarked in an undertone.

"What makes you think he's not resting at home on the sly," said David dryly.

"The nurse isn't, and she was ill, too."

"How do you know?"

"Almost everybody is—the gas-meter man, Bobby's maths-teacher, even the butcher."

"What do you do, go around asking people?"

"No, they tell you—like our taxi driver. I hear someone moving around the surgery," she broke off, "I think he's come in."

An instant later the door opened, and Dr. Geiger beckoned David from the threshold. Claudia rose to follow, but Dr. Geiger stopped her with a gesture of his hand. "If you please, Mrs. Naughton, I prefer to see your husband alone."

David threw her a triumphant smirk. "That'll learn you," he said under his breath.

She returned the smirk, but inwardly she was chafing. An active dislike of Dr. Geiger moiled within her. A physician should exude warmth and understanding and reassurance, but instead he was impersonal to the point of being ruthless. He didn't even look like a doctor, much less act like one, for he was as undistinguished as Watkins, with sparse brown hair and little if any overtones to his bloodless voice. She strained to hear some murmur of conversation behind the closed door, but not a sound came through. There was nothing to do but wait out the suspense, and count the minutes until the door finally opened again.

She was scarcely aware that another patient had come in until a voice beside her made her look up. "I said I hadn't seen you here before."

"Oh, I'm sorry. I didn't hear you." She found herself meeting the friendly smile of a pleasantly middle-aged woman who was thumbing through the magazines on the

3

centre table. Claudia forced herself to smile back. " No, this is only the second time I've been to Dr. Geiger's surgery."

The woman laughed. " This is about my hundred and second, I guess." She picked up an uncompromising treatise on hygiene and sat down with it unopened on her lap. " Are you from New York ? "

" Yes. How did you know ? "

" I'm pretty good at spotting people. I work in the bank here, and that gives me a lot of practice. I'm from Indiana, myself."

" Oh," said Claudia, and added politely, " I've never been there."

" I haven't been back there either for a couple of years," the woman forgave her readily. " I'm planning to go home for a visit this Christmas, though."

" That's nice," said Claudia. She felt a twinge of envy. " It must be wonderful to be able to go to work every day."

" My goodness but it certainly is," the woman eagerly agreed. " Sometimes I swear I can't believe I'm the same person who came here five years ago next April. I was too sick to even get in the Sanatorium. Lordy, I wasn't even allowed to so much as knit for the first six months."

" Really ? " Claudia breathed. (This was something to tell David.)

" So don't you fret, my dear. Dr. Geiger's a perfectly marvellous doctor. By far the best in town if you want my candid opinion."

" That's what we were told," said Claudia doubtfully.

" Honestly, I just think he's God Himself." the woman rushed on, with the same tremble in her voice that Julia used to have when she spoke of her Medium. " If he told me to jump out of the window, I wouldn't stop to ask why, I'd just go ahead and do it, and know that he meant it for my best good. All his patients feel that way about him, I'm not the only one."

"I wonder if I'll ever get to feel that way about him," Claudia murmured, incredulously.

"You will. Just put yourself in his hands, and he'll have you fat and rosy in no time."

It was on the tip of Claudia's tongue to explain that she didn't have to be fat and rosy because she wasn't ill, but it seemed in bad taste to flaunt a sound body at this point. "Would you excuse me," she said hastily, "I have to make a phone call—"

The nurse's desk was tucked into the small oblong of hall, and there was a telephone on it. "Will I be bothering you, Miss Reynolds?"

Miss Reynolds kept on filing some cards. "No, go ahead, it's all right."

Claudia dialled the number. It was funny to dial a number that she'd never used before, and call it home. Bobby answered, with a heated argument in the background. "Matthew, quit that! You know Mother doesn't like children to answer telephones!"

"And what do you think you are?" Claudia opened up in lieu of a "hello." "Where's Bertha?"

"She said to answer her hands were in dough. Matthew's a pain in the neck. Where are you, Bertha told us you went to the village."

"We'll be home soon. How was school?"

"Pretty good. Is Dad at the doctor's getting examined?"

Claudia hesitated. Bobby was sentient to a degree that sometimes startled her. She couldn't tell him an untruth any more than she could lie to David. "Yes," she said, "but everything's fine, I'm sure. (Would she ever be strong enough not to touch wood.) Good-bye, darling, I just wanted to see if you and Matthew got home from school all right—"

"Don't ring off, Bertha's here now, she wants to talk to you. . . ."

Bertha said, cautiously, "You don't know anything yet?"

"No, he's still in with the doctor. If it doesn't get too

late, he wants to stop at the barber's, he needs a hair-cut."

" Don't hurry back, everything is fine. The boys had a little something to eat when they got home from school, and now they will go out on their sleds for an hour. And don't worry, I will keep a good eye on them out the window."

Claudia didn't know how Bertha's good eye out the window could keep them from crashing into a tree, but she refrained from saying so.

" Oh, and also you had company as soon as you left," Bertha remembered in a rush.

" Company—who ? "

" Mr. Dexter."

" Oh, yes, he said he'd stop in some time. I'm sorry we missed him."

" He said to tell you he was sorry too and he will try to stop off on his way back again from Lake Placid. I showed him the baby. He thinks he is more beautiful even than your other babies were. He is a lovely man, Mr. Dexter."

" Just because he admired your baby, he's lovely."

" No, no," Bertha protested. " I always liked Mr. Dexter."

This was no time to discuss the merits of Philip Dexter. " Bertha, I'm holding up the doctor's calls," Claudia interrupted. " I have to ring off now."

She was hanging up the receiver as Miss Reynolds ushered in another patient. " *Good* afternoon," she said brightly.

" Hello dearie, how's tricks ? "

" Fair to middling," said Miss Reynolds. " How are things with you, Mrs. Jenkins ? "

Claudia turned. Mrs. Jenkins recognised her at the same instant. " Well, look who's here ! " she cried voluminously. " If this isn't a surprise, bumping into you like this ! "

" I'm awfully glad to see you—" Claudia exclaimed, and

the surprise to her was, that she meant it. "I didn't expect to bump into you here, either."

"Oh, I drop in every month or so for a check-up," said Mrs. Jenkins, unwinding one of last year's Christmas presents from around her neck. "You know what I told you, nobody's ever cured of this thing," she added blithely. "Arrested, maybe, but not cured." She folded the bright scarf and stuck it in the sleeve of her shaggy coat. "How's Mr. Naughton doing?"

"Very well. At least I hope Dr. Geiger's going to think so."

Mrs. Jenkins patted Claudia's shoulder. "If he doesn't, God forbid—I mean, if your little cottage doesn't work out right, always remember that I'll turn myself upside down to make room for you if you ever want to come back. We missed you when you left. You weren't with us long, but we all said after you left how much we missed you."

"I missed you too," Claudia returned, finding to her increasing surprise, that this also was true. Mrs. Jenkins and all the people in the boarding-house suddenly became old friends, friends who shared what outsiders could not possibly share. They seemed closer, all at once, than Julia, or Phil Dexter, or even, in a way, than Candy and John. "How's Mr. Barwell?" she asked. "Is he up and around again?"

"Oh, sure," said Mrs. Jenkins. "He's not back on exercise yet, but he's down to his meals every day, bright as a daisy, making jokes the same as always. He's a caution. He certainly is a caution, that man."

Claudia wasn't sure what a "caution" really was, but there was a wealth of affection in Mrs. Jenkins' voice every time she spoke of Mr. Barwell. Mr. Barwell, with his many hæmorrhages and abounding spirits, was something of a prize boarder. "He'll just be tickled to death when I tell him I saw you," Mrs. Jenkins went on. "They all will, for that matter." She peered into the waiting-room. "Well, sure that's Mary Brooks! I've been saying to myself, is that Mary Brooks without my eyeglasses?"

"I was waiting for you to get around to seeing me," said Mary Brooks, putting away her magazine. "Come on in, sit down, make yourself at home."

Mrs. Jenkins sat down in a slim maple chair that creaked beneath her weight. "If this isn't a coincidence," she said. "Would you believe I went to the bank a little while ago to deposit some cheques and I didn't see you around and I said to myself, 'I only hope Mary isn't cutting up shinanegans of some sort.'"

"Look, don't you wish anything on me," Mary returned with a nervous laugh, and a tiny cough. "I've been wonderful, cross my fingers, except for a little bit of a feeling of feeling fagged, so I thought I'd find out if it meant anything. You know I'm planning to go home for a visit over the holidays and the last thing I want is a flare-up."

"I don't blame you," said Mrs. Jenkins. "You're smart, remember the old saying, a stitch in time—"

Claudia's heart sank. So even Mary Brooks, who worked all day at the bank, was living in the shadow of an eternal fear, no different than Mrs. Jenkins. She lingered at the desk, held back from joining them by a sense that her good health was an intrusion upon their intimacy. "I'd like to pay for my phone call," she said.

"There's no charge on local calls," Miss Reynolds told her.

"Thank you." She was conscious once more of her clammy hands, and a heavy pulse beating up into her throat and against her ear-drums. She looked at her watch. David had been with Dr. Geiger almost half an hour. Why was it taking so long just to weigh him and go over his chest with a stethoscope?

"Does a routine check-up always take this much time?" she asked.

"It depends," Miss Reynolds replied, riffling through a pile of notes. "Sometimes they're in and out before you know it, and then again it's just as likely to be half an hour or more. It all depends."

Claudia lacked the courage to find out what it depended

upon. She dropped into a chair beside the desk. "I think I'll wait out here, if you don't mind."

Miss Reynolds glanced up. "You look sort of white," she noticed. "Don't you feel well?"

"I'm all right, it's just that it's very warm in here."

"That's funny, I thought it was cold." Miss Reynolds rose to squint at a thermometer on the wall. "I was right," she discovered with a trace of relief, "it's only sixty-eight. For a minute I thought I was running a fever, I was so chilly. I hope you're not running a fever."

"No, I'm all right," Claudia insisted.

From the waiting-room, she could hear, without listening, the low buzz of talk going on between Mrs. Jenkins and Mary Brooks. "I don't like it when it hits them that young," Mary was saying. "It's so treacherous, you can't tell which way it's going to jump."

Mrs. Jenkins gave a small crackle of amusement. "Don't waste your sympathy, she's not the patient. Not that I don't feel sorry for her anyway," she amended soberly. "It's no joke to have the worry of a sick husband and three children."

It dawned on Claudia that it was herself they were talking about. A sick husband and three children. It was like seeing her image, remote and unfamiliar, at the far end of a telescope. It seemed such a little while ago that she was a silly young bride, yet what a richness of experience had crept into the years between. She wondered toward what end life was shaping her so quickly. Or was it any different, in its sum total, than the living and loving of any human soul? "It only seems different because it's me," she told herself philosophically, "so don't get filled up with self-pity."

"Here's your husband now," Miss Reynolds broke into her thoughts.

There was David, practically at her shoulder. He'd come through the door that led from the office into the hall, and already Mary Brooks was dropping her purse and her gloves all over the waiting-room floor in her haste to answer

Dr. Geiger's beckoning nod. " I'll be with you shortly, Mrs. Jenkins," he called out. " I'm a little behind schedule this afternoon."

" I'm in no hurry, Doctor," Mrs. Jenkins called back cheerfully.

" Oh Lord, let's get out of here," David muttered. " Mrs. Jenkins is the last person I feel like talking to—"

He had hung his hat and coat on a rack near the doorway, and it was but an ignominious step out to the vestibule. " But I wanted to see Dr. Geiger ! " Claudia protested.

" There's nothing to see him about," said David shortly. " Besides, if he'd wanted to talk to you, he'd have said so."

She glanced at his face apprehensively. It was set and grim. " Tell me—" she whispered. " What happened ? "

They were already on the sidewalk, looking up and down the street for a taxi. " I'm going to get that haircut," he decided abruptly. " Nothing happened. What would happen ? I'm all right—it's only a block or two to the barber shop, come on."

She followed him blindly. " David, if you don't tell me what Dr. Geiger said, I'm going to stand stock-still where I am and open my mouth and scream."

" I told you, there's nothing to tell. He said it's too soon, and anything he might say would be premature. The rales are clearing up but that doesn't necessarily mean anything. Chart looked good, but that doesn't mean anything either. Of course it's better than the other way around, but—it's too soon to say."

It wasn't hard to get the flavour of Dr. Geiger's attitude from the bitter overtones of David's voice. There was one thing he didn't tell her though, and she was afraid to ask.

" But why did he keep you so long if that's all he said ? " she led up to it.

" He was on the phone most of the time."

" While I sat outside and stewed my head off ! "

" Serves you right. Next time stay home."

" What else did he say ? "

" Nothing. Except that the bastard didn't put me on exercise, if that's what you're driving at. I'll get back to work in a couple of years at this dandy rate."

" Oh," said Claudia. " Any special reason that he didn't ? "

" None that I could see. Just to continue as is."

" At least, he doesn't want you to go back to the boarding-house, and us to go back to New York, that's one thing I'm grateful for."

" Don't be an ass," said David. " Even if he did, do you think I would ? He's not God, you know."

" I know he's not God, but if you're not on exercise yet, do you think you should be walking to the barber shop ? " she suggested in a small voice.

" No, I'll have the barber shop walk to me."

" Don't be an ass," said Claudia.

Telling each other not to be an ass was better than admitting the heavy disappointment in both their hearts. She wished she hadn't suggested telephoning John and Candy and Hartley. What little they had to report could as easily be written on a penny post card.

FIVE

THERE WAS NO GETTING away from it, her mattress was a beast, and the longer she slept on it the worse it got, and now she was waking up every morning with a pain in her back. Fortunately, the mattress on the porch seemed to be quite good, and the children's mattresses, having been bought new, were passable, except that they were made of cotton and after many weeks of hard use, were beginning to show signs of getting lumpy. " Never mind," said Bertha, " they will last for as long as we need them, and they are better than what they slept on at camp last summer."

Claudia hated to think what Bertha's mattress must be like because she was the soul of generosity, and yet she'd never offered to change with anybody. One thing was certain, though, it couldn't compete with Claudia's, which, in addition to being everything bad that a mattress could be and still be called a mattress, had a hollow spot in the middle completely surrounded by broken springs. Bertha didn't know it, of course, since you couldn't see the hollow when you made the bed, only when you slept in it. The mattress on the other twin bed was almost worse. It had no springs at all, and was flat as a pancake and hard as a rock. " Mr. David is lucky he sleeps on the porch," Bertha puffed one morning, when in a burst of sheer, perverse energy, she decided to turn it. " It almost broke my wrist, it is so heavy."

" Don't look to me for sympathy," Claudia told her heartlessly. " It's positively indecent to go round turning mattresses that are never slept on."

" I had a reason," Bertha confessed. " I was planning how we could put Miss Candy and Mr. John up when they come."

" We can't," said Claudia. " They'll have to sleep at the hotel in the village."

" Everything is crowded in the village, the butcher was telling me how the hotel was turning people away."

" Bertha, the butcher told me the same thing, but that was during Christmas, when everyone had friends and relatives visiting them. The holidays are over now, there'll be plenty of room."

Bertha would not admit defeat. Her continental hospitality stood up on its hind legs. " When people travel all the way from New York, and will only be here a few days, it is not right to make them go to a hotel," she maintained.

" What makes you think they won't be more comfortable in a hotel instead of this menagerie ? "

" They are not coming for comfort. They are coming to be with you and Mr. David."

" Well it might be too much excitement for Mr. David if they stay here," Claudia revealed her chief reason against it. " He'll be talking business from morning until night."

" He will do that anyway," said Bertha, " but maybe he will do it not so much if Mr. John has more time to spend with him."

" Well, maybe," Claudia conceded. " But, Bertha, you big-hearted, half-witted woman, we haven't got a spare inch in this cottage, we can hardly fit ourselves into it, much less two extra, one pregnant."

" Miss Candy is very little pregnant. And no matter how small a house is, there is always room for people you love and who love you."

" You sound positively biblical," said Claudia. " Would your saintly spirit tell me how we can manage with one tiny bathroom ? "

" It is not for ever," said Bertha largely.

" No, but it might seem like for ever at moments."

" There are always ways," Bertha persisted stubbornly, and refused to divulge what alternate solutions she had in mind. " It is time enough to meet trouble when it comes," she said. " And as for eating, we can move two tables together in the living-room."

" Eating," said Claudia, " is my least worry. What about sleeping ? "

" That is simple. Your room has two beds, even if one mattress does not happen to be so good."

" That's what you think."

" Miss Candy can take yours, with the springs in it."

" The good one," Claudia amplified.

" They will know how to arrange it," said Bertha delicately.

" Then they're better men than I am," said Claudia. " And now that you've laid your plans in such a wily manner, where do I sleep, please ? "

" In Bobby's bed."

" And Bobby ? "

" That is also simple. On a little folding cot I found in the attic. We can put it in the living-room."

" I'll take the little folding cot," said Claudia firmly.

" No, no ! " cried Bertha.

" Yes, yes ! I'd rather take it than sleep in the same room with Matthew."

" But it is not a good mattress on the cot ! "

" Ha ! " said Claudia.

" I would say you should use my bed, and I would sleep in the living-room," Bertha mentioned as an afterthought, " but the baby might disturb you."

" Don't make excuses," said Claudia. " I'm on to you. You have the best bed in the house, and you don't want anyone to know it for fear you'll lose it."

" That is it," said Bertha, with a poker face. " So, it is all decided."

" It's not decided. Do you realise how much extra work you're asking for ? Three meals a day for eight people ? "

" I would rather cook for eight people than for one person," said Bertha.

" You have a fresh answer for everything," Claudia told her, " but I'm not going to stand by and let you kill yourself."

Bertha not only had an answer for everything, but she went about getting her own way by surrounding herself with allies.

" Yippee ! " Claudia overheard Matthew shout between tangerines that very same day after school.

" Boy," said Bobby, " that's swell."

" Yippee, what, and swell what ? " she demanded suspiciously from the doorway. " Don't gulp that milk so fast, Bobby."

" I'm thirsty. Bertha says Candy and Uncle John are going to live here when they come."

Bertha pretended to be busy straightening the grocery cupboard. " Your back," Claudia remarked coldly, " looks guilty as hell."

" ' Hell ' is a bad word," Matthew observed virtuously.

" Shut up," said Bobby. " I don't mind sleeping in the parlour on a cot. I'd rather do it than sleep with Matthew."

" I got in ahead of you on that," said Claudia. " And as I'm older than you are, I have first choice." She tweaked Matthew's ear to make him think she was joking, but she needn't have had any qualms about it, he was very pleased at being the object of discussion.

Bertha must have got in first with David, too, because that night at supper he said, " We're quite a crowd as we are, we'll have to fit Candy and John in with a shoe-horn." Nevertheless, he looked as pleased as the children at the prospect. Except that Matthew, as usual, picked a delayed flaw in the situation. " Why didn't they come for Christmas, the way they promised ? " he demanded in brooding retrospect.

" You got your presents, didn't you ? " Bobby remarked.

" Nice talk," said David, hiding a grin in his soup.

" It's what Matthew was thinking," Bobby insisted. " He thinks he might have got a lot more presents if they didn't have to send them by mail. I know the little stinker."

" Bobby ! " Claudia reproved him in earnest. " I simply loathe that word ! "

" Besides which, he does not," Bertha bridled from the direction of the stove.

" It doesn't mean he smells," Bobby explained impatiently.

" Then you should not say it," said Bertha.

" He always calls me bad things." Matthew looked as if butter wouldn't melt in his mouth. " Why didn't they come for Christmas ? "

" You were told why," said David. " This ceases to be funny."

" But I forget again."

" Uncle John's mother got sick, you dope," Bobby hissed at him.

" Did she die ? " he asked with interest.

" I don't think so," said Bobby, wondering whether he too, might have missed something. " Did she, Mother ? "

" No," said Claudia shortly. " She did not."

It occurred to her, with increasingly concrete evidence, that Mrs. Payne's attacks of illness were invariably spaced in exact relation to her son's activities. She had, in fact, become suddenly and alarmingly indisposed on John's wedding day, a year ago this very month, and she hadn't regained her strength since. It worried John quite a bit. " Mother's always been so well and so active," he said. " I can't understand what's happened to her all at once."

Claudia had a fair idea of what had happened to Mrs. Payne all at once, but it was hardly the sort of thing that you could say to a devoted son, and better left unsaid to a not so devoted daughter-in-law. " If I ever get that way, shoot me," she invited David, when John had had to call off their Christmas visit at the last moment.

" With pleasure," David had accepted.

In the long run, however, the postponement worked out for the best, because Dr. Geiger had continued to keep David off exercise in spite of his gaining two and a half pounds over a period of as many months. " Do you know what I think," Claudia hazarded, with double intent, " I think he knows you cheat anyway."

" What do you mean I cheat anyway ? " David demanded belligerently. " I'm glued to that blasted chair from morning until night."

" Except when you're not. Darling, there are so many little things you do around the house, from taking Bluff out on the sly, to fixing a tap, also on the sly, that it all adds up to more than a fifteen-minute walk. Dr. Geiger knows that. He's no fool. It's a marvel to me that you've gained any weight at all, the way you take advantage."

" What did you expect would happen to all the eggs and cream you and Bertha slip into one scrambled egg every morning ?—on the sly, I might add."

" Just what did happen," she gloated. " They're stuck to your ribs exactly where they belong."

They weren't stuck very hard, though, because, like a Christmas present in reverse, and for no good reason, two of the precious pounds vanished into thin air. David pretended to be pleased that he was getting his figure back (as if those few ounces had made him portly), but secretly he was as fearful as Claudia that it would mean another couple of months of complete inactivity.

And then, when they least expected it, it happened. Dr. Geiger examined David early in January, and made no issue whatsoever of the loss of weight. As usual, he pumped David's hand in terse dismissal, and remarked from the threshold—so that Claudia could hear it from the waiting-room, " By the way, begin exercising twice a day. That means you can take a fifteen-minute walk morning and afternoon, and always choose a road that's downhill on the way back."

They couldn't believe their ears. They left the office, floating on air, with David forgetting all about his customary hair-cut. " To look at your face," he poked fun at her as they drove home in the taxi, " you'd think someone had left you a million dollars."

" What's a million dollars next to this ? I feel as if God had come down and kissed me on both cheeks."

" You wouldn't mean Dr. Geiger, by any chance ? "

" If anyone had ever told me I'd ever get to love that man, I'd have told them they were crazy."

" He's not a bad sort," David admitted. " He had the good sense to realise that the weight I put on was just so much blubber."

" Are you sure he saw it on the chart ? I mean that you lost most of it ? "

" He looked straight at it. I thought, ' This cooks my goose.' "

" You must have fallen off your feet when he said, ' Begin on fifteen minutes twice a day '—I know I did ! "

" Except that you were sitting down."

" Do you think he waited until he got to the door, so that I could hear ? Could he be so human after all ? "

" He's a good sort," David repeated.

She sighed deeply. " I don't think I've ever been so happy in my life——"

" It doesn't take much to make you happy, I must say."

" This is a lot," she said simply.

He pressed her hand. " One thing about it, I'm glad I'll be able to get off the porch a little when John comes."

" So am I. Isn't it perfect the way his mother messed things up ? It's so wonderful how everything always works out for the best."

" There's a great fallacy in that kind of thinking," David stopped her short.

" I know. And I've often tried to get to the bottom of it. It really doesn't make sense, because in order to work out for the best for some people, other people are bound to get it in the neck."

" Exactly," said David.

" And then again," she concluded thoughtfully, " maybe they only think they've got it in the neck."

" Exactly," said David again.

She gave him a little shove. " Make up your mind ! "

" Make up your own," he said.

She fully expected the exercise to go to his head, especially with John and Candy coming. " Watch. Give him fifteen minutes and he'll take an hour," she unburdened to Bertha. " We'll have our hands fuller than before."

" I am afraid so," said Bertha.

They were both wrong. Out of a perfectly clear sky, he turned over a new leaf and became a model of good behaviour, and to Claudia's utter amazement, John and Candy's arrival only made him more of a model. It was as if he had disciplined himself to the point where he wasn't even excited over their coming.

They took the night train from New York on the Thursday evening following his visit to Dr. Geiger, and got in the next morning in time for breakfast. It wasn't much different than any other morning, except that Claudia and Bertha hustled to make all the beds instead of letting them air, and there were pancakes and sausages instead of oatmeal and bacon. " You probably won't get out on the porch until away after ten, but that won't hurt for once," Claudia remarked magnanimously, as she bent to light the fire in the living-room fireplace before Candy and John arrived.

" I'll get out on time," he said. " Nothing's going to come between me and my cure-chair."

She had to look at him twice to see whether he was serious. She decided that he was, and suddenly she wished, for his own sake, that this right-about-face might have been put off for another day or two. " I don't really think Dr. Geiger would object if you weren't so conscientious just this one week-end," she suggested tactfully.

" Look," he said, with a new intensity, " I've made up my mind to get well and be out of this place, and the quicker the better."

It was the first time, it occurred to her, that he had admitted he was ill by saying that he wanted to get well. She couldn't help wondering, although it was a contradiction to all that she had asked of him, whether he was going about it in the right way. Now, however, was not the moment or the place to discuss the subtleties and gradations of his emotional behaviour, for Matthew burst into the room with the information that there was a taxi coming down the road. " Why couldn't Bobby and me wait to have breakfast with you ? " he catechised them. " Why did we have to eat already ! "

" For the simple reason," said Claudia, " that the train might not have been on time, which would have made you late for school."

" You don't have to apologise," said David, hurrying to the window. " You gave an order, and that's sufficient."

" Don't be stuffy," she exhorted him. " Move aside a little and let me see out too."

Already the taxi was turning in at the drive, its chains crunching over the hard snow. She rushed to the door. A shaft of thin, clear sun had broken through the winter sky, turning the mountains to a golden white. " Oh, it's going to be a lovely day," she breathed.

" The thermometer read three below zero this morning at seven," David asserted behind her.

" Who cares ! " she hugged his arm in quick contrition. " I'm so excited——"

" You certainly seem to be."

Her hug turned into a shove. " Well, aren't you excited?"

" Sure," he said. " But I'm not turning somersaults."

She knew, without looking at his face, that something had gone dead within him. She couldn't explain it. She didn't know when it happened, or how it happened. The thought flashed through her mind that part of it was having the outside world—his own world—walk in at his door again. And then she thought, in swift loyalty to all of them, " It can't be. It mustn't be."

A moment later, John and Candy were piling out of the taxi on to the porch and everybody was talking at once, with Candy crying, like an idiot, because she was so happy. " Look at me blubbering," she gulped, fishing for John's handkerchief. " I didn't know I missed you as much as I did until now that I see you again ! "

To Matthew, this sounded like sheer nonsense. " We have to catch the bus," he injected, with a bid for immediate attention.

He got his attention. John tossed him in the air with one sweep of his long, thin arms, and Matthew put on a great show of loving it, although he was a little beyond that sort of thing. " Do it again ! " he clamoured. " Daddy never lifts me like that any more, do it again ! "

Bobby grabbed his arm. " Come on, you, we're late."

" You kicked me," Matthew protested. He recovered his dignity by bustling off down the porch steps with immense importance. " Ill see you when I get home ! " he threw back nonchalantly.

" I'll see you when I get home ! " Bobby parroted in a rage. " You dope—— ! "

" No fighting on the road ! " Claudia called after them.

" They look wonderful," Candy exulted. " Bobby's growing like mad, he's getting to be the image of David."

" And what do you think of my baby ? "

They were still on the porch, but Bertha couldn't contain herself another instant, so she came out with Michael plastered to her hip. She had put on his best rompers, and carefully brushed his hair into a soft little tunnel of gold up the middle of his head as if she didn't have enough to do without making extra work for herself. Candy's squeal of joy was ample reward though, and John said, " If we have one half that good I'll be satisfied." Then they both kissed Bertha plumb on the cheek and everybody went inside.

It wasn't until they were unpacking that Claudia had a chance to ask John what he thought of David—they'd talked at great length about the children and the dog and the cat and Bertha and the house, but nothing beyond a cursory discussion of David's vastly improved appearance had entered into the conversation.

"I kept watching my step," John admitted, "after that fool stunt I pulled with Matthew. Bobby had more sense than I did."

"I adore Matthew but I could have pinned his ears back for calling attention to it," Candy blurted out. "Nobody would have noticed, if the little monkey hadn't said anything."

"Matthew gets object-struck," said Claudia. "David's used to it by now, so don't think another thing about it. How do you find him in general?"

"Splendid," said John, with an enthusiasm that left her oddly unsatisfied.

"I can't get over him," Candy marvelled, "you kept writing us that he just wouldn't buckle down to obeying orders, but no sooner did he finish breakfast than he was off to his chair without one bit of argument."

John smiled. "Claudia probably gave him a stiff lecture before we got here."

"No," Claudia denied lightly, "it's quite a recent change in him, I'm just as surprised as you are."

Candy laid a lacy night-gown in an empty bureau drawer. "I should think you'd be terribly relieved."

"I am. That night-gown's awfully thin, you'd better count on sleeping in a pair of John's pyjamas."

"Oh, I'm never cold, it's a shame to waste twin beds on us."

"The other bed is just a spare, you might like to switch," Claudia suggested blandly.

"Oh, don't be silly," said Candy, "once we're asleep, we never budge."

David and I never used to budge either, thought Claudia. Using a single bed was the prerogative, the sweet, everlasting wonder of love, and it made no difference how long you were married. . . .

"You've shocked Claudia," said John. "Look how disapproving she looks."

"I wasn't disapproving, I was envious."

"I could bite my tongue off," Candy wailed.

"Listen, you two," said Claudia sensibly, "stop this business of trying to spare our feelings or your whole visit will be spoiled. When we get back to New York, do you think anyone's going to handle us with kid gloves?"

"Claudia's right," said John. He shrugged into his overcoat, and picked up a bulging brief-case. "I'm off to join my partner in his outside office."

Claudia handed him a woollen cap that belonged to Bobby. "Wear this," she advised, "or you'll freeze your ears off."

"It's not my ears I'm worried about."

"It's his hands," Candy explained. For no good reason, probably because he looked so absurd with his angular face peering out from the fuzzy red wool, they doubled up in groans of helpless laughter, and laughed until the tears rolled down their cheeks.

"Here I go again," Candy dabbed at her eyes. "It must be my condition."

"I can't blame it on my condition," said Claudia. "Let me borrow your handkerchief a minute."

Candy gave a final sniff. "I think it's because you're so wonderful, that's why I can't bear it. I can't even manage little things in my life the way you manage big things."

"I think that you're handling at least one little thing extremely well," Claudia complimented her.

Candy preened, and stood profile for inspection. She looked not an ounce different from those summers at Eastbrook, when she'd come over to the farm in blue jeans, with her hair in a stiff braid behind each ear. Now it hung page-boy fashion, in a honey-coloured frame around her shining face, and instead of blue jeans, she wore with an exceeding gaucherie of grace, no-heeled slippers beneath the longist flare of a wool-plaid skirt.

"Were you ever so huge at three months?" she demanded proudly.

"Never," Claudia told her with a solemn face, knowing that when, in due time, Candy became really huge, she'd be equally convinced that she didn't show at all. " Is John's mother very pleased about the baby ? "

" Frightfully, although she says she won't live to see it." Candy closed her suitcase with a bang. " My, but you were lucky David never had any family but Hartley."

" I know. How is Hartley, anyway ? Do you ever see him ? "

" We were there for dinner last week. He didn't look awfully well. John says he has prostate, which is sort of a pain in the neck, I imagine, but not serious."

" It's serious to Hartley," said Claudia. " What's Julia doing these days ? "

" She's planning to go away on a trip all by herself as soon as Hartley feels better. I think to Tibet. . . . Or could it be Tibet ? "

Claudia weighed it. " It could be. Julia's at that stage."

" I don't get it," said Candy flatly. " How can a woman go away alone if she doesn't have to. I wouldn't even have a soda or go to a movie by myself."

" Neither would I," said Claudia, " but I guess neither one of us has lived that long."

" And I hope to heaven I never do. What are you looking so twinkly about ? "

" Because you remind me so much of me when I was young."

Candy hooted. " Oh, you're so old, I suppose ? "

" Yes, age seems to have crept up on me without my knowing it," Claudia returned flippantly. What she meant was that she found herself understanding things she had never understood before, without knowing why she understood, or how. It was probably as good a definition of age as any, but it was too obscure to explain to Candy, who was so full of youthful passions and contempts. " I discovered a whole batch of grey hairs," she said instead.

Candy gave another hoot. " I don't believe it. Not that you haven't been through enough to turn you grey. Funny, I was talking about your miscarriage on the train last night."

" Didn't you have anything better to talk about ? "

" No, but really, I said to John, if anything happened to this baby, I don't think I could bear it."

" What did he say ? "

" He said, ' You'd bear it, and have another, the same as Claudia had Michael.' "

" I didn't bear it too well," Claudia told her honestly.

Candy leaned forward, and lowered her voice. " Look, I've never breathed this to a soul, but it's stuck in my mind all these years. Tell me it's none of my business if you don't want to talk about it——"

" What is it ? " Claudia asked curiously.

" Well, one day in Eastbrook," Candy began, " about a month or so after you'd lost the baby, I heard Nancy Riddle tell Mother you had a nervous breakdown from the shock, and might have to go to a sanatorium. Mother was wild, and told Nancy off—Nancy always was, and always will be an awful old gossip. But anyway, the word ' sanatorium ' had such a dreadful sound in connection with a normal person like you, I simply died at the thought. It wasn't really true, was it ? "

" It was pretty nearly true," said Claudia slowly. " I hardly ever think of it any more, it's like a bad dream that never really happened. I suppose it wasn't just the miscarriage, I can see that now; it was a combination of a lot of things—the war, and losing my mother—I suppose I didn't want to assume the responsibilities that come with maturity—" She stopped herself from going on. So much had become clear to her with the passing of the years and the settling of the muddy waters of her being, and yet she resisted the temptation to hold forth from her pinnacle of wisdom. Besides, it was fairly obvious that Candy was leading up to her own problems. " Everybody," Claudia summed up in one-syllable words, " goes through things."

Candy caught at the opening. " At least you went through something big that made you a better person. But I let little stupid ignoble things get the best of me. If John wasn't as wonderful and understanding as he is, I could certainly have made a mess of things these last few months."

"Oh come, you're not that bad, a lot of women get temperamental in the beginning of pregnancy."

"Pregnancy might have aggravated it," Candy acknowledged, " but the fact remains that I discovered a streak of jealousy in me that's enough to dish any marriage."

"John's mother?"

"No, that's behind me, we're working through John's mother together. No, I mean just plain ordinary garden-variety jealousy. Of another woman."

Claudia could feel her jaw drop. John and another woman? It wasn't possible. "Candy, no!" she cried aghast.

"Naturally, no," Candy cheerfully agreed. "John was perfectly innocent, it was just something I cooked up in my own mind. I'm ashamed to tell you, it sounds so silly."

"Go ahead," said Claudia. "I won't listen."

"All right. It was this way. John got a new secretary. He didn't want to worry David, so he never even wrote that the old one left. She really was old, too. Anyway, the new one was young and awfully pretty, and well-bred and charming—decayed aristocracy bravely making its way. I didn't see why John shouldn't fall for her. And I suffered, just like a bad movie, I suffered. I hated myself, but I hated her more, and I could have killed John with my bare hands. You don't know what that kind of jealousy can do. John explained that it was just my own insecurity, but that's too nice a name for it. You must be disgusted with me," she broke off. " I wish I hadn't told you, because that kind of jealousy is one thing you'll never be able to understand in a million years. You can't, unless you've gone through it yourself."

"Well? Who says I haven't?"

"You're not that kind of a person."

"I'm not? Maybe I oughtn't to disillusion you, you seem to think I'm so wonderful in all my departments."

"You're pulling my leg. There couldn't have been anyone else with you and David."

"There was. Twice."

Candy's eyes popped. " I don't believe it ! When ? "

" You were only twelve. A high-busted little girl with skinny legs——"

" I was a mess at that age, my glands were all over the place," Candy recalled.

" And you had the measles in a most unpretty fashion, and David asked me to buy you something—' Elizabeth Van Doren's youngster has the measles—' It grew in me, like a poison. Why should he care about another woman's youngster ? "

" My mother—" Candy breathed incredulously.

Claudia nodded. " Your father had just died, and she was very sad and alone and very lovely. I didn't blame David for wanting to put his arms around her."

" But she was older than he was ! "

" Not much. Only thirty. As old as I am now. And wiser and finer than I could ever be. If she knew how I felt, she never told me. Neither did David."

" Surely there wasn't anything to it—there couldn't be ! "

" Of course there wasn't. I cooked it up just like you did."

" And what about the second time, you said there was twice ! "

" Well," said Claudia, " there was part two of the same bad movie. Suddenly, one day, you came home from college, all grown up from that awkward, high-busted little girl into a slim, sweet seventeen——"

A slow red suffused Candy's face. " I fell awfully in love with David that summer on the farm," she confessed. " But I didn't think anyone ever dreamed it."

" I did."

Candy's voice fell to an abashed whisper. " Do you think David knew it ? "

" If he did, he never said so. I was carrying Michael, and I felt so clumsy and unattractive beside you. Oh, how I hated you, like you hated John's secretary, only worse, because I loved you, too. And then Elizabeth died. And almost immediately afterwards, you fell in love with John."

Candy wet her lips. "What was it all for?" she asked softly.

"The way I look at it now," said Claudia, "David was a kind of instrument. He helped Elizabeth to the realisation that love is a stream that doesn't stop flowing unless you let it, which is the greatest sin there is against love. And then I think he helped you to grow up and be ready for John. He certainly was a little boy scout in those days," she added flippantly, to cover her emotion.

Candy, however, couldn't shake off the spell that the past had woven around her. "No wonder we're all twined up so close, the four of us. There's a lot of richness packed into simple-seeming lives, isn't there?"

"A lot," said Claudia.

"Do you mind if I tell John?"

"Yes, I certainly do," Claudia answered promptly.

"But think what respect he'll have for me, if he knew you were jealous of me——"

"If you breathe a word of this," Claudia threatened, "I'll call you a liar."

Candy giggled, and a moment later they were both hysterical again. And then the sudden sound of David's coughing wiped the laughter from Claudia's lips. Her legs refused to take her to the window to look out to the porch. She sat, frozen with fear, waiting for the paroxysm to pass. Please—oh, please—let it be nothing more than a wrong swallow . . .

She was aware that Candy, who hadn't noticed the cough, was carrying on a one-sided conversation. "If we can get off the fascinating subject of ourselves," she was saying, "I forgot to tell you that Jerry's finished his book."

"He has? He's never mentioned it in any of his letters, and we rather imagined he'd given up the idea of writing it."

"No, he wrote it," said Candy, a little tensely. "He's sending me the manuscript to read. I don't see why I should put myself through the ordeal, though, because he doesn't intend to publish it."

" What's the matter, isn't he satisfied with it ? " Claudia asked, with one ear still on the porch. (There. David was talking again, it was over with.)

" Yes, I think he is satisfied with it," said Candy. " That's why he says it's served its purpose, and he doesn't have to publish it. He says that just getting it out of his system has been like a catharsis to him."

" Read it," Claudia suggested gently. " Maybe it will be like a catharsis to you, too."

Candy bit at her lips, distorting the soft, crimson outline. " I could use one," she admitted. " No matter how hard I try, I can't get over the feeling that if Mother hadn't married him, she might be alive today."

Claudia shook her head. " I don't think it would have worked that way, Candy, really I don't. I think it was a beautiful marriage, short as it was, and it completed a beautiful life."

" But why couldn't she have lived to see her first grandchild ? " Candy demanded rebelliously. " Now is the time I need her so terribly. I sound as if John weren't enough to fill my life," she amended swiftly. " He is, it isn't that."

" I know," said Claudia.

" I can't begin to tell you what he's been to me these last few months. It almost seems as if—and this is a dreadful thing to say—but it almost seems as if your having to go away was the best thing that could have happened to us. It's not only given John a chance to prove himself at the office, but it's meant our moving back to the apartment away from John's mother, and getting down to rock-bottom all by ourselves. You mightn't have suspected it, but I was beginning to get awfully dependent on you."

Claudia smiled faintly. " I suspected it."

" A sort of mother transference, I guess."

" You sound pretty much up on Freud," said Claudia, amused because she had, herself, been so careful to eschew the easy jargon of a little knowledge. But Candy made no bones about it.

" Oh, I've read the whole shooting match," she acknowledged shamelessly. " Everything I could lay my hands on at college. I always ended up by having all the diseases, too. I was a paranoiac during my junior year and a manic-depressive in my senior. If John hadn't happened to come along, I'm sure I'd have gone in for nymphomania. Well, look who's here," she broke off. " Oh, you big fat angel ! Bertha, give me that baby this instant ! "

" He just woke up," said Bertha, handing him over with his best foot forward.

" Oh, he smells so sweet ! " Candy nuzzled her nose into his fat neck. " I hope I'm going to have a sweet baby, I'd hate a smelly one."

" All babies are sweet," said Bertha. " Like pigs. It depends on how they are taken care of."

Claudia left them to the ramifications of Bertha's seasoned opinion, and went out to the porch. David was still hacking a little, being a trifle self-conscious and apologetic about it, but John didn't seem to notice any more than Candy had noticed. He was putting a stack of papers back in his brief-case, arranging them as well as he could with fingers that were numb with cold. " Well," he greeted her, " we got through quite a bit of work, considering it's zero, or thereabouts. I must say, though, it doesn't feel it."

" That's because the air's so dry," said Claudia. (How inane one could become about the weather.) " Anyway, I think you've had enough for the first time."

" So do I," said David. " I just told him to go inside and get thawed out while I take my walk."

" While *we* take your walk," Claudia corrected. " What's the matter, are you too good for my company ? "

" I thought you'd want to stay home and visit with Candy," David commented, as they started off down the road, with Bluff keeping sedately at their heels and Shakespeare a few yards behind pretending he wasn't going along but just happened to be around.

"I wouldn't miss this walk for anything," said Claudia. "It's become the big event in my day. I look forward to it."

"Funny," David mused, "how we used to tramp for hours at the farm."

"And never stopped to think how lucky we were. I suppose nobody does."

"I suppose not," said David. They fell silent for a space. The crackle of snow beneath their boots made a pleasant sound, a sound they would always remember, like they remembered the smell of burning leaves at the farm, and the sweet, warm steaminess of the barn at twilight. The snow, and the mountains and the dry, clear cold, had already become a part of their very lives.

"It was that old briar pipe I've been smoking," David said suddenly, out of the blue.

"Oh," said Claudia, "I was afraid maybe you were coming down with a cold or something."

"No, that pipe always makes me cough, it's time I threw it out."

"High time." She was very close to being happy and, glancing at David's face, she saw that he also was at peace. It was strange that they never once spoke of John and Candy. It was good to be with them again, but they belonged to a world that was far away.

"When I get half an hour exercise," David was saying, "it ought to bring us pretty close to the San gates."

"Yes," said Claudia, "it will." They reached a piece of broken fence, half-hidden beneath a drift of snow, and turned around and walked slowly back.

Bertha outdid herself at lunch, with John's favourite dish of kidneys and corn fritters. She was devastated because he ate so sparingly. "Have at least another fritter," she coaxed.

"Bertha, I couldn't possibly."

"Didn't you like them?"

"Like them? They were superb. I ate twice as much as I usually eat in the middle of the day."

David used to eat that way too, Claudia reflected, with a polite consideration of his digestive tract and a healthy horror of overweight. Now he was eating as a business, intent upon padding his ribs with that extra ten pounds of insurance that Dr. Geiger wanted him to carry. Comparing the two of them across the table, John looked much the sicker, actually. "I remind myself of the people in the boarding-house," she caught herself up in dismay. She would have given anything if David hadn't come out with almost exactly the same thing a moment later. "Only a healthy man," he remarked with a grin, "could afford to look as spindly as John. A couple of days more out on the porch and he might work up an appetite and some colour in that gaunt and interesting face of his." It was strange, and a little disturbing, that people who were ill were ready to read illness in others. It was an illness in itself.

Perhaps John and Candy also felt the constraint and the strangeness of a different world and a different point of view, for John said, directly after lunch, "Let's take a walk and see the countryside, while David's resting."

"Let's," Candy complied with alacrity.

Claudia watched them sprint off, throwing snowballs at each other, gay as children. At the gate they paused for an instant and then swung right. David and she had never gone in that direction, because it was uphill on the way back.

On an impulse, she decided to go out on the porch and lie in the empty chair beside him. His eyes were closed. He gave no hint that he knew that she was there, but after a few minutes he reached over and put his hand on her knee.

"Why didn't you go with them?"

"Why would I want to go with them when I can stay here with you?"

"You picked a great bargain," he said.

She wanted to tell him what a fool he was, but her voice choked up and she was afraid to talk.

The next day was Saturday, and Bobby and Matthew were home from school, and there were bottle-necks all

along the line. "It's my fault," Candy apologised, "I had
no right to soak so long in a hot tub."

John took Claudia aside. "I hate to bother you," he
said, "but Candy woke up this morning with an awful pain
in her back. If the hot bath doesn't help it, maybe she
ought to see a doctor, what do you think?"

"I think it's nothing that a good mattress won't cure
when you get home," said Claudia.

He looked relieved. "I thought maybe that was it. We
tried both beds. How on earth do you manage to get a
decent night's rest?"

"Oh, I've grown rather attached to the one with the hole
in the middle. Listen, I warned Bertha you'd be more
comfortable at the hotel in the village. Should we try to
get you a room?"

"Would it be easier for you if we went?"

"No!" she returned emphatically. "Unless you want
to?"

"No!" he replied with equal emphasis. "Candy says
she hadn't even begun to talk herself out—and neither
have I."

"John, now that you've had a chance to be with David,
how do you find him, really?"

They were standing in the small hall outside the living-
room; it wasn't the ideal place to ask the question, but it
wasn't likely that a greater degree of privacy would offer
itself over the crowded week-end.

John hesitated. "The same as I told you yesterday, only
more so. He looks fine, and he acts fine."

"But . . . ?"

"But nothing."

"How do you think he is mentally?"

"Resigned," said John. "I expected him to be restless
and impatient to get back in harness, but not a bit of it."
He gave a small laugh. "As a matter of fact, there's been
quite a revival of interest in the Iceland project. I wasn't
going to mention it, but when he asked about it, I told him
—and he didn't seem at all upset. 'Well,' he said, 'that's

nice to hear, but there's nothing I can do about it at this point.' "

" And there isn't," said Claudia. Their eyes met for the briefest instant. She turned away quickly, lest she reveal some strange confusion of her loyalties. " I have to phone the marketing list," she murmured, " or it'll never get here on time."

It was a very long marketing list. " A rib-roast large enough for eight, please—" Even the baby was getting meat chopped up in tiny bits. " And a knuckle-bone or two, for the dog, if you have any around to spare, and about a pound of yesterday's fish for the cat."

Although Bertha wasn't too in love with the rib-roast when it came, she showered all kinds of endearments on the bones and the halibut, for which there was no charge. She boiled the bones to get the marrow out of them—and a little soup on the side—and Claudia obligingly agreed that it was not good for Bluff to eat anything that wasn't cooked. At supper, however, there was a delicious barley broth, and some excellent patties. " Crab flakes in sherry," Candy exulted, as she tasted the filling. " With mushrooms ! "

" Oh," said Bobby, gaining enthusiasm. " I like lobster and crab ; and what's those other little things we have sometimes, Mother ? "

" Shrimp."

" I like shrimps, too."

" We're very pleased to hear it," said David.

" I wish it didn't have the mushrooms," Bobby decided vaguely. " Maybe that's why I don't like this so much."

" This is fish," Matthew stated explicitly. " And I hate fish."

" No comments about food," David reproved him.

" I hate it anyway."

John averted an open battle by saying quickly. " You don't know what's good, my lads."

" There is more," Bertha coaxed, with quite flushed cheeks. " Let me have your plate."

" Shame on you," Claudia muttered under her breath. " Taking halibut out of a poor little cat's mouth."

It might have been sheer coincidence that Shakespeare did not return when he was let out that evening. Bertha must have had a guilty conscience, because she went looking for him with a flashlight, and calling him with all sorts of implied overtures in her voice. " That's funny," she said, " there is no sign of him."

" You've destroyed his faith in human kind," said Claudia. " He's through with us."

Nobody was actually worried about his disappearance except Bobby. " I don't want to get undressed until he comes back," he said. " Maybe he's lost."

" Cats don't get lost," said David.

" Maybe he's stolen."

" Look," said Claudia, " Shakespeare can take care of himself, he's older than you are."

Candy was intrigued. " He isn't really, is he ? "

" David bought him for me the first month we were married, so figure it out for yourself. I'll never forget how tiny and sweet he was. He fitted into a candy-box."

" How long do cats live ? " Bobby wanted to know with an anxious frown.

It was a new thought, and Claudia didn't like to think about it. " Oh, eighteen years or thereabouts," she answered casually.

" Do they ? " she asked David, after Bobby had been cajoled into going to bed.

" Rarely," said David. " You know something ? Bluff's no youngster either," he added soberly.

She heard him whistle softly from his bed on the porch long after he was supposed to be asleep. She went to the window. " Did he come back ? " she whispered.

" No," said David. " Don't worry about it, we'll probably find him at the kitchen door tomorrow morning."

He was. And without so much as an excuse-me. Bertha poured cream into his saucer of milk; he turned away from it, his amber eyes opaque with some hidden secret.

4

" You crazy cat ! " cried Bobby, in mingled anger and relief.

" I'm certainly glad he came home before we left," said Candy. " I couldn't bear leaving not knowing what had happened to him."

Matthew's lower lip thrust out. " Are you going back to New York today ? "

" Yes."

" When ? "

" This afternoon. Late."

" You can't go. I want you to stay here with us. Why can't you live in the mountains like we do ? "

Bobby gave him a kick in the shins. " Because Uncle John has to go back to the office, stupid."

" Why ? " Matthew persisted. " Daddy doesn't."

Claudia was grateful that David was out of earshot. " Some day, Matthew, when I have the time," she promised him, pleasantly, " I'm going to wring your neck."

She spoke in jest, but his perversity was beginning to be something of a problem. Even Candy admitted it when they were alone in the bedroom, packing. " Much as I adore him, I must say he's a handful. How long did it take Bobby to grow out of that stage ? "

" Bobby was always more like David," said Claudia. " Good and naughty, but you knew where you were at with him."

" That's the trouble," said Candy. " You never know where you're at with Matthew. But I guess you can't have three children, and have them all alike. You take what you get and like it." She rolled her lacy night-gown in a ball and wedged it in the corner of her suitcase. " It goes in the laundry anyway. I can't believe we've been here three days already. The time's just flown. Before we know it, you'll be home."

" Yes," said Claudia.

" One thing I'm happy about, you're sure to be back by June. I refuse to have the baby without your being there. Just on general principles."

" June is the perfect time for us to get back, weather-wise," said Claudia. " I only hope David will have the patience to stay that long."

" He hasn't mentioned a word to John about coming home, so maybe he will," said Candy. " John was really surprised he didn't bring it up."

" No more surprised than I," said Claudia.

The long hours of the afternoon limped along, filled with the indecisiveness of approaching departure. Finally Bertha cajoled the children into going out on their sleds, and in turn Matthew cajoled John and Candy into joining them. " One sloppy kiss of yours," Candy gave in, " and I'm your devoted slave, like a fool."

They were full into it when Claudia and David got back from their walk. Candy was yelling like a hoodlum on the side-lines, while the others belly-wopped down the steepest hill, with John steering and all of them landing in a heap. Over and over, up the hill and down they went, until even Matthew was out of breath. Claudia stole a look at David. It was impossible to know what thoughts were going through his mind because his face told nothing. He just stood there, watching. Then finally he said, " John's a damn fool, nobody who's over twenty ought to tax himself like that."

It was the last thing that she'd expected him to say, and she knew that the hurt within him must have been very bitter to have made him want to cover it up.

A few minutes later, John caught sight of them. " Come on, ruffians," he stopped the children hastily, " that's enough. Time to go in." Claudia thought, " This visit's been a strain on all of us." She was glad it was over, and David was glad that it was over, although he didn't say so.

The taxi came at five o'clock. Suddenly there was a great deal of excitement, piling luggage in and saying good-bye, and then just as suddenly there wasn't any excitement at all. The cottage seemed empty, and quite large. It was hard to realise that it had ever seemed so small that they didn't think that they could all fit into it.

That evening, Bertha decided that it was as good a time as any to wash hair and cut toe-nails. " I couldn't do anything with her," Claudia expostulated to David. " She's cleaned up all three of them like a lunatic, even though she must be dead on her feet."

" She misses John and Candy," said David. " There's not enough for her to do, all at once." He took off his coat, and hung away his trousers. Claudia gathered her towels and toothbrush and pyjamas, and went into the bathroom, still warm and steamy from Bertha's ministrations. Bobby followed her disconsolately, pale with an overdose of cleanliness. " Shakespeare's gone again," he said.

" Dear me, he's getting very gay in his old age," said Claudia. She kissed him. " Don't worry about it, darling, he knows his way back. Get a good night's rest, tomorrow's school."

When she got back to their room, David had turned down the other twin bed, looking as self-conscious as Matthew. She tried to hide the soft tumbling of her senses. " Shakespeare's gone again," she said inanely.

He didn't seem to hear her. " You look like a little boy in those pyjamas," he said.

" If I'd known I was going to have company I'd have worn a night-gown."

His eyes were bluer than they'd been in months. " It's not too late to change, is it ? "

She could feel her cheeks grow warm. No, it wasn't too late. The bottom drawer of the bureau was full of Julia's lovely cast-off lingerie that was just lying there in utter waste. She selected a gown, sheer and lacy, like Candy's, only prettier. She put it on, and dabbed perfume behind her ears, the way women did.

She felt David's arms around her. " You're shivering."

" I'm not used to night-gowns any more," she answered tremulously.

It was light as a cobweb in his gentle hands. He tossed it aside. " You ought to wear this sort of thing more often," he whispered. " It's very becoming."

Fear came, unbidden, to share their happiness, although David was afraid to call it fear. First he said that it was hard to get accustomed to sleeping indoors again, and then he said that the mattress was enough to scare anybody away.

In a little while, after he thought she was asleep, he crept out to the porch.

SIX

THE JANUARY THAW came in February that year, and
Matthew, as always, took for granted that the elements
functioned for his especial diversion, and literally threw
himself headlong into the sudden onrush of spring. He
wallowed through rivers of melting snow, flung off his coat
during intervals of baking sun, and promptly got himself
pneumonia. Of course nobody knew what he'd been up
to until he came down with a cold, and then one damp
shoe led to another until finally the whole series of his
indiscretions came to light.

It was Bobby who wakened Claudia early that bleak, chill
morning when, without warning, Matthew's cold slipped
down from his nose into his chest. Sleep—a fugitive visitor
at best these past months—vanished instantly. She sat up
in bed, with her heart banging drunkenly against her ribs.
" Bobby ! What's wrong ? "

" It's Matthew. He's coughing, and he says it hurts."

" Shhh. Don't let Dad hear us from the porch." Already
she was fishing for her slippers, with her bath-robe across
her shoulders.

" Maybe he's just putting it on," said Bobby.

" I hope so." She pulled back the blankets of the empty
bed beside her. " Here, pop under the covers and try to
go to sleep again. It's only half-past six."

" First I didn't want to wake you up," Bobby regretted.
" I was going to call Bertha instead but he said he didn't
want Bertha."

" You were right to call me. Now go back to sleep until
it's time for school."

She was used to Matthew cutting up shinanegans in
the middle of the night. Sometimes he'd waken with
a bad dream, sometimes he'd complain of excruciating
aches and pains that were invariably gone by morning.

But one look at him now told her that this time he wasn't crying wolf. " It hurts," he whimpered, " it hurts."

" Where, darling, show me."

His hand fluttered vaguely toward his chest. " I want Daddy."

" Daddy's asleep, we mustn't disturb him."

" Who says ' Daddy's asleep we mustn't disturb him ' ? "

The sound of David's voice was as welcome as a strong arm around her. He moved toward the cot, jerking the cord of his dressing-gown into a knot against his flat, firm waist, and silently gauged the shallow quickness of Matthew's breathing. " It might be nothing but a heavy bronchitis," he said at last.

" A heavy bronchitis is bad enough. I'm going to call Doctor Craig. He's supposed to be the best child specialist in town. Thank heaven we haven't needed him up to now." She had her usual impulse to knock on wood, but it seemed ironic under the circumstances.

Dr. Craig's housekeeper reported that he was away, and that his assistant was ill. Nobody was available. " Call Dr. Geiger, he'll be able to recommend someone," David suggested. He glanced at his watch. " You'd better wait until seven before you disturb him, though. I'll get some clothes on."

" David, please," Claudia begged him. " What am I thinking of to let you stand here, go back to bed, you oughtn't to be up for another hour."

" Yes, I'm so delicate," he said.

It went through her mind that with her need of him, he was his old self again. It was as if the core of him had remained whole and healthy, while only the outer shell of his being was touched by illness. After long months of standing alone, it was good to know again this sense of leaning and reliance.

" I want some water, some cold water—I want Daddy to stay here—I want Mother to stay here too—" Matthew's voice held the chant of fever, at once petulant and unearthly.

" Yes, darling," Claudia soothed him.

Bertha came bustling in a moment later. She was on her way to the kitchen to start breakfast, neat as a pin in her blue house-dress, bulging with tidy bosoms and girdled thighs. It was a gift in itself, something Bertha had learned throughout the years, to wear each morning the freshness of a new day, with no harried left-overs of the day before. Claudia was suddenly conscious of her tousled hair and trailing bath-robe, she could feel strain and apprehension distorting her face. "Never mind breakfast, stay with Matthew, Bertha, while I get dressed."

Bertha took over, blaming herself angrily. "Never again will I sleep with my door closed, I could not hear a thing."

"Don't be silly, you have to have it closed, or there's a draught all through the house," said Claudia. "Besides, he seemed fairly normal last night."

"Yes he was," Bertha conceded. "This happened suddenly, so quick ! Have you called the doctor yet ? "

Bertha was always the last one to want to call a doctor, so Matthew must seem pretty sick to her, too, thought Claudia, with a sinking heart. "We're waiting until seven."

"It is almost seven," said Bertha. "I wouldn't wait any longer."

Dr Geiger sounded, over the telephone, as if he were awake but not up. When he heard Claudia's voice, he seemed relieved that it was Matthew rather than David she was calling about. "I'm so sorry to bother you—" she faltered, "but we didn't know anyone else to turn to."

"I'll be there within the hour," he answered shortly and to the point.

His examination was short and to the point too. He talked to them while he washed his hands in the quickly tidied bathroom. "That's a sick child," he told them bluntly, "you can thank God for penicillin, let's hope it does its work. But we've got a different problem with you, young man." He turned squarely on to David. "I don't want you to minimise the seriousness of this situation. You must stay out of the sick-room completely, and not relax on any detail of your daily routine. There is a definite danger of contagion, and a physical setback at this stage of your cure is apt to add months to your eventual recovery. I can't impress this upon you too strongly."

"I understand," said David in a white voice.

"Would it be better," Claudia asked, "if we moved Matthew to the hospital?"

"Under ordinary circumstances," said Dr. Geiger, "by all means. But we're overcrowded at this time of the year, and low on facilities. I think the boy will have a better chance where he is. I noticed that your maid handled him very competently."

"Bertha's family," Claudia corrected him instinctively. "She's been with us on and off ever since we were married."

Dr. Geiger gave a warm and unexpected smile, which changed his face completely. "Well, my child, at least you're fortunate in that department, anyway." He put his arm around her shoulder for the barest instant. "Try not to worry too much. I'll look in again around two."

"It's wonderful of you," Claudia told him gratefully. "I can't thank you enough."

He smiled again. "I've got a double stake in this little household," he said.

Bertha had the nerve to take advantage of good nature. She waylaid him on the way out, and showed him her baby. To Claudia's astonishment Dr. Geiger mellowed even more and chucked Michael under his fat chin.

It was hard to keep David from feeling that he was nothing but an added responsibility. "A lot of help I am," he accosted her at lunch, "stuck out on the porch, building up my confounded strength."

"There's nothing to do," said Claudia, "nothing for Bertha or me to do, either, except watch and wait." A lump blocked her throat. "The worst part is seeing him lie there so quietly. There isn't a saucy word in him. I'd give anything in the world for him to be naughty again——"

"He'll be plenty naughty again," David promised her, "and you'll be wanting to wring his neck."

She gave a watery smile. "Who said you weren't a help?"

When Bobby came home from school that afternoon, he asked in a muted voice, " Is Matthew very sick ? "

" Yes," said Claudia, " but he's going to be all right."

" Did the doctor say so ? "

" Daddy said so."

" Oh," said Bobby. He too, gave a watery smile. " I believe Dad, don't you ? "

" Yes, I believe Dad," said Claudia. " And by the way, Dr. Geiger came back after lunch to see Matthew, and he sat with Dad a little while on the porch and looked at his chart and felt his pulse—and what do you think ? "

" What ? "

" He said Dad didn't have to go to the surgery this week for his check-up, he seemed in such good shape he could take another fifteen minutes' exercise."

Bobby's face brightened. " Boy, that's good, isn't it ? "

" It's more than good," said Claudia. It was, she realised, a timely injection of encouragement just when David needed it. " And the nice part of it is," she went on aloud to Bobby, " you're back from school just in time to go with him."

" Aren't you going to go with him ? "

" I want to stay with Matthew."

" Sure," said Bobby eagerly. " I'll go. Oh, boy ! "

She watched them from the window as they walked down the path to the road. It was the first walk with David that she had missed. How they had looked forward to this extra fifteen minutes. She was glad that he did not have to go alone, that Bobby could take her place.

At the gate they turned and whistled for Bluff. He bounded after them, horizontal in his haste. Then Shakespeare, who had recently returned from one of his inexplicable absences, emerged from the bushes and followed daintily. It was a picture to treasure in her mind for always.

Matthew was very ill, but not for long, and a week of anxious days and nights faded quickly into something to look back upon with a reminiscent shudder and a wonderment that all was well that ended well.

At the end of a fortnight he was able to get up, looking like he'd lost pounds and grown inches. He was mildly interested to note that winter once again lay piled in white drifts against the door and windows, but he showed no desire to go out on his sled. He was content to sit in an easy-chair and play with the books and games that Candy and Julia had sent him from New York.

Claudia couldn't get used to the change in him. "He gives me the rather awed feeling that he's gone places and done things," she told David.

"He very likely has," said David, "but I guess wherever he went, they didn't want him and sent him back."

"Well I want him," said Claudia, "and I wish he'd take off his hat and decide to stay and settle down in his skin again."

Eventually, Matthew did just that, and it became increasingly difficult to treat him like a hero. Bobby was the first to revert to normal reflexes. "You used my tooth-brush!" Claudia heard him shout hoarsely the evening before Matthew was due to go back to school.

"I did not!" Matthew's voice rose in an affronted whine. "Let go, you're hurting my arm!"

"Then why did you use my tooth-brush?"

"I said I didn't!"

"And I say you did. Mine is blue and it's wet!"

"I only began to use it," Matthew defended. "I thought it was green."

"You're a little liar, you knew it was green—I mean blue!"

Matthew came off the easy victor. "You don't even know what you're talking about!" he remarked disdainfully.

"You!" Bobby choked on his indignation. A chair turned over.

"Now see what you've done," cried Matthew virtuously.

Claudia sought out David in the bedroom, where he was

rubbing oil on his heavy boots. " Well, the house has returned to normal," she reported cheerfully. " They've just had a fight."

He looked up. " Do you know what tomorrow is ? "

" Yes, Wednesday," she replied promptly, " and exactly four weeks to the day that Matthew took sick."

" It also happens to be seven months to the day that we landed in this god-forsaken place." He placed the boots on the floor beside the chair that held his heavy sheep-skin coat, and corked the bottle of oil. " Seven months," he reiterated with grim emphasis, " and I haven't had my comparative X-rays yet."

" That's because of Matthew," she pointed out. " Dr. Geiger examined you at the house, and his X-ray machine is in his surgery."

" That explains exactly once," said David. " I've come to the conclusion that Dr. Geiger is giving me a fine runaround. First I was going to be here three months——"

" That was your own interpretation," Claudia broke in.

" ——then it was six months," he swept on, " and now where am I ? Kidded along until I'm in the same boat as all these poor devils up here. I know what his game is. The longer he postpones the X-rays, the longer I stay. Well, I've had my fill. I'll give the Herr Professor Geiger until the first of April to stop shilly-shallying around, and then by all that's holy, I'm kissing this town good-bye, and to hell with what the X-rays show."

She was unaccountably happy at his outburst. Matthew's illness had done wonders to him, it seemed to have given him back his old spirit. She recalled that the six months' mark had passed just before Matthew was taken ill, and David had forgotten to remember it was half a year since he had left New York, half a year since he had turned his back on the hopes and dreams that had made up so large a part of his life. He had been concerned chiefly, that morning, with a sudden rise of temperature that had turned out to be nothing at all, and Claudia had avoided any mention of the day, torn between relief and dismay that he was so engrossed in his symptoms that it had slipped his mind.

Now, a month later, he was showing a tonic impatience, a healthy impulse to return to work. She played along with it gladly. " I look at it differently," she said. " I don't think Dr. Geiger's trying to put anything over on you, I just think he thinks there's no rush about the X-rays, because you can't go back to New York in the middle of winter, anyway. Besides which, we haven't even talked about a place to live, we haven't got a roof over our heads, literally."

" We'll find a roof," said David, " don't you worry about that end of it. All I want to do is to get back to the office. If worst comes to worst we can live at Julia's and Hartley's until we find an apartment. . . . Is his Royal Highness out of the bathroom yet ? "

" I don't know, I'll see."

Matthew was reading. She caught him at it with his pants down, so to speak. " Matthew," she reproached him, " how many times do you have to be told—" Secretly she was full of rejoicing because he was well enough to be disobedient again. God had been so generous—surely, she gave up a little prayer, He wouldn't be a piker when it came to David's X-rays. . . .

Matthew's first day at school was fruitful with all sorts of exciting incidents. For one thing, " a boy " gave him a fountain pen; for another, " a lady " came up to him in the street while he was waiting for the bus, and said she knew him and sent her love to his mother and father.

Claudia felt his forehead. " Begin from the beginning," she suggested. " What boy and what lady ? "

" I told you already," he resisted indignantly.

" But it doesn't make sense. Firstly, why should a boy give you a fountain pen ? And secondly, we don't know any lady who would send us her love. What was her name ? "

" I don't remember," said Matthew. " But she did, she said, ' Give your mother and father my love.' "

Claudia wondered if it could have been anyone from the boarding-house; yet it couldn't have been, because they'd left Mrs. Jenkins' before the children had arrived from New York, and nobody at the boarding-house knew them. " I think you're imagining things," she said.

In answer, he dug the fountain pen out of his rear pocket, and showed it to her. It was a very excellent fountain pen, one that she wouldn't have minded owning herself. She went in search of Bobby, who was bolting a glass of milk, and sharing a plate of buns with Bluff. " Don't drink so fast," she adjured him, " and Bertha will be wild if she finds you giving her good butter cookies to Bluff. What's this about a fountain pen and a lady ? "

Bobby disclaimed all knowledge of the pen. " Let's see it," he challenged distrustfully. " I don't believe it."

" I saw it, and you can take my word for it. However, we'll get to the pen later, what about the lady ? "

The lady he admitted to be true. " She heard me yell Matthew's name because he was going too near the gutter, and she stopped and looked at us and then she asked me if my name was Bobby."

" And what did you say ? "

" I said it was."

" That was extremely knowing of you," she complimented him dryly. " I mean, what happened after that, you goop ? "

" Nothing. She just said we'd grown a lot, but she recognised us anyway after she heard Matthew's name, and she wanted to know why we were in the mountains instead of on the farm."

Claudia's curiosity was biting its nails. " Well, who was it, certainly if she knew you at the farm it must have been someone you knew, too ? "

Bobby looked blank. " If it was, I don't remember her. I forgot who she said she was too," he added helpfully, " because we had to hurry, the bus driver almost went without us."

"I can't bear it," said Claudia speechlessly. "Was it Nancy Riddle by any remote chance?"

He regarded her in disgust. "You must think I'm dumb," he said.

"Frankly, yes; a little."

"As if I didn't know Mrs. Riddle. She has red hair."

"Didn't this person have red hair?" she wheedled, as if she might surprise some information out of him behind his back.

He thought a moment. "It was sort of grey, with glasses."

"Sort of grey with glasses," she mulled. "Fat or thin?"

He thought another moment. "I couldn't see. She had a coat on."

"I'm going crazy," said Claudia. And then, all at once, she remembered something. "Was it a beaver coat?" she asked eagerly.

"What's beaver?" said Bobby.

"Oh, God," said Claudia.

She appealed to David. "Who on earth do you think it could be?"

"I wouldn't know," said David. "What difference does it make?"

"The same difference," she returned hoarsely, "as when the telephone bell stops ringing before you answer it, and you never find out who it was."

"And——?"

"There are times when I could honestly cheerfully murder you. It's inhuman not to care."

"Go ahead and brood about it," he invited her cordially.

"I shall," she said.

It was only logical to expect some sort of communication from this unknown woman who seemed to know the whole family so intimately, but several days passed without a single clue to her identity. The mystery of the fountain pen, however, was cleared up the following afternoon. It appeared, according to Bobby's sober tale when he came home from school, that the registrar had had her pen stolen from her desk, and a general assembly of the lower grades had been called to trace the culprit. Claudia listened to the story with a nod of enlightenment. " So that accounts for the pen being such an expensive one," she figured it out. " It belonged to the registrar. It must be a great blow to parents to have a thing like that happen."

David cleared his throat. " It's nothing to get tragic about. All children go through a stage of thieving in one form or another."

" Did I ? " Bobby asked in a small voice.

" No," said Claudia flatly, " you did not."

" I stole a tennis racquet from the boy next door when I was a youngster," David volunteered, with an air of bragging about it.

" You mean you borrowed it," Claudia corrected him icily, so as not to set Bobby a bad example. She didn't want Matthew to have a first-hand acquaintance with stealing, either. " I'd rather not explain to him," she said, " that whoever gave him the pen wanted to get rid of it so he wouldn't be found out. I'll just tell him to return it tomorrow, without mentioning any names. At least let the boy have the chance to own up."

" It seems a little involved," said David. " I'd better talk to Matthew."

" No, I'd rather do it," Claudia insisted. " You seem to have got a little too mellow about dishonesty. It might be the modern approach, but according to my old-fashioned ethics, stealing is stealing, and there's no two ways about it."

" I'm sorry you feel like that," said David quietly.

Bobby fiddled nervously with the top button of his shirt. " Mother, do you know what I think, I think maybe you'd better let Dad talk to Matthew."

Claudia looked from one to the other of them. What were they trying to tell her ? What were they trying not to tell her ? She felt sick in the pit of her stomach. From the next room she could hear Matthew lavishing extravagant caresses upon Bluff, as if a few hours' separation had caused him untold anguish. She shook her head numbly. It was difficult to speak. " I don't believe it. I just don't believe it."

" I'm afraid it's true, dear, from what I can piece together."

She clutched for a flaw in his reasoning. " But how did Matthew get to the registrar's office? What would he be doing in there? "

" Bringing his excuse for being absent," Bobby explained without triumph.

" Other boys bring notes, it still could have been someone else."

" It couldn't, Mother, because when nobody confessed in Assembly, the Principal went through the notes that were brought in yesterday, and Matthew's was the only one. She told me I shouldn't worry Dad about it, though, on account of being up here for his health. She said she'd telephone you tomorrow, but I thought maybe I'd better tell Dad first, and then he said we'd better tell you before the Principal did."

Claudia sank down in a chair. " Does Matthew know you told us? "

" No, he doesn't know I know. He didn't say anything coming home, so I didn't say anything either."

" I'm glad," said Claudia. " I'd rather he told us himself."

Bobby seemed doubtful. " He won't, I don't think. He was pretty fresh on the bus. I don't think he cares."

" He must, Bobby, don't say that ! "

David put his hand on her shoulder. " It's tough to take, darling, I know that. The youngster needs some handling. He's always been a little of a problem, we might as well face it."

" I'm facing it," she said.

" Get your things on, it's four o'clock, we'll go for a walk and talk it out."

" All right," she said, with dry lips.

She had to pass Matthew's room to get her coat. He was

alone, singing loudly as he took off his shoes. He caught sight of her. " Bertha says I have to rest; how long do I have to keep on going to bed in the afternoon ? " he demanded belligerently.

Claudia regarded him with a great and incredulous sadness. He was born of her, and yet how little she knew of him. What vast mistake had she committed to have caused him to become this small, complex creature with no awareness of right, no awe of evil ? Or was it not of her doing ? Could it be any one of a half-dozen glib and easy explanations ? The middle child ? Or the insecurity of giving up the farm ? Or David's illness ? Or was it rather some pattern within Matthew's own soul that needed to be worked out ?

It was as if he felt the weaving of her thoughts about him. Vigilance masked his face like a curtain. " How long are you going to make me rest ! " he repeated angrily, putting her in the wrong instead of himself.

" Until you're strong," she told him in a low voice.

" I'm strong," he declaimed with arrogance. " I can lick any boy in my class, I can even lick Bobby, if I want to. I can."

She wanted to take him in her arms because he was so transparent in his swaggering, so pitifully frightened underneath his bold front. She moved swiftly to him, and knelt beside him, not daring to touch his small, fierce body. " Oh, Matthew—" she whispered. " Matthew, darling—"

Suddenly his poor little defences crumbled away. He flung himself against her and began to cry. It wasn't ordinary crying, it was a ripping open of the tightness in him, and the fear. David and Bobby came to the door. After a moment, they tip-toed down the hall again, leaving her to know the way to Matthew's heart.

SEVEN

HE WASN'T WICKED, she tried to make him see that he
wasn't. The real part of him, the Matthew that they loved
and respected, was honest and loyal and fine. But tucked
far inside of him, there was another Matthew who was the
enemy of the Fine Matthew, and who led him into doing
things that were wrong—such as taking fountain pens that
didn't belong to him. Therefore the Fine Matthew had to
become strong enough to withstand the evil influence of
the Naughty Matthew—

"And that's what you told him," David interrupted.

"Yes," said Claudia.

"Very beautiful," said David. "It must have all come
to you like an inspiration from above."

"A little," she confessed.

"I bet," he said.

Her eyes narrowed in suspicion. "You bet what?"

"Nothing. I merely said 'I bet'."

"I heard you the first time," she returned tersely. "And
how would you have handled him? Kissed him on both
cheeks and told him that you stole too when you were a
little boy, and loved every minute of it?"

"Or words to that effect," said David. "But I'd have
gone one step further. I'd have guaranteed him a good old-
fashioned whipping if it ever happened again. On the
bottom of the Naughty Matthew, mind you. I wouldn't
dream of laying a finger on the Fine Matthew."

"And leave him with a trauma," she disapproved.

"A red one, I trust."

"You're cruel."

"You're soft," he came back at her. "Soft as mush.
The Fine Matthew, my eye. What's he doing now, patting
himself on the back?"

"He's busy."

" Communing with his soul, I dare say."

" After a fashion, yes."

" What's the mystery ? "

" None," she said.   " Come on, it's after hour, let's take our walk."

When they returned, Bobby met them with the information that Miss Grigsby, the Principal, had telephoned while they were out.   " She said you could call her back at the school, she'll be there until late today because there's a teachers' meeting."

" Better still," said Claudia.   " I'll go down to the school and see her."

" You'll do nothing of the sort," said David.   " It's not that important, it can wait until tomorrow."

" Psychologically, it's better not to put it off.   Bobby, run and tell Matthew I'm home and then telephone for a taxi like a good boy."

" Look," said David, after Bobby had strutted off on his double mission, " Matthew needs a strong hand.   You'd better let me attend to this, I'll go down and see Miss Grigsby."

" Please," said Claudia.   " Let me go through with it as long as I've begun it."

" By the time you get finished filling him with fancy ideas about himself, he'll think he's wonderful.   Beyond reproach."

" Hush," said Claudia, " he's coming."

She had to admit that there was some truth in what David said, because Matthew wore an unmistakable air of pride in his dual personality.   " Here," he said quite cheerfully, offering the pen and a sheet of note-paper.

Claudia took the pen, and unfolded the paper.   She read the words that staggered across it in large print.   " Dear Miss Grigsby.   The bad part of me stole this.   I am sory. I am sending it back.   I am sory.   Matthew Naughton."

" You spell sorry with two ' r's,' not one," said Claudia.

" He used it twice so it comes out even," David remarked under his breath.

Claudia ignored him. " However," she continued, " I'm sure that the registrar will be very glad to get her pen back."

Matthew eyed it wistfully. " It's a nifty one," he said, as if reluctant to relinquish it. " It writes in two colours."

" It sure is," Bobby chimed in, with envy. " I'm going to save up and buy one just like it some day. How much do you think a pen like that costs, Dad ? "

" About fifteen dollars," said David sternly.

Bobby's face dropped. " That's a lot," he said.

" Which reminds me," Claudia discovered suddenly, " I haven't got enough money."

David dug his hand in his pocket. " How much do you need ? "

" About fifteen dollars," she answered silently. Aloud she said, " Never mind, I have to cash a cheque anyway, and I've got enough for the taxi down."

" Matthew's expensive," Bobby commented. " He ought to have his tail kicked."

" I'm in complete accord," said David.

Claudia didn't trust the glint in his eye. She took him aside before she left. " Promise me," she begged him, " that you won't lose your temper with him while I'm gone."

" I'll promise nothing," he said.

It was dark when she came home. Lights from the little cottage blinked at her as the taxi turned up the drive. She was relieved to see that David was still on the porch, but the way he got up from his chair showed that he wasn't curing, he was waiting for her. " It's about time," he greeted her. " What did Miss Grigsby have to say ? "

" I didn't talk to her. She was still at the teachers' meeting, so I left the letter and the pen on her desk."

" What kept you so long then ? "

" It wasn't so long."

" It's pitch dark."

" I can't help what time the sun goes down. Very well, I did a little shopping if you must know. Tooth-paste, and the like. Where's Matthew ? "

" In bed. And without his supper, if you must know."

" That's heartless. You promised——"

" I promised nothing. Come back here, where are you going ? "

" To see him, of course."

" Be sure you tell him he's wonderful ! " David threw after her. " Go ahead and spoil him ! "

" I might," she said. " And then again, I mightn't."

At any rate, Matthew got no supper. " He ate enough when he came home from school to last him, so do not worry," Bertha confided to Claudia, as they cleared the table together.

" I'm not worried," said Claudia. " It's better for him not to eat too much when he's upset. Give me the peas for baby's lunch tomorrow. I'll do them in the living-room."

David was reading on the stiff sofa. She sat down beside him and began to shell. " This is cosy," she said.

" Very cosy. I suppose you smuggled something in to him ? "

" Into who ? "

He returned to his book with a grunt. " It's a good thing children are born with fathers."

" Oh, very good," she agreed readily. " I don't see how we could manage otherwise. What is it, Bobby ? " she broke off. " Come in, don't stand at the door like company, what do you want ? "

" Matthew's crying," said Bobby.

" Crocodile tears," said David. " He's not to have anything to eat, and that's final."

" He's not hungry," said Bobby. " He's acting funny."

" Funny how ? " said David.

Bobby shifted his weight uncomfortably. He looked at Claudia, not certain whether to divulge the exact nature of Matthew's behaviour. " Speak out," Claudia invited.

" He gave me this," said Bobby. He opened his hand. David leaned forward to see what was in it. " It's the pen," Bobby explained.

" So it appears," said David in an ominous voice. " I thought you said you returned it, Claudia."

Claudia popped a pod so that the peas made a small tattoo against the side of the pot. " I did," she said.

" This is a new pen." Bobby gave a large swallow. " It's just like the old one except that it's new, and Matthew says he doesn't want it, the dope. Can I really have it, Mother ? "

" ' *May* I really have it, Mother,' " Claudia corrected pleasantly. " No, dear, you mayn't. Matthew had no right to give it to you. It's his, and he's to wear it to school in the top pocket of his coat. And use it."

" But he doesn't want to, he says he hates it ! "

" Good night, dear," said Claudia.

" Good night," said Bobby, vastly bewildered, and not a little awed. " Gosh."

She stole a look at David's face. Once more his eyes were fixed on his book. To all intents and purposes, he was absorbed in what he was reading.

" It worked with Bluff that time on the farm," she ventured in a small voice. " You tied the goose around his neck and he never killed another one."

David closed his book with great deliberation. " It certainly takes a woman to be cruel," he said.

" It certainly does." She rose quickly and started for the kitchen with the peas. He caught her hand, and pulled her down on to his lap. " I'm not crying," she denied.

" Who said you were. Let me have your handkerchief." He dabbed with a gentle touch at her streaming eyes.

" I'm glad you're soft underneath," she gulped. " I couldn't bear it if you weren't."

He smiled. " That makes us even," he said.

It was idiotic the way she let the thing get hold of her. She woke up the next morning with—of all ignominious ailments—an earache, and she knew that it was nothing else in the world but the pen—and maybe the cold blustery ride into town and back, the evening before. She'd never

had an earache in her life, the children weren't given to
ears either, thank goodness, so she had no idea how much
it could hurt. It was far worse than a toothache, actually,
since you could always have the tooth taken out.

She didn't mention it to David, and went walking with
him as usual, but the sharp March wind was an excruciating
torture.

" Why's your face all screwed up ? " he noticed half-way
home.

" I have a pain in my ear," she mumbled.

" Your *what* ? "

" Ear."

" That's what I thought you said. This is a nice how-
do-you-do. You're going straight to bed when you get
home."

" You don't go to bed with an ear."

He took no monkey-business, however, and while she was
in the bathroom getting undressed, he telephoned Dr.
Geiger behind her back. " Dr. Geiger says he'll see you
tomorrow if you're not better. In the meantime, he'll
leave a prescription at the drug-store to relieve the
pressure."

" It's not necessary, that's ridiculous. Anyway, who's
going to pick the prescription up ? "

" I am," said David. " It'll be dull walking by myself,
so I'll go down to the village this afternoon and get that
haircut I've been needing for a couple of weeks."

It was all a little too pat, especially in view of the fact
that he came home without the haircut. " Both barber
shops were busy," he told her.

" Then what kept you so long ? "

He gave her back her own routine of the night before.
" It's not so long," he said.

" Only an hour and a half, which is quite a time to get
no haircut in."

" Oh, I did a little shopping on the side," he said. " I
picked up your medicine and bought some tooth-paste and
the like."

" You're hiding something. You stopped in at the school and saw Miss Grigsby."

" I can't think of anything I would enjoy less than exchanging theories of modern education with Miss Grigsby," said David, and Claudia saw no reason to doubt his word.

The next morning, however, she got to the bottom of his trip to town. Her ear was much better but not well enough to go outdoors—in fact, she must have been half deaf, for she didn't hear Dr. Geiger's car drive up, and it wasn't until he walked into the house, with David behind him, that she realised that they had been talking on the porch together for quite a while. " Oh, this is unforgivable to have you come all the way out here for nothing," she cried. " David should have phoned you I was all right."

" I didn't mind the trip, I rather enjoyed it," said Dr. Geiger. " You see, I have no surgery hours on Saturday." He opened his satchel, and withdrew the usual paraphernalia. " Besides, a bad ear is nothing to trifle with," he continued leisurely. " It's just as well to have a look at it." He put his little light together, and squinted through it. " How's Matthew coming along ? " he asked.

" Quite chastened," she said. " The goose worked." Then she remembered that Dr. Geiger didn't know anything about what had happened yesterday, he was referring to the pneumonia. " Oh, fine," she corrected herself hastily. " He's out sledding with Bobby, just as if he'd never been sick. Ouch ! "

" Hurt ? "

" A little."

Dr. Geiger withdrew the instrument. " Considerable inflammation," he said, " but no bulging. Stay in the house over the week-end, and I'm fairly certain it'll clear up in a day or two."

She threw a disgusted look at David. " I don't see what you're grinning about. Dr. Geiger is being nice about it, but he doesn't particularly enjoy wasting his time like this.

It would serve you right if he went over you too while he's here."

" That would be an excellent idea," Dr. Geiger agreed, as he closed his satchel with a decisive click. " Rather like killing two birds with one stone. Except that there wouldn't be much point in it, since I examined him yesterday at my house."

" But he isn't due for a check-up until next week," Claudia explained. " Why did you go without my knowing, David—is anything wrong ? "

" Not a thing," Dr. Geiger assured her in haste. " Your husband stole a march on you, and we got the X-rays over with at the same time."

The word X-ray exploded against her brain, and caused the room to recede in dimming circles. No wonder people fainted, it was a good way to duck out of facing the things you didn't want to face. And then she saw that David was still wearing that broad smile, and his eyes were very blue. " It's good news, darling," he told her jubilantly. " Don't look so scared."

Her voice was hardly more than a croak. " How good ? "

" Cured ! "

" Hold on a minute, not so fast," Dr. Geiger objected. " I told your husband on the porch just now that the pictures showed a definite healing of the lesion——"

" And the tests were negative, what more do you want ? " David interrupted.

" I want you to be sensible," said Dr. Geiger, " and face facts as they are, and not as you'd like them to be. Yes, I'm very pleased with the X-rays, and the tests, too, although they're less conclusive than the pictures. But—" He stood a long time on the small word, and made it say a great many things. " I can only go so far as to say that the progress of the disease has been arrested. As for a cure—" He shook his head. " With the perfected use of surgery and drugs we might some day be able to say that we've found a cure, but at the present time no honest physician will allow a patient to return to normal living under that assumption."

"Just the same, darling," David broke in again like an eager schoolboy, "Dr. Geiger says we can go home around the middle of May, or the first of June, depending on the weather."

She couldn't take it in. It was too much to take in. She knew that she ought to say something, but when she began to speak, she found that for the second time in two days, she was crying like a fool.

"Hey, darling," David protested. "This isn't like you, darling—"

Dr. Geiger smiled one of his rare and wonderful smiles. "Let darling alone," he said. "It's been a long, hard pull. She's entitled to a few nerves."

Bertha didn't cry, exactly, but she acted pretty much like a fool, too, and burned the spinach. "Yippee!" said Matthew, when he saw canned corn.

"Chew it and chew it," she impressed upon him. "I would be in a fix if I didn't have some strained peas left from yesterday for the baby."

"I hate strained peas," Matthew tossed in gratuitously. "Can we take an airplane home?"

"We'll need a truck," said David.

"Or Julia's limousine," said Claudia.

"It seems like last week only that we drove up with the children," Bertha marvelled. "How time flies."

"Yes, and no," said David. "Mostly no."

Claudia nodded. That summed up her feelings, too. The past year might be but a moment in time, but it was an eternity in living. It had been the same with the war. Perhaps all great suffering boiled down into a capsule of experience. It tore you to pieces while you lived through it, and then all at once, you were put together and made whole again, sometimes better than before. Certainly David had never looked as happy as at this moment. He looked as if the world were suddenly laid at his feet. It was only

Bobby whose eyes held no looking-forward. She was pretty sure that she knew what was bothering him—Shakespeare had disappeared again and this time he hadn't come back. " Of course, we've another six or eight weeks before we leave," she mentioned, casually.

The cloud on Bobby's face lifted. " That crazy cat certainly ought to be home by then," he said.

" He's been gone a pretty long while, Bobby," David said gravely. " I'm afraid he's not going to come home."

" I keep hoping," said Bobby.

" I keep hoping too," said Claudia.

" So do I," said Matthew. " Could I have some more corn ? "

" Please—" Claudia supplied mechanically.

" Please."

" No, you've had enough."

" I bet anything," Bobby went on, with stalwart conviction, " that somebody stole Shakespeare off the road, and he'll find his way back."

" I bet he doesn't," said Matthew. " I bet he's dead. Pass the pepper—' please '."

" You can get along very nicely without pepper," David interposed.

Matthew gave up in utter frustration of his each and every desire. " Oh, shoot," he said.

Claudia refrained from admonishing him that " shoot " was a bad word, since, strictly speaking, it wasn't. " How would you like to go walking in my place this afternoon ? " she offered, purely on behalf of his badly battered psyche. " Dr. Geiger said Dad could add another fifteen minutes to his exercise."

Matthew could see no particular pleasure to be derived from trudging along the countryside for three-quarters of an hour. " When can I have a bicycle ? " he said.

" That's all I need," said Claudia. " You'll walk and like it."

" Is Bobby going with Dad ? "

" Yes," said Bobby. " Any objections ? "

He pondered it, trying to decide whether there was more éclat with or without his elder brother.

"Make up your mind," David injected curtly. "You're doing us no favour."

"Oh, all right, I'll go," Matthew finally elected. His tone implied that although it was no great shakes of a way to spend a Saturday afternoon, it was, nevertheless, the best offer he'd had to date. He didn't have the remotest idea that company would come the minute he turned his back, or wild horses could not have dragged him from the spot. Matthew liked the general excitement of company, no matter who.

It wasn't five minutes after they started off that Claudia saw a car drive up. It wasn't a delivery, so she concluded that it couldn't be anybody except someone looking for some place else. A moment or two later, Bertha knocked at the bathroom door. "Mrs. Naughton, it is a lady to see you."

"What kind of a lady?" Claudia opened the door on a cautious crack, but Bertha was too fast for her. "Mrs. Naughton, you are not going to wash your hair with a bad ear!" she decried, aghast.

"Of course not, I was going to take it off first. Who is it?"

"She says to tell you it is ' Miss Carey.' It is the worst thing for an earache to shampoo!"

"It won't hurt me, and don't go telling tales to Mr. David. I have to do it while I can get a whack at the bathroom. I don't know any Miss Carey, is she selling something?"

"She has nothing in her hand; she seems to know you."

"They all seem to know you. Intimately. ' Carey.' I don't remember any Miss Carey, only my old trained nurse when I had the miscarriage. Is it?"

"That I could not say," said Bertha. "That was the year Lisa died and Fritz took sick, and you had Jane to help you."

"Oh, yes. Well, tell whoever it is I'll be right in."

"I am glad whoever it is stopped you from taking a shampoo," Bertha had the last word.

" Whoever it is," Claudia muttered, " I'll get rid of her quick, and take it later."

Whoever it was, was standing with her back to the door looking out of the living-room window, but Claudia recognised at once the beaver coat, which finally cleared up the mystery of the phantom woman on the Sanatorium grounds. Then Miss Carey turned, and her eyeglasses solved the problem of the stranger who had sent her love through the children the previous week. " You have been driving me crazy ! " Claudia expostulated without preamble.

Miss Carey laughed. " You know, it wasn't until the bus had gone that I realised I hadn't told the youngsters my name. So I made it my business to find out where you lived, and here I am. I've only kept you in suspense a few days, so don't hold it against me."

" You've kept me in suspense for months," said Claudia. " Were you at the Sanatorium around November ? "

Miss Carey thought back. " November. Yes. I came up for a few days around that time, but I couldn't have spent more than half an hour there."

" Some time within that half-hour I drove by in a taxi with David and saw you. It's been bothering me ever since. I can't get over your being here ! "

" I can't get over your being here, either," Miss Carey said. She sat down, and Claudia sat in a chair near by, and they looked at each other across a sudden, small silence, at a loss all at once to bridge in a few short moments everything that had happened to each of them in the intervening years. They made no pretence of not studying each other. Miss Carey was smaller than the picture Claudia carried in her mind, but that might have been because the starched white of a nurse's uniform lent stature to even the plainest of women. And Miss Carey was plain, her greying hair and spinster-face lost in the undistinguished brown of hat and coat. Yet the brusque approach of her forthright voice could have belonged to no one else."   " You haven't changed," said Claudia.   " You're just the same."

" You've changed."   Miss Carey's eyes held a candid

interest as she searched Claudia's face. "A lot of things
have happened to you. I kept tabs on you through Dr.
Rowland until I went overseas toward the end of the war."

"Dr. Rowland told me when you went," said Claudia.
"I asked to have you again when Michael was born, but
he said you'd stayed in Los Angeles with your sister."

"I did, for almost a year. That's why I didn't know
about your husband until I saw Bobby and Matthew."

"Hardly anyone knows," said Claudia. "At least that's
what David hopes, he's still so sensitive about it."

"Most people are," said Miss Carey, "until they realise
how many thousands and thousands either have it, or have
had it. I don't have to ask how he's coming along, I passed
him walking down the road with the boys and the dog. I
waved, but they didn't see me. He looked very well."

"He's wonderful!" Claudia said jubilantly. "Dr.
Geiger told him today to increase his exercise slowly up to
an hour by the first of May, and if all went well—" She
wasn't taking any risks at this point—she bent to knock
loudly and firmly on the wooden rung of the sofa— "we
could go home around the first of June."

"That is wonderful," Miss Carey acknowledged heartily.
"And he wants to go home," she added, more in question
than in statement.

"Wants to?" Claudia echoed. "My biggest job is
going to be to make him wait the time out until the weather
settles."

"That's really wonderful," Miss Carey repeated. "You'd
be surprised at the number of patients who want to stay
on whether they have to or not. They have a fear of going
back to normal living. It's a disease in itself."

"Well that's one thing I don't have to worry about with
David," said Claudia. "He's counting the days until he
can get back to work."

"You've been through a great deal." Miss Carey's eyes
again searched Claudia's face. "I said you'd changed when
you came into the room a few minutes ago. You haven't
actually, you've just lived up to yourself. And you're fine."

"Oh, I've had a little earache," Claudia returned casually, although she knew that Miss Carey was looking deeper than ears. Miss Carey had helped her find the way through a long black tunnel that had led from the hospital bed back to the wide sunny meadows of the farm. It was incredible, and a little disturbing to realise that this quiet stranger knew more about her than any other living creature, including David. David had only glimpsed the agony of those nightmare weeks, but he could not share in the fullness of knowing, because he had never experienced fear, and weakness and confusion. David was strong, he would always be strong.

She was aware that Miss Carey had risen to her feet. "I've got to get back to my patient," she said. "I only meant to drop in for a minute or two, and I've stayed longer than I should have."

"Oh," said Claudia. "I'm glad. I mean, I didn't want to ask straight out—I thought you were up here because you were ill. I mean, I didn't know you took anything but obstetrical cases."

"I don't," Miss Carey said. "But this is an exception. It's a little girl I brought into the world ten years ago—"

"Bobby's age—how dreadful," Claudia breathed.

"It is. Her parents are getting a divorce, and the Sanatorium had no place for her, so I found a little apartment for us, and she's doing fairly well. The cleaning-woman's with her now, so that's why I have to hurry back. Maybe you'll bring Bobby to see her when she's a little further along—I'll call you in a week or so—"

"Please do," said Claudia.

"Could I have a peep at the baby before I go?"

"Could you? You must. I'm surprised that Bertha hasn't brought him in already, she's such a show-off. I'll see what's keeping her." She started for the hall, and then hurried to the window at the sound of a car pulling up in front of the door. It was a bright yellow car, full of sport, with its exhaust pipes springing out of the motor and over the hood, like mighty entrails. It came to a stop behind

Miss Carey's dun-coloured coupé, and made the driveway look very social indeed. " This is absolutely unheard of," said Claudia. " We haven't had a visitor since we've been here. Excuse me, I'll see who it is. . . ."

It turned out to be the Trents. They had driven down from Lake Placid to see some friends, and were merely stopping by on the way home. " I told Byard we simply had to come in if only for a minute, I'm so thoroughly ashamed, all these months, and after I told Julia I'd keep an eye on you. But you know how it is, one thing and another—*what* a sweet little place—this is fun, we drove past it twice, looking for it—" Lydia paused for breath. " Byard dear, don't take off your coat, I see Mrs. Naughton has company, and we shouldn't have barged in without telephoning first—but it was such fun."

" I have to take off my coat, it's warm in here," Byard said, a trifle petulantly. " Where's your husband, taking his exercise like a good lunger ? "

Claudia winced. " Yes. Do come into the living-room, won't you ? "

Lydia clung to the clear spaces of the hall. " Julia told me you had a cat. I loathe cats—I mean to say, I'm terrified of them——"

" You can relax," said Claudia ironically. " we've lost our cat."

" Oh good," said Lydia, which endeared her immeasurably to Claudia's heart. She remembered not liking Lydia very much, and now she liked her less. Fun, indeed. Where did all the fun come from ? There wasn't much fun about Byard. He was a sullen-looking man, with a dark moustache and a round, full chin, the sort of man who had to be well-bred not to look ill-bred with that kind of a face. Lydia had a lot of chin, too, but it went in a different direction. It was quite long, and jutted out, and gave her face an unfurnished expression, as if she hadn't had time to move into it and settle down.

Claudia introduced Miss Carey, who said she was just about to leave, and in the flurry of incoming and outgoing,

5

Bertha nonchalantly appeared with Michael, just as if she hadn't spent the last twenty minutes making him look beautiful. He did look beautiful, too, in the blue silk rompers that Candy had sent the day before, with a note pinned to the sleeve, saying : " To be returned in one year for further use."

Miss Carey won Bertha's heart at once by reaching out her arms. " Bless it ! " she cried, in the deep tone of a 'cello.

" How sweet, what fun," Lydia piped, like the chirping of a bird. " How old is he ? " She didn't wait for an answer. " Oh dear," she discovered, " look outside, it's beginning to snow, I think we'd better shove off, Byard, we haven't any chains on the car."

Byard said they certainly had better, and hustled back into his coat. " Wouldn't like to get stuck on a hill," he said.

A few moments later, both cars were driving off. Lydia took one perfectly gloved hand off the wheel to wave it back. " We'll be driving down again soon, now that we know how to find you ! " she called back.

" Do ! " Claudia shouted under her breath. " And what fun if you find us in New York ! "

David turned in at the gate while she was still standing in the doorway. He said, " Whose two cars just drove out?"

She stared at him. " Two cars ? Darling, you're crazy, mad. Bobby, what's happened to your poor father ? "

" He must be seeing things," Bobby played along.

" There were two cars ! " Matthew swaggered. " There were so, one was yellow ! "

" You're a fool," said Bobby. " Shut up."

" Would you like to tell us of your own accord, Mamma?" David enquired pleasantly, " or shall we use force ? "

He was in too high spirits to take any chance, he had the look in his eye of being ready to pick her up and swing her around. She edged away from him. " Some people have all the luck," she grumbled. " You missed the Trents."

" Splendid," said David. " They've been hanging over our heads for months. Did they drive down in separate cars, or what ? "

" No, but I wouldn't put it past them. Guess who it was at the bus ? "

" The bus driver."

" Very witty. Miss Carey."

" Who's she ? "

" My old trained nurse. Remember ? "

" Oh," said David. " Yes. She was quite a guy, as I recall. Matthew, stop kicking at that chair ! "

Matthew desisted sullenly. " Why did I have to take a walk when company was coming ? " he demanded rebelliously.

" I didn't know company was coming," Claudia explained, " or I'd have gone for a walk, too. . . . The Trents are definitely not our type," she elucidated to David in an aside.

" I could have told you that before they came," said David.

" Everything's fun with Lydia and nothing really is."

" I know the type. What's Byard like ? "

" Not like you."

" Did you tell them we were going home ? "

" I didn't want to brag. There wasn't time, anyway. I told Miss Carey, though. She was so happy for us."

" I'm so happy for us, too," said David simply.

He slept indoors that night. " I might as well get used to it," he said. " I can't take a sleeping-porch back home with me."

Claudia nodded. She couldn't speak. She knew that tonight he would not leave her.

He sat down on the bed beside her, and turned her face toward his. " Don't look so frightened," he said in a low voice. " Everything's all right." Slowly, he placed his lips on hers. " I'm well, darling," he said huskily. " I'm well."

EIGHT

IT WAS A LOAD off her mind that he didn't get too big for his breeches. Still, working up to an hour's exercise twice a day was as much as anyone could ask for. Twenty-five minutes carried them through the north gate of the Sanatorium, almost to the south gate, which meant their first real contact with the patients, because only a few of them ever took the road past the house, on account of its being a long uphill climb on the way back.

The grounds of the Sanatorium were beautiful at this time of the year. The trees were beginning to put out leaves, and some of the shrubs were already in full flower. It was a happy enough place. On the surface, anyway. Often the women carried baskets back to their cottages from the workshop, with the gay colours of the raffia streaming out behind them; the men, however, made things that had to be finished at the shop—things of leather and metal and wood. Some of the projects were quite ambitious. For example, Dr. Healey was making a desk set of seven pieces, including the copper-cornered blotter. He was a professor of Physics from a mid-western university, and David got to talking to him one day about molecular beams, and they struck up quite a friendship.

" How'd you like me to make you something? " David asked Claudia, half in jest. " I can double my exercise time, and it's a good way, Healey says, to work yourself into unlimited." Dr. Healey had just been put on unlimited, which meant that he could walk as far as he liked, and stay in the shop as long as he wanted. " I think," said David, " I'll start on an ash-tray, just for the fun of it."

" I can imagine nothing I'd like better than an ash-tray," said Claudia. " Suppose I make you a sewing basket? "

No one could have been more surprised than they were when the shop began to get under their skin. " Really, I forget everything while I'm doing that silly basket," said Claudia.

" So do I," David admitted sheepishly.

Occasionally, they had to miss a morning or an afternoon, because they could never be sure that they could thumb a ride down to the Sanatorium and back. If they couldn't, it turned out to be a walk and no workshop, but even so, David turned out the ash-tray in no time, and began on a leather wallet for Bobby. " I'll make another basket," said Claudia. " I'm a one-trick pony."

They hadn't quite finished their second enterprise when Dr. Healey stopped coming to the shop. For a day or two they thought nothing of it, but when he kept on not coming, they asked one of the patients whether he had gone home.

" Not much he hasn't, he's in the infirmary," said the patient with an hysterical giggle. She was a perpetual girl with her bleached hair bobbed long, and wrinkles, which proved that everyone who was sick wasn't wonderful, which was David's contention about dead people, too.

" Infirmary ? " David echoed. " What for ? "

She shrugged. " What do you think for ? Flare-up, of course."

It was shocking to both of them. " Poor devil," said David, " that's a pretty tough break just when he was ready to leave. The workshop won't be the same without him."

She suddenly realised now much he must have missed male companionship during all these months. " Do you know something ? You've had an awfully big dose of two females and three children," she said.

" It wasn't too bad," he replied. " There was always the dog."

They laughed a little, but neither of them felt like laughing. They didn't even work out their time at the shop that morning. " Let's leave now," David suggested, " and walk home, instead of getting a ride."

" All right," she agreed. It was going overboard a little, but she could see that he was restless and perturbed.

When they got back to the cottage, they found Bertha bustling around, trying to hide boxes of winter underwear and leggings and heavy sweaters. " I did not know we would have company, or I would not have started to pack all over the place," she apologised.

" Oh, oh," said David. " Another visitation from the Trents."

" Also Mr. Dexter is coming, he is staying with them for a little while," Bertha went on with a pleased smile. " Mrs. Trent telephoned just after you left, and I said you would be home around noon and she said that would be about the time that they would get here."

" She has a nerve, just at lunch," said Claudia.

Bertha looked worried. " I hope the grocery man comes with the order soon," she said.

" They are not staying to eat," David stated firmly. " What's more, I'm going out on the porch to rest from my morning's labours. If anyone should ask you, Mrs. Naughton, our exercise today added up to approximately an hour and twenty minutes."

" I know it did," said Claudia, " but I let you get away with it—I'm exhausted," she threw in casually, " aren't you?"

" Not especially," he said. " But I'm going out on the porch anyway, and whoever wants to see me, can see me there."

" My sentiments exactly," said Claudia. " I'll join you as soon as I change to a decent dress. Lydia's gloves challenge the woman in me."

" I hate to think what her husband will challenge in me," said David gloomily.

One thing that could be said for Byard, however, he was an easy guest to entertain. The moment he set foot on the porch, he flung himself into the chair next to David's with a satisfied grunt. " I can use a little rest cure after that ride," he announced. " Phil drives like a demon. That's a big animal you've got there. Hey, get away from me."

" Down, old boy," said David. " Come over here and behave yourself."

" That's better. He's too much dog for my taste. Have you got an extra blanket around ? "

" Take this one, I'm not using it."

" You're not ? You're asking for trouble, old man, this warm weather's treacherous."

" Yes, David, it is, I'll get another one," Claudia urged. " Come along inside, Bluff."

" He's all right," said David. " Let him stay. And I don't want a blanket, I haven't used one for a week."

Phil and Lydia had already made themselves at home in the living-room. " Did your cat come back ? " Lydia asked.

" No, he didn't," said Claudia shortly.

Phil turned to her in solicitude. " That beautiful orange Persian, what happened ? "

" We don't know. He began to go away for a day or two at a time, and one night he went off and never came back."

" Perhaps somebody liked beautiful orange Persians," said Lydia.

Claudia shook her head. " He wasn't stolen. David says that when cats grow old they often find a place where they can go off by themselves and die."

" More sporting than humans," Phil commented. " The boys must miss him."

" Bobby's heartbroken, he was devoted to Shakespeare. But Matthew takes it in his stride. Nothing bothers him for long."

" Lucky Matthew," said Phil.

Bertha sidled up to the door, full of unction. " Mr. Dexter, would you like to see my baby eat his dinner all by himself ? " There was a definite pointedness to the invitation, which implied that she was not casting pearls before swine. Lydia, however, took no umbrage. " Of course Mr. Dexter wants to see your baby," she said. " It's the main reason he came."

" It really is, too, I do believe," she went on laughingly to Claudia, as Phil sprinted off in Bertha's wake. " That man is absolutely out of his head about children."

" I know," said Claudia.

" He should have had a whole houseful of them—if Edith hadn't been such a selfish fool of a woman."

Claudia found it embarrassing to allude to Phil's dead wife in such terms. " But Edith was so devastated after the loss of her son," she offered in justification.

" It was Phil's son too," Lydia maintained dispassionately. " And he worshipped the boy. But did she ever think of that? No. She ruined her own life, and damned near ruined his. It's a dreadful thing to say, but he's been a different person since she—— Well, everyone knows that it was suicide, so why mince words."

" He is changed," Claudia conceded. " There was a time when he'd got so——" She sought for a word. " Bloodless," she ended lamely.

" Precisely," said Lydia. " And why? Because Edith hung herself around his neck like a mill-stone."

" I suppose that's true," Claudia murmured.

" I think we've got him interested in buying a strip of property across from where we are. Phil always wanted a place of his own in the country, but Edith hated the country, she said the quiet frightened her. But Phil loves it, and the only thing *he's* afraid of is the social aspect because everyone is beginning to build or buy at the Lake. But it would be the best thing in the world for him to go to a few dances and dinners. Why be a hermit? Life's too short."

Too short for what, thought Claudia. Certainly too short to waste on dinners and dances.

" Whom have you met interesting up here?" Lydia swept on, hardly pausing for breath.

" What? Oh, nobody, really." (Nobody, that is, that you'd call interesting.) " David's been too busy getting his health back."

" Yes, of course. This dreary routine. It must be simply ghastly for you."

" Not now. It's almost over with. It must have been pretty ghastly for you, too." A note of warmth invaded

Claudia's voice, she felt a sudden sense of contact with this remote and talkative woman. "After all," she said with compassion, "your husband's been up here a great deal longer than David."

"Oh, it wasn't so bad," said Lydia cheerfully. "You see I knew lots of people in this neighbourhood, and of course I used to fly to New York every month or so for a few days, so it was all rather fun, actually. . . . As a matter of fact, I've just got back from New York. I met Jerry Seymour at Hartley's—Julia's still away, but Hartley asked me for dinner, knowing I'd seen you—and he sent you his regards. Jerry, I mean."

"I'm very fond of Jerry, he's an old friend," Claudia managed to get in edgewise.

"Strange man," said Lydia. "Sensitive, I suppose you could call it."

"Very sensitive," said Claudia, "and very fine."

"I suppose so," Lydia repeated vaguely. "I hear he's got a book coming out shortly. Autobiographical. All about his marriage to Elizabeth Van Doren."

"Yes. Candy wanted him to publish it. She feels that it's a tribute to her mother."

"I'd never met Candy," Lydia digressed, "until that same evening. Poor child, she was horribly pregnant. I knew her mother-in-law, though, we used to summer at the Vineyard, our places were practically in each other's laps, you know how the Vineyard is, it's fun if you're brought up to it. And of course I knew John from the time he was knee high to a grasshopper. I never realised he was your husband's partner until the other evening. Small world. I hear he's very good, too. Some friends of ours wanted him to do their camp at Placid but he turned it down. He was foolish, it could have led to any number of things."

"It really isn't that sort of a firm," Claudia explained.

"What's the difference what you do," Lydia argued, "as long as you're an architect, and it's something to build." She yawned in the back of her throat, suddenly weary of the whole discussion. " I'd like to wash up before we go, may I ? "

" Of course." Claudia led the way to the tiny bathroom, clean and tidy, but festooned with its carefully separated towels, and a large assortment of oddments and endments. She could sense the impact on Lydia's fastidious soul, as she left her to make out as best she could over the hurdle of the baby's equipment.

She found Bertha bustling around in the kitchen. " Michael has had his dinner and is asleep," Bertha opened up in a propitiating way. She never called Michael Michael unless she was ill at ease about something.

" May I ask what you are doing ? " Claudia enquired distrustfully.

" Fixing lunch. It will not be much because the order did not come, but they will understand."

" WHO will understand ? "

Bertha rolled her shoulders and her eyes. " We cannot let people leave at this hour without eating, surely."

" Oh, can't we, surely ? Well, I'll show you how it's done. Bertha, seriously, don't you realise Mr. David would have a fit if they stayed ? "

" Mrs. Naughton, I think he would like it," said Bertha flatly. She drew Claudia to the window. " Look out at him. Is that a man who does not want company ? "

By straining a little, Claudia could see the porch. There was Phil, lean and tan, sitting on the rail, while David and Byard Trent were still in their chairs, wrapped in blankets. All three of them were talking with interest and animation. " I'll ask them," said Claudia.

Phil was against it. " We'll snatch a bite in the village the way we intended to do."

" Nonsense," said David, as if he meant it. " Bertha thrives on this sort of thing."

" You won't get much," Claudia warned them quickly, " the deliveries haven't come——"

" Whatever it is," Byard accepted with alacrity, " it'll be better than eating at one of those inns. Got plenty of milk?"

" Quarts," said Claudia.

" Fine," he said, " just beat a couple of eggs into mine."

Claudia returned to Bertha. " I hope you're satisfied," she said. " You have five people to feed, not counting yourself."

" What shall I do, sit all day in a rocking-chair and rock ? " Bertha retorted. " I am having a beautiful lentil soup and a chicken liver omelette."

" Mr. Trent wants two eggs in his glass of milk."

" The omelette is eggs," said Bertha doubtfully.

Claudia got out the beater. " I'll do it anyway," she said. " He acts like he'd like it."

Bertha nudged her slyly in the ribs. " While you are about it," she said without moving her lips, " beat one into Mr. David's milk, too."

Claudia was greatly tempted. " No," she decided. " He'd be wild." David was very proud of the fact that he had both his health and his shape.

A feather could have knocked her over when he asked for an egg-nog before he went to bed that night. " Byard says he's found that it's the most painless way of putting on weight," he explained. " How much do you think that fellow's gained ? "

" Judging from his chin and his stomach, quite a lot."

" Twenty-two pounds."

" Well, well," she remarked lightly, " he seems to be making quite a career of getting well."

" He's a pretty old hand at it, he ought to be, he was here a year before he decided to settle in Placid for good. He's very keen about Placid, by the way."

" So is Lydia. She says she hasn't been out of a dinner-gown the whole season."

Again, he didn't seem to catch the irony in her voice. He sat on the bed and drew her down beside him, like the evening that Dr. Geiger had told them they could go home around the first of June. Another few weeks, and it would be the first of June.

" Claudia," he said, " what would you think of our
changing our plans and spending the summer in Placid ? "

At first she thought she hadn't heard him correctly, and
then she thought he was joking. " What fun ! " she
answered banteringly.

" It would be extra insurance for me, and a good rest
for you, before you begin looking for a place for us to live,"
he went on quite seriously.

" You don't really mean it, do you ? " she asked with
difficulty.

" Certainly I mean it," he said. " There's not much
activity in the office during the summer, and there happens
to be a lot of building going on in Placid. I could take on
a commission or two and gradually get myself back into
the swing of work before the autumn. It'd be good for the
children, too," he added. " Byard says there are a number
of boys' camps around there. What do you say ? "

She didn't know what to say. It all made very sound
sense, and she had every reason to jump at the suggestion,
and be happy that he was being sensible about not plunging
back too quickly into normal living. She probably owed a
lasting debt of gratitude not only to Byard Trent, but to
the unwitting contribution of poor Doctor Healey as well.
Except for one thing. David's lips were eager and smiling,
but fear looked out at her from his eyes. She tried to turn
away from it, make herself believe that it wasn't there. But
it was there. It had been there for weeks, for months—
a hidden adversary suddenly to be reckoned with.

Matthew bustled into her room early the next morning,
dangling a broken shoe-lace. " Here," he said accusingly.

" Thanks," said Claudia. " What would you like me to
do with it ? "

" I have to have another one right away, or I'll be late
for school." He took in the unopened bed beside her own.
" Why didn't Daddy sleep with you again " he demanded.

Trust Matthew never to miss a trick. " It was too warm
indoors," she told him, which, in fact, had been David's

rather faltering explanation last night. That, and the mattress. He'd given her credit for just about as much sense as Matthew, for the mattress was no worse than it had been all along, and the weather, if anything, had turned cooler. She'd let him go without question, however, knowing that he wanted to be alone. She could see how hard it was for him to acknowledge this newness of fear within him. He, too, was trying to pretend that it wasn't there.

She led Matthew's interest back to the shoe-lace. "If Bertha hasn't got another one for you, wear your black shoes."

"I can't. I wore them yesterday. . . . Is Daddy still asleep outside?"

"Yes, so don't talk so loud."

He lowered his voice greatly. "Could I have a shoe-lace from his shoe?"

"Your father would be enchanted. No, you may certainly not. And anyway, there's no law against wearing your black shoes two days in succession, and also, anyway," it came over her, "why did you wear them yesterday? You know you're to save them for your good blue suit when you get back to New York."

"I had to wear them. My brown ones were wet."

"Your brown ones were wet," she repeated significantly. "You wouldn't have stepped in a puddle by any chance?"

"I didn't see the puddle."

"It's your business to see where you're walking," she informed him sharply. "You got yourself pneumonia once this winter by getting your feet wet, will you never learn a lesson? But no. Puddles seem to be your meat and drink."

"What?"

"Nothing. Go ahead and wear your black ones today, and be a little careful not to scuff them, kindly."

"Bertha won't let me wear them."

"Tell Bertha I said it was all right."

"But Bertha says ' no,' " he reiterated hoarsely. "She says she doesn't want me to catch cold because they're not dry enough yet."

Words failed her. She said, " Matthew Naughton," and found that she couldn't go any further without losing her voice completely. Matthew was made of the stuff that had undoubtedly given birth to Teachers' Meetings. Although he now specialised in honesty, for the benefit of all and sundry, she could see him going through life, stepping into one puddle after another, and being written up in small print as a case-history. On the other hand, it was probably better not to redirect this aquatic tendency into more immediate channels of expression, but just to let him work it out in the great outdoors. " Give me the lace, and I'll tie it together for you," she capitulated with ominous patience.

" I tried already. There isn't room any more."

" Let's see."

He gave it over reluctantly, a diminished brown string knotted raggedly in several places. She examined it for breathing space, and gave it back to him. " This seems to have been going on for years," she concluded grimly. " Go and ask Bobby if he has an extra lace."

" I did, and he said to ' shut-up,' he didn't. Is Daddy always going to sleep on the porch, even in New York ? "

" Do we have porches in New York ? " she requested icily.

" I hate New York," he mentioned free of charge.

" You just hate on principle. You hated it here, too."

" I like it here now," he said. " I wish we didn't have to go home."

" Shame on you. I should think you'd be happy that Dad is well enough to go home."

" Maybe he'll get sick again if he goes home," he suggested blandly.

Her nerves jangled. " Stop dawdling and go and eat your breakfast."

He lingered, graceless and belligerent. " But I have to have a shoe-lace," he persisted.

She had, some minutes past, washed her hands of the shoe-lace. " Matthew, get out," she said slowly, in many syllables.

This time he read the handwriting on the wall. In his haste to depart he bumped into David, who was coming in from the porch with the thermometer in his mouth. " Watch where you're going ! " David commanded thickly.

Matthew regained his equilibrium and his flair for gain at one and the same instant. " If you break the thermometer, save me the quick-silver," he said genially.

He was gone before David could find his tongue. " What was all this jabber about a shoe-lace ? " he mumbled, in a substitute grievance.

" Nothing," said Claudia hastily, wondering what else he had overheard of the conversation. She experienced a small sense of shock that he had taken his temperature in front of Matthew, careful as he always was to hide any evidence of illness from the children. Even when Bluff occasionally got out of bounds and leaped up with his massive weight, David resented protection. " Let him alone, the dog's all right," he would say, making it sound as if Bluff were the one to be protected. Claudia knew that it was the pride in him, yet now, all at once, his pride seemed to have vanished. He withdrew the thermometer and studied it intently for a moment. " Damn," he said.

" How much ? "

" Ninety-nine. On the nose."

She was aware, as she swallowed the sick lump of fear in her throat, that their roles were suddenly reversed, and she was the comforter, not the comforted. " Ninety-nine's no fever," she said.

" It is at this hour of the morning," David returned with a kind of anger. " It'll probably be a hundred by four o'clock, and I'll be flat on my back again."

" That's ridiculous. You talk as if a tiny rise of temperature meant something."

" It means enough. It means that this is the first time in months that I've gone over ninety-eight three or four."

" You might have washed it off in warm water and not shaken it down."

For answer, he shook the thermometer hard and stuck it

in his mouth again. She busied herself making the bed while he sat on the edge of a chair and counted his pulse. Ordinarily she would have let the bed air until after breakfast, but she had to do something to keep him from seeing that she was as shaken and disappointed as he was. This was the sort of thing that had happened at the boarding-house all the time—" So-and-so's off exercise. Running a temp." And of course it had happened to Dr. Healey, that was usually what a flare-up meant.

" Pulse is eighty-four," David informed her after an intolerably long minute.

" That's only because you've been moving around."

He squinted at the thermometer. " Same thing. Damn it."

" I really don't think it means anything," she insisted. " Maybe that long walk yesterday and company on top of it was too much."

" That's very encouraging. I can't even have a little normal social intercourse without paying for it the next day."

It took courage to poke fun at him at this point. " ' A little normal social intercourse,' forsooth. What fancy language you have, Grandma. Only you seem to forget that Candy and John were here for a whole week-end, and your temperature never budged."

His mouth twisted ironically. " That's also very encouraging to think I was better in January than I am now." He gave a small mirthless laugh. " From present indications I'm about as ready to go home as—" (she thought he was going to say " Dr. Healey " but his thoughts fished further afield) " that chap Barwell at the boarding-house," he brought out.

" That's an idiotic comparison if ever I heard one. Tom Barwell's a really sick man."

" Well, give me time," he retorted with the same harsh laugh, " and I might work myself up into his class."

Bewilderment overcame her apprehension. He wasn't himself, he didn't talk like himself or act like himself. This was more than a reasonable discouragement, this was a complete surrender to fear. She was at a loss to understand what had made him so suddenly lose confidence, so suddenly desert the philosophy that had always dictated his great sense of proportion. "Look," she said, marvelling that her voice came out from a closing throat, "you're making a mountain out of a mole-hill, excuse the cliché. I bet you what you like that this tiny little elevation of temperature and pulse has nothing to do with your general condition. You're working yourself up into a stew over nothing. Not that I blame you," she added fairly, "coming at the very tail end like this."

"I don't like it," he insisted doggedly.

"I don't like it, either, but I'm not in the least worried about it," she lied. "If it'll make you feel any easier, though, call Dr. Geiger."

"Why waste his time, he'll just tell me to go off exercise and wait and see what happens."

"Well, that's sensible. Do it, why don't you?"

He gathered up his towel and tooth-brush, without saying that he would, or wouldn't. "I hope Bertha's out of the bathroom with the baby," he remarked as he left the room, ready to be irritated if she wasn't.

"She always is out at this hour," said Claudia genially.

She felt anything but genial. The palms of her hands were wet, she had to wipe them with her handkerchief before she fluffed the pillows. Her movements slowed. She could hear him say something to Bobby in the hall, and a moment later, Bobby came in, wearing the air of just having eaten breakfast. "Hello," he said.

"Hello," said Claudia. There was a satisfying quality in Bobby's undemonstrative adolescence. "What did Dad ask you just now?" she enquired after a pause.

"Where, in the hall? Oh, just did I leave Bluff out."

"And did you?"

"Yes." He walked to the window, and peered out toward the fence that bounded the property. "He's still sniffing," he reported. "He's so slow."

"He sees no hurry," said Claudia, observing that Bobby was registering the opened bed on the porch. She half expected him to say something about it, but he was old enough not to. "That crazy fool, Matthew," he blew off, as he turned back to the room. "Him and his shoe-lace."

Claudia couldn't help smiling. Such delicacy of instinct deserved recognition. "You know it was almost as warm as summer last night," she remarked conversationally. "I was so glad Dad could sleep outside and get a little air."

"What's he going to do when he gets back to New York?" he asked her thoughtfully.

He was so different from Matthew in his thinking. She could talk to him like a grown-up. "I suppose he'll just have to get used to it," she answered.

"I suppose so," said Bobby. "Bertha says we might live at Uncle Hartley's and Aunt Julia's until we find some place of our own. Will we?"

She didn't tell him that the picture had changed since Bertha had talked to him. His young mind had enough to cope with. "We'll have our hands full keeping Matthew out of the lift," she replied obliquely.

"Who runs it?"

"Anybody. You just press a button."

"Why does Aunt Julia have to have a lift?"

"Because there's five flights of stairs to walk up."

"I'd like to run it," he confessed.

"We'll see if it can be arranged," she smiled. "But look," she cautioned him in good earnest, "don't you ever dare get in it alone, unless you ask first."

"We're not there yet," he reminded her drolly.

"So we're not."

He felt like talking. "Is Aunt Julia home? I mean from that place in India?"

"Tibet? No, she couldn't get there. She went to Australia instead."

"Does she know people in Australia?"

"I don't think so."

" Then why did she go ? "

" For that reason, I imagine. Because she didn't know anybody."

" Oh," said Bobby, not quite seeing. " I wouldn't like to be all alone in a strange country," he remarked finally.

" Some people need to be alone sometimes."

" Do you like to be alone ? "

" No, I hate it," she responded at once, and vehemently. She sounded the image of Matthew. " What are we going to do about that silly shoe-lace, anyway ? " she reverted.

" Bertha wants me to wear my black shoes, so Matthew can have a lace from my brown shoes, and Matthew says if I do I can have his pen. He can't write anyway, and he's beginning to lose it all over the place."

" I noticed that," said Claudia.

His lips twitched in half a smile, and made him look like David. " So I'd better take it before Dad takes it. He has an eye on it, too."

" Fair enough," said Claudia. She ruffled his hair in lieu of the kiss he was too big for. " Hey," he protested, " now I'll have to comb it all over again ! "

" Tough luck," said Claudia. She gave it another ruffle. Bobby almost made her forget that David's temperature was ninety-nine.

NINE

DAVID CAME BACK from the bathroom, exuding an agreeable aroma of tooth-paste and shaving lotion, but still unready to meet the day's demands. "They haven't stopped gabbling about Matthew's shoes in there," he said with growing irritability. "What's it all about?"

"It's about Matthew's shoes," she returned mildly, and explained the situation with a high coloration of its comic aspects.

David listened with one ear, and that one not tuned to comedy. "Very well, if he hasn't got sense enough to keep out of puddles, let him stay home from school until his shoes get dry," he decreed largely.

"And just who do you think you'd be punishing?" Claudia wanted to know. "Anyway, don't bother about it, it's all settled." She thought that it was, with Bobby coming off exceedingly well in the deal; and then the whole lot of them came trooping back—unfortunately just as David was prancing into his trousers.

"Oh excuse me," Bertha apologised, stopping short on the threshold with averted eyes. She picked up the baby, who was giving a good imitation of walking, and started to retreat in embarrassment.

David buttoned his fly with exaggerated composure. "Think nothing of it," he calmed her, "I wouldn't know what to do with privacy if I had it."

"I'm not even sure you'd like it," said Claudia. She regarded the group with foreboding. "What's the matter now?"

"I can't wear these black shoes," Bobby stated baldly.

"What do you mean you can't wear them, you've got them on," said David.

"The trouble is, they don't fit any more," Bertha explained. "Let Papa feel, Bobby."

With mingled pride and discomfort, Bobby extended one foot upwards. David, however, was in no mood to feel, and let him hang in mid-air. Quickly, Claudia felt. It was only too true. Bobby's big toe was jammed up to the very tip of his shoe. It was an occasion of sorts—David really ought to rise to it. " Listen, you've simply got to feel the way this good-for-nothing has grown," she exhorted him.

" I'll take your word for it," he said as stubborn as a mule, and disappeared into his closet for a jacket.

" My shoes still fit," Matthew remarked virtuously.

Bobby threw him a look of contempt. " That's because you're a shrimp."

" I am not a shrimp ! "

A good fight was all that David needed to complete a happy morning. " Bobby, do they hurt very much ? " she interceded hastily.

" They pinch."

" Maybe it will not do harm if for just once you wear them," Bertha wheedled.

" I'm wearing them," Bobby assured her.

" You are a good boy."

" Hell," said Bobby in David's voice, " I want the pen."

" Bobby said ' hell,' " said Matthew.

" Go put your wings on, and fly to school," said Claudia. She pushed him out while David was still in the closet, looking for a certain belt among the ties on his tie-rack. It was an unhappy coincidence that, as he emerged, Bluff should have come bounding into the room, wondering where everyone had disappeared to. In his exuberance, he kissed the wrong person. " Damn it, down ! " David shouted in a sudden burst of temper. He kicked out at the dog, and Bluff gave a small yelp of surprise. A startled silence fell upon the room. Claudia felt sick, abashed. David had never kicked an animal in his life. She tried to cover the nakedness of his fear by acting as if it hadn't happened.

" What's today, Thursday or Friday ? " she queried brightly.

"Friday," said Bobby.

"Good. Then tomorrow's Saturday, I'll go down to the village with you, Bobby, and we'll get a new pair of shoes for you."

"That is fine," said Bertha. Agitated, she removed a cherished ornament of pink china from the baby's hand, barely in the nick of time. "Come, we will get out now, and let Papa finish dressing," she said, and piloted them from the room as fast as she could.

"Thank you," said David, in a nice, nasty tone. He gave himself a moment to cool off before he started on something else.

"Why don't you wait until we see what our plans are, before you buy Bobby another pair of black shoes?"

"No matter what our plans are, he'll need two pairs."

"Yes, but he won't need black ones, unless we go back to New York."

"That's true. I'll get him brown ones. Are you almost ready for breakfast? I'll start your eggs."

He wasn't hungry. She could see that he could scarcely swallow the food that was set before him, and she knew, from experience, that there was nothing like anxiety to twist one's inside into a hard knot of rejection. "David, don't force yourself," she advised him compassionately.

"Yes, this is the very time to strip off weight," he returned, ironically. "You'd better telephone the Trents, will you?"

Her heart laboured. "What about?"

"That we can't go today."

"Go where?"

"Didn't I tell you last night?"

"No, what?"

"Byard said that if we were interested in a place for the summer, we'd better not lose time in looking, so I said we might hire a car this afternoon, and drive up. We were to let them know early in the morning so that they could arrange for an agent to show us around."

" You never told me," she said, with neither reproach nor rancour.

" I thought I did. Anyway, there's nothing lost, I can't go anyway with this temperature."

" It wouldn't be too wise," she agreed levelly, " at least until you see if it goes up at four o'clock."

He didn't wait until four o'clock, he didn't even wait until noon, he checked it again at eleven. It hadn't budged from ninety-nine. " That's funny," said Claudia, not really meaning it, " it should either go up or down. Maybe it's broken, try another thermometer."

" We haven't got another one," he answered, wholly serious.

" Certainly we have."

" Not on your life, not that one."

" Sweet little innocent children ? "

" You took Bluff's temperature with it last week."

" Nonsense, that was a month ago."

" The passage of time has nothing to do with it. I will not use the house thermometer," he baulked. " Anyway, it's ninety-nine all right, because my pulse is still high."

" Eighty-four's not high."

" It is for me."

" Darling, if I were to check on myself three times a day every day, I wouldn't be normal every minute either. Nobody would."

" It wouldn't signify anything in a healthy person."

" And you're not healthy ? You're bursting with health——"

" That's why I'm here," he said. " For my eyes."

She kept feeling more and more bewildered and sick at heart. " I didn't mean that, I meant your last X-rays. You've got a convenient memory to forget how pleased Dr. Geiger was."

" I remember that he said no one's ever cured of this damn disease," he reminded her a trifle sharply. " You know that as well as I do, so what's the sense of fooling ourselves ? "

" Then you're ' arrested,' if you're so much of a purist.
. . . David, listen, maybe it would be a good idea for you
just to forget that you have ninety-nine——"

" And end with a nice juicy flare-up. You talk like a
lay-person."

" You didn't let me finish. I was about to say, let me
phone Dr. Geiger and ask him if it would be all right to
drive over to Placid this afternoon anyway."

" Since when are you so anxious to go ? "

" It's not that I'm anxious to go, but I think it might be
a good thing to do. All around."

" Well, don't bother to ask him, he'll say ' No '."

" I'm not so sure."

The faintest note of petulance came into his voice. " Let's
drop it, Claudia, I don't feel like making the effort."

She turned away in mystification and defeat. " I'll phone
the Trents."

" I thought you had, what's the idea ? "

" The line's been busy every time I tried. Lydia's quite
a talker."

" Tell them I hope I can make it next week."

" I will."

" And Claudia ! " he called after her, " I'll have a glass
of milk, please."

" Lunch is at twelve, it's after eleven now, it'll spoil
your appetite, won't it ? "

" I'd better have it," he said.

Bertha couldn't get over that he asked for milk between
meals. She brought it to him while Claudia telephoned
the Trents. An over-trained maid informed her that Mrs.
Trent was playing tennis, and Mr. Trent was resting.
Claudia hated to waste a toll-call. " Is Mr. Dexter
there ? "

Phil came to the phone. He said he was getting his
tackle ready for a fishing trip the following morning. " I'll
be back here Monday night," he said, " and I won't be
leaving for New York until Wednesday, so I could drive
down on Tuesday and pick you up, how's that ? "

" That's lovely," said Claudia, " if it isn't too much trouble for you."

" I'd enjoy it. I might buy a piece of land up here, and I want David to see it. Maybe he'll design a little fishing lodge for me, nothing elaborate, just a place to get away to for an occasional week or two."

It sounded like a perfect set-up, thought Claudia—masculine and hearty, with one foot in New York and the other in a trout stream. Perhaps some day David would be able to afford that kind of living. It would mean that his life would dominate his illness, instead of the other way around.

" Suppose I get down to your place around ten-thirty," Phil's pleasant voice went on, " we can stop somewhere for lunch on the road."

" Around two would be better," said Claudia. She didn't say that David preferred to rest in the morning, and she blessed Phil for not making her say it. " Splendid," he concurred at once. " Two on Tuesday."

How really changed he was, she reflected, as she hung up the receiver. He had got back to where he was years ago when she had first met him at a dinner party at Julia's, hard of limb, and vigorous and gentle. She could understand a woman falling in love with him.

She went out to the porch to tell David that everything was arranged for Tuesday at two. He said he hoped he'd be in shape to make it that early in the week, and she said that she was sure he would, what nonsense. She picked up the empty milk glass, and then she put it down again so that her arms were free. " Do you know you're quite handsome ? " she whispered with her lips against his cheek. " That old blue sports shirt's very becoming."

" Glad you like it," he said, but nothing else answered from within him. She withdrew her arms, hoping until the last split second that he would catch her hand and pull her back to him. He made no move. When she left him, he was staring up and out across the mountains, and it was as if he did not know that she had been close, and gone away again. It came to her to wonder how often it had happened that way to Lydia. You could never judge. . . .

She found Bertha in the living-room, finishing the packing that she had begun the day before. She stood for a moment, indecisive. Then she said, " Bertha, I wouldn't pack too much until we know definitely what our plans are."

Bertha kept on folding a bulky sweater. " No matter what they are," she said, " we will not need these heavy things until next year."

" We really ought to have moth-balls."

" We will," said Bertha, " I already told Bobby to buy some when he buys the shoe-laces today."

" Can't I ever beat you to anything ? " Claudia reached for a chatty one. " Isn't it wonderful that he's grown-up enough to send on errands ? "

" Bobby has grown up in every way, not only his feet," said Bertha. " This winter has done him good. It has done everyone good. Mr. Dexter could not get over yesterday how big the baby was." She shook her head in unspoken censure. " It is a pity that such a man who loves children has no children of his own."

" Yes, Mrs. Trent and I were talking about it. His wife was never very well after their son died."

" I remember she committed suicide."

" You sound as if you blamed her."

" Many times in my life it would have been a pleasure for me to commit suicide too," said Bertha curtly.

" I'll bet it would. Pretty good for me you didn't. Whatever would I have done without you ? "

" You could do without me. You are stronger than you know ! "

" I wonder," Claudia said. She picked up a pair of woollen socks and rolled them into a ball. " Bertha, about our plans. Mr. David thinks it might be a good idea to stay on in the mountains for a few months longer, and put off going back to New York until September."

" It could be a good idea," said Bertha judiciously.

"You see there's not much doing at the office during the summer," Claudia went on a little lamely. "The Trents said we could rent a place in Placid quite reasonably."

"Surely it does not hurt to look," said Bertha, unrolling the socks.

"We were going today, but Mr. David woke up with ninety-nine."

Bertha weighed the fact. "Ninety-nine is no fever unless it keeps up. It could come from anything, even from worry. I would let him go, anyway," she said.

"I'd let him go, but he doesn't want to. I think he's a little bit nervous about himself all of a sudden."

"I think so, too," said Bertha quietly. "It is not so sudden, either. It has been there on and off, but he did not give in to it."

Claudia nodded mutely.

"Miss Candy will be very disappointed if you are not with her when the baby is born," Bertha remarked after a pause.

Claudia nodded again. It was not as much of a *non sequitur* as it sounded. Bertha meant, without putting it into words, that the time had come for David to leave his mountains.

All day there was an inarticulate prayer in Claudia's heart. "Don't let it go up—don't let it go up. . . ." At four o'clock it was as if the prayer were answered. David's temperature was ninety-nine. "Let me see," she insisted, sceptically.

"You can believe me," he said, holding the thermometer out of her reach.

"I can't." She managed to get it away from him.

"It isn't ninety-nine!" she exclaimed. "It's under, it's only ninety-eight nine!"

"Ninety-nine."

"No! Look at it again."

"What difference does it make?"

"A great deal," she replied indignantly. She remembered

the times he had fooled himself the other way around, and she'd let him get away with it. She couldn't let him get away with this, though. It was a different kind of symptom, and one that was more frightening.

"We'll see what it is tonight," he said, "before I get too cocky."

They sat together on the porch after supper, and each of them tried not to seem conscious of the hour. "Well," said David finally, with an indolent yawn, "I guess it's almost eight o'clock."

"I guess it is," said Claudia. She circled his wrist lightly with her fingers. "Your pulse is disgustingly slow," she gloated.

"A lot you can tell, without a watch," he mumbled with the thermometer bobbing from his lips.

"I don't need a watch. What do you want to bet? Sixty-six. On the nose. Go on—count with your second hand." He counted a full minute, and admitted, a little shame-faced, to sixty eight.

"I refuse to be made a liar for two beats. Now let's see what your temperature is—I bet that's normal, too."

It was a fraction under normal. She felt like slapping him in her immense relief, the same way she sometimes felt like slapping Matthew when he fell down and didn't hurt himself after scaring her to death.

She hugged David's arm against her. "You devil," she exulted. A kind of peace came over them. The night was warm, and still, and full of the sweetness of new cut grass. The old man up the road, who had shovelled their snow all winter, had brought down his mower that afternoon, and gone over the lawn around the house. "It's not a bad patch," David had commented. "It's large enough to stick up a croquet set for the children."

"It wouldn't pay for the little time we'll still be here," Claudia had demurred. "The children can live without croquet."

"But I was thinking," he'd gone on, "if we don't find a reasonable house at Placid, this little place mightn't be half bad in summer. It's very pretty with the trees shading it from the road, and it's bound to be cool."

"It's all of that," she'd acknowledged, with an odd sinking in the pit of her stomach. Did he really mean that he would be willing to stay on ? She couldn't believe it. And yet, as they sat on the porch this evening, with their very happiness hanging upon the exact fraction of his temperature and pulse, it occurred to her that they were right back to where they'd started nine months ago. Except that nine months ago she had been the fearful one, and David had done all the minimising. Now it was the other way around. She tried to trace back the subtle beginnings of this disturbing change. Had it been her fault, had he taken on the colour of her apprehensions ?

"What are you thinking of ? "

She put her hand out to him. "Nothing. And everything."

"I think we're in for a storm," he said.

"I thought I heard thunder before."

The storm was on them before they knew it. It was a wild storm, with lightning carving up the heavens and the world crashing savagely around them. Bluff got up and crept inside. "Sissy," Claudia called after him. Then Bobby came out. He was in his pyjamas. "It's nice, isn't it ? " he said with relish. He sat with them until they went inside. "I love a storm," he said.

"I'd bat your ears off if you didn't," said David. "What's Matthew doing ? "

"Playing parcheesi with Bertha. He's too scared to go to bed."

"He's no son of mine," said David.

"I don't want him either," said Claudia. "And now if you don't mind, my very brave lad, what about a little privacy while we get undressed ? Are you all out of the bathroom ? "

"Except my teeth," said Bobby.

"Well go get them out and hurry up. Good night, darling."

"What time do we leave in the morning ? " he asked.

" Leave in the morning ? "

" My shoes."

" Oh, your shoes. I forgot. We'll leave about ten o'clock, I guess." An idea came to her. " How'd you like to stop in and visit a nice little girl ? "

" I don't like girls. What's her name ? "

" Marian. Miss Carey's taking care of her, she's just about your age."

" Gosh," said Bobby, undecided. " Do we have to ? "

" We don't have to, but I promised I would, some day, and this might be my last chance. Anyway, we'll talk about it tomorrow."

" While you're down in the village you can get me a haircut," said David, running his hand across the back of his neck.

" I will. But maybe you'll decide to get it for yourself."

" I'll see how I feel in the morning." He went to the window and closed it quickly against a driving sheet of rain. " The wind's changed," he said.

" It's a beautiful night to sleep indoors," said Claudia shamelessly. She opened a bottle of perfume that Julia had given her some time ago, and dabbed a little on the tip of each ear. " I wonder why women do it there," she said. " Why ? "

" I don't know," said David. He was getting into his pyjamas as fast as he could. " Just listen to it blow," he exulted. " It's getting worse, it's like all hell breaking loose, I wouldn't miss sleeping out in it for anything."

He dropped a kiss on her head. " Good night, darling —I can open the bed on the porch, don't dare go out in that thin gown. . . ."

He was gone, into the vast impersonal solace of the storm, like a man hurrying to his love. Claudia put the bottle of perfume back into the drawer. It was a shame to have wasted such expensive stuff.

She slept, fitfully, and in the morning she didn't like her face. The tiredness around her eyes, and the lines around her mouth told of an uneasy body and an unfilled heart. David had always complimented her on waking up with radiance and bloom. "I'd hate to be married to a puffy woman," he'd said, "who takes until noon to go down in her face." She'd known exactly what he meant. Even young girls sometimes had that look.

She was afraid that he would notice, but he didn't. He was too perturbed about himself. "My temperature's only ninety-eight," he greeted her, "but I've got a sore throat."

"I hope you didn't catch cold sleeping out in all that weather," she said, ruling everything from her voice except concern.

"It isn't a cold, I haven't got a sign of a cold," he said. "I wish I could be sure it was a cold."

She knew what he was thinking. There was a patient in the boarding-house who had been "on silence," which meant he hardly ever talked, and when he did it was in a grating whisper. "If you're worried about it," she said, "call Dr. Geiger, and we'll go down and see him."

"I'll give it another day or two."

Was it possible that he was afraid to go to Dr. Geiger? Fear was begetting fear, until all of him was fear, and there was no telling where it began or where it would end. She did not dare to say to him, "David, be honest with yourself, you don't want to leave here, you want to stay on and not face going home and all that it means." But how could she be sure whether that was the truth of it? The thing to do was to see Dr. Geiger herself, for this that was happening was more serious than a matter of physical symptoms. A month ago, a week ago, even yesterday, a little temperature or a sore throat was of paramount importance, a lurking threat to the course of their lives and the solidity of their future. Now something greater was at stake. The flame that was David was more important than his body. There was astonishment in her heart that she could feel this to be so. She must have come a long way beyond herself, she realised suddenly, to have been able to even think the thought.

She telephoned Dr. Geiger while David was shaving. He said that he would not be at the surgery, because it was Saturday, but if it was urgent he would be glad to talk to her at his home.

" I think it is urgent," she told him after a moment's indecision.

" Then make it as near ten-thirty as you can," he said.

That meant an early start. She stood on the porch with Bobby, waiting for the taxi. Matthew was there, too, loud in his protestations that he didn't want to go along. " Nobody asked you to," said Claudia.

He mightn't have heard her. " I'm going to play my radio all morning," he announced.

" Why don't you take him ? " David suggested abruptly.

For an instant, she thought that he was being funny in his old dry way, but he was serious about it. She smothered the laugh that bubbled to her lips. " I couldn't possibly, you'll have to put up with him," she said. " I told you last night I want to see Miss Carey."

" Oh," said David. " I forgot."

Subterfuge was a strange companion to their marriage. She felt soiled, knowing that her visit to Dr. Geiger would probably mean that she wouldn't have time to see Miss Carey. " Here comes the taxi," she said in relief. " No it isn't, it's the mail. Run down to the gate and get it, Matthew, and save the postman coming in. Go on, get a move on, I want to read my letters before I go."

Matthew hurried slowly. " Look at him taking his time," David boiled.

" It's nothing you can put your finger on, he seems to be rushing," said Claudia.

He came back eventually, dropping a letter here and there, and stopping to pick it up. Bobby lost patience and went to meet him. " Oh, come on, give them to me, you dope," he said.

There was quite a lot of mail for a change—a note from
Candy, on the thin blue English stationery that she always
used, a letter from John, on David's thick white office paper,
and a card with Nancy Riddle's careless uphill scrawl.
Claudia glanced at it and read it aloud. " Hear you're
coming home. So glad. If you want to stay at the farm,
I've let my herdsman go, and the house is empty and you're
more than welcome to use it for as long or short as you
want. Affec'ly, Nancy."

" ' Affec'ly, Nancy ' and her penny post cards," said
Claudia. " You'd think she didn't have a couple of million
dollars. It's nice of her to ask us though, isn't it ? "

" I can think of nothing I'd like less," said David.

" No more can I. Oh, David, look," she broke off. She
picked up a thin oblong package with a publisher's imprint.
" It must be Jerry's book, Candy said he was sending an
advance copy." She tore at the heavy paper. " Why do
they wrap these things like crazy," she complained. " What
does John say in his letter ? "

" Nothing. Things are quiet down at the office. Everything's running smoothly."

" That's good." She drew out the book, a slim little
volume, with the single word " Elizabeth " spilling like
liquid gold across the black cloth. " It's so chaste," she
breathed. " And it's dedicated to Candy. I'm glad." She
riffled the pages. " It's not very long, and quite large print,
you'll be able to finish it easily while I'm gone."

" When you've done looking at it, I'd like to see it,"
said David tersely.

Bluff began to bark. " The taxi's coming," said Bobby.
He seemed a little uncomfortable. " Doesn't Dad feel
well ? " he asked, as they drove off.

" It's nothing, just a little scratchiness," Claudia assured
him cheerfully. She was glad to see his face brighten, and
his spirit take on the colour of happiness. " There's a baseball game at school this morning," he said. " Could I watch
for a little after I get my shoes ? "

" Yes, because I have to do an errand or so anyway."

6

" Swell," he said.   He began to whistle, not as well as he thought.

" How much extra would you charge if you didn't ? " she enquired.

" Didn't what ? "

" Whistle."

" Thirty-five cents," he came back promptly.   " For some marbles."

" It's a deal," she agreed.   " And very cheap at the price."

Her heart lifted.   Being with Bobby was relaxing and easy, like being with David had used to be.

" Wait a minute ! " Bobby suddenly exclaimed, turning backwards.

" It wasn't Shakespeare," said Claudia.   " It was a yellow cat, not an orange one, and short-haired."

" Did you see him, too, in those bushes ? "

" Yes.   And darling, I think if Shakespeare were this close to home he'd have come back."

" I guess so," Bobby admitted reluctantly.   " I think somebody who lives pretty far from here must have him."

Claudia shook her head.

" You mean you think he's dead."

" I'm afraid so."

" I think he's alive," said Bobby.

She put her hand on his knee.   " I never knew you loved Shakespeare so much."

" I never knew it either," said Bobby, " until he went away."

" When we go home, we'll get another cat.   Maybe a Siamese cat.   Would you like a Siamese ? "

" I don't think so," said Bobby.   He looked out of the window without talking for a while.   " Why did Uncle Jerry write a book about Aunt Elizabeth ? " he asked.

" Because he loved her."

" Is it to tell everybody how sorry he was when she died ? "

" I think it's more than that. I think it's to say that they were only married a few months, but it was such a happy, full few months, that it was like a whole lifetime."

" She didn't know she was going to die, did she ? "

" No. It was very sudden."

" But don't you have to be sick to die ? "

" Lots of people who are sick live a great deal longer than people who are well," she told him. It was easy to see what was in his mind, David's illness was a shadow across his days, although he gave no hint of it. He must have discerned her motive, because he gave a quick little grin and said, " That doesn't make me feel very good about you, Mother."

He was growing up so quickly, she realised, that she could no longer treat him as a child. " Darling, what's going to happen is going to happen," she said, " and you can't stop it from happening."

They fell silent again. In a little while he began to whistle, first under his breath and then louder and louder. Claudia smiled. It was a wonderful sound, the sound of the whistling of a person who was happy. She wondered when David would whistle again, and not know that he was whistling.

" I want my thirty-five cents back," she remarked. They looked at each other and laughed, pleased to be together.

Bobby said, " I'm glad Matthew didn't come along."

" So am I."

" He's a pain in the neck."

" A little of a one," she conceded.

She thought, suddenly, what a lovely day it was, with the sun coming up out of a grey morning, and great shadows stalking across the mountains like giants. They were passing through pure country, with no cottages along the road to remind her that this quiet village held sickness and suffering. This might be a moment of time, nowhere and anywhere, suspended in space, perfect and complete. Long afterwards she thought about it, and that was the way it stayed in her heart.

TEN

IT WAS ONLY A SHORT WALK from the shoe shop to Dr. Geiger's house, and an equally short walk but in the opposite direction to the school. "I can go by myself," said Bobby.

"Then I'll pick you up later at the playground," said Claudia. She watched him go, walking a little gingerly in his new shoes. "Be careful crossing!"

She couldn't help feeling an enormous satisfaction in his independence and his competence. It was a rewarding thing to raise a child and have him turn out to be like Bobby. It certainly didn't look as if she'd have that kind of luck with Matthew, and Michael was too young to be able to tell at this point, just what problems he would present. He'd taken to storing his dinner in his cheeks like a squirrel, but so had Bobby at that age. . . .

Pleasant, fragmentary memories carried her to the stark reality of Dr. Geiger's square white house. A maid with a dish towel in her hand answered her ring. "Doctor has no surgery hours," she said.

"I telephoned," said Claudia. "He expects me."

"Just a minute then, I'll see."

She disappeared through a door on the left, and after a short time she reappeared. "It's all right, you can come," she said.

Claudia followed her through the door, into another kind of living. So this was Dr. Geiger's private world, a piano, and books, and a dining-room, and the quick glimpse of his wife, presumably, whisking through the hall, and the clatter of pots and pans from the kitchen.

"Right out here," the maid beckoned, and Claudia found herself on the porch, extending along the back of the house, and hidden from the street. It was a pleasant place, with comfortable wicker furniture and a radio. Dr. Geiger was lying in a long chair. Her first thought was that he was ill, and that she had disturbed him, but he told her no, he always tried to get in as much resting on a Saturday as he could, and that he was glad to talk to her if there was something on her mind.

" There is," she said, and then found that it was difficult to begin, because anything she told him would make David appear less than he was in strength and courage. Dr. Geiger seemed to sense that she was in some sort of conflict, so he gave her an opening. " Well, I suppose you're about ready to pack up and go back to New York, aren't you? Let's see, what did I say, the end of May? "

" Or the beginning of June, depending on the weather."

" Today's like summer. Did you have much of a storm up at your place last night? "

" Yes, it was pretty bad." She cleared her throat. She couldn't go on taking up his time like this without saying anything. "Dr. Geiger," she plunged in. "David ran a little fever yesterday. That is to say he woke up with ninety-nine but it went down in the evening, and this morning it was under ninety-eight."

Dr. Geiger gave one of the unexpected smiles that lit up his appealingly homely face. " In that case, I think he'll live. Seriously, though, I'd stop this business of checking his temperature three times a day. If he takes it at four o'clock, it's sufficient. And I think you'll find that he'll stick pretty close to normal."

" He has, all along," said Claudia. " But now, of all times, he's starting monkey-shines. I mean, he had a little sore throat today, too. Could that possibly be anything? "

" Anything can be anything," Dr. Geiger returned with a slight acidity. " But look here, you can't watch every little ache and pain in a sick person any more than you can in a well person. If you keep this up, you'll make your husband into a first-class hypochondriac, and then you'll really have a problem on your hands. It's perfectly natural for you both to be nervous about going home—there's always a certain amount of adjustment to be met, believe me." Dr. Geiger's voice became a little more gentle. " But you'll have to help him through it, instead of adding to his difficulties."

" I realise that," said Claudia, in humble willingness to take the blame. " I think another thing that was upsetting, was that a patient we know at the sanatorium, a Doctor Healey, was ready to go home, and we heard that he was in the infirmary with a flare-up."

" Who told you ? "

" Another patient."

" And the moral of that is, don't listen to other patients. I know Lewis Healey very well—as a matter of fact I saw him yesterday. Merely to set your mind at rest, my child, his present difficulties are complicated by an ailment that is quite removed, in a general southerly direction, from the area of his lungs."

" Oh, I'm so glad," Claudia blurted out. " I'll tell that to David, the idiot." Dr. Geiger was saying exactly what she wanted to hear, and exactly what she had felt, instinctively, to be the truth. Never mind whether he thought she was the idiot, instead of David. She rose to her feet, to let him see that she didn't intend to use up his whole morning plying him with silly questions. " Just one more thing," she besought him. " We were wondering—I mean —what would you feel about our not going home quite yet ? Spending the summer at Lake Placid ? "

" Why Lake Placid ? "

" We know some people there, and there's quite a bit of building going on, and David thought he might start in doing a little work."

" That's a very sound idea," Dr. Geiger approved at once. " It's just that much added insurance, and all to the good, if he can afford the extra time."

Claudia's face fell. How had she got herself into this unequivocal position of having sold Dr. Geiger a bill of goods with David's point of view ? And now how could she unsell him with the less healthful aspects of such a move? "The trouble is that David isn't that kind of an architect," she tried to explain. "He'd never be happy building houses with leather bars and rumpus rooms."

"That's too bad," said Dr. Geiger a trifle dryly. "Let him leave out the bars and rumpus rooms."

"That was only a figure of speech," Claudia stumbled on. "What I mean is that before we came here, he'd almost landed a commission to go to Iceland on a very important project. And before we were married he wanted to build a modern cathedral. I can't ever forget the way he looked when he'd talk about it. As if candles were lit behind his eyes."

"When I was first married," said Dr. Geiger, ignoring the candles, "I wanted to be a great brain surgeon." There was neither regret nor amusement in his voice, merely an acceptance of what life had done to him. Acceptance was the very thing that she was fighting against, but she couldn't say, "I don't want my husband to relinquish high hopes and full living." It was not the thing to say to a man who lay in a cure chair every Saturday so that he could face the week ahead of him. "I see what you mean," she murmured. She glanced at her watch. "I mustn't keep you any longer. And I could kick myself for barging in on you like this."

"Not at all. I'm glad you came. And again, if you want my advice, by all means go to Lake Placid for the summer. Who knows," he added with a smile, "perhaps you'll like it so much you'll want to settle there permanently. It's getting to be quite a community, I understand. It would be good for the children, and certainly your husband could only benefit by a way of life that would take him out of New York."

"Yes," she agreed falteringly, "I see that. And thank you." There was nothing more to say, Dr. Geiger was a good friend and a good physician. He had helped David to regain his health and had, upon occasion, been a source of encouragement and comfort. But he wasn't God. He was a man with a sad heart, who had given up his dream.

She found Bobby in the courtyard yelling with a group of boys as they watched the ball-game. The deserted school looked prim, remote, its shaded windows discreetly closed against the ribald shouting. He caught sight of her and took his leave regretfully. " What did the doctor say about Dad ? " he asked.

" I didn't tell you I was going to the doctor."

" I know, but I thought you went, anyway."

She couldn't tell him an untruth. " You're too smart. . . . Dad's fine, not to worry about him."

" That's good."

She glanced at her watch. " It's only a quarter to eleven, shall we stop in and see Marian ? "

" O.K.," he said, although he wasn't crazy about going.

" It's not far, I know where Oak Street is, we can walk."

They started off. " I don't remember Miss Carey much." He dropped his voice. " Was the baby born dead ? "

" It lived a few hours."

" Why did it die ? "

" I don't know, Bobby. I wish I did. Maybe it was the strain and worry of Dad being in the war, and—oh, a lot of things."

" Maybe the baby just wasn't supposed to live," said Bobby.

" Maybe."

" If it had, though, we'd have had a little sister."

" Yes."

" Michael's not so bad. I guess we're more of a man's family anyway."

" It looks that way."

He held her elbow over a crossing. " Marian can't play or anything, can she ? "

" Not until she's well again."

" I would hate to be sick," he said.

" I would hate to have you sick," said Claudia. " I think it's the next block over."

They found the house at last, a modern-looking apartment building, low-built, with porches all around it.

" Here's the name, they live on the second floor," said Claudia. " I hope they're not out. I suppose I should have let Miss Carey know that we were coming but I wasn't sure we'd be able to make it."

Miss Carey was home, and in her forthright hearty way she said Claudia had more luck than brains. " We were just getting ready to go for our fifteen-minute walk, but sit down, and have a little visit, we can put it off a while, you probably can't stay long anyway. Marian ! Company ! " she called. " Come on in."

Marian came in from the porch, the picture of health, and large for her age, with a round sweet face. She reminded Claudia of the way Candy had used to look when she was a child.

" This is Bobby," said Miss Carey.

" Hello," said Bobby. They shook hands limply, and stood staring at each other in an agony of bashfulness.

Claudia took pity on them. " Why can't they go off for a walk together ? " she suggested. " Bobby's very careful of crossings."

" That's an idea," said Miss Carey. " How about it, Marian ? "

" I'd like to," Marian assented in a baby's voice.

" O.K.," said Bobby, trying to look like a man of the world.

Claudia watched them go, with an air of being hand in hand, although they kept a discreet distance from each other. " It would have been wonderful to have a daughter," she said.

" Try until you get one," Miss Carey advised cordially.

" I can't. Not now."

" On account of your husband ? Don't listen to that sort of old wives' talk, he'll be as good as new. Better."

" It's not David. I'm the one. After Michael was born, Dr. Rowland said I could never have another child."

" I didn't know that," said Miss Carey soberly. She gave one of her healthy shrugs. " Well, adopt a little girl."

"I don't think I'd be big enough, I don't think I could love her as if she were my own."

"People do."

"I know. I suppose if the need is there, you rise to it."

"Well, one way or another, I'm not going to feel sorry for you with three magnificent sons. Bobby's quite a youngster. Do you know he's shot up in the few weeks since I last saw you?"

"He has. When I think of Marian, I'm so grateful."

"You ought to be. How's your husband?"

"Oh, fine."

"Then why do you look like hell?"

Claudia was taken aback. "Me look like hell?" She laughed nervously. "I didn't sleep very well last night, but I didn't think it showed."

"I'm a trained nurse, remember? When do you go to New York?"

"I don't know. We might even stay on for the summer."

Miss Carey raised her brows. "Really? I thought David was so anxious to get back to work."

"He was. He is."

"Then be smart. Don't hold him here if Dr. Geiger says he's well enough to leave."

"I'm not. And he is well enough. But he doesn't particularly want to rush things."

"Scared?" The word shot out at her like a pistol going off. It took her unawares.

"Terribly," she acknowledged in a choked voice. "He's so different, almost overnight. He's lost his courage, and the healthiness of his outlook on life."

"You're giving the perfect description of a nice little nervous breakdown," Miss Carey observed.

Claudia recoiled. "Don't say that!" she cried sharply. "David's the last person in the world to be neurotic!"

"That may be. As long as he's got his previous T.B. to hang his troubles on," said Miss Carey unperturbably. "You went through the same thing after the baby died, and it wasn't the baby, any more than it's David's lungs.

Everyone needs a good house-cleaning sooner or later. It's a nicer name for nervous breakdown, if you like the sound of it better."

" I like it much better," said Claudia. " I'd almost forgotten the agony of those months. I was so full of fear, I remember I didn't want to go in the subway. It was even torture to go out and see people."

" And I remember," Miss Carey injected tartly, " when you were afraid to get out of bed, without my holding on to you."

" Poor David," Claudia whispered. " It brings it all back."

Miss Carey snorted. " That sort of talk doesn't get you anywhere. ' Poor David ' nothing. He's just building his muscle for a long productive life. He'll be well again, and stay well, if that stinking pride of his—excuse the language —doesn't get in his way, and land him on his ear again. A lot of it is up to you, my girl. And why not ? You've been through it, so pay up for the privilege, and get to work."

Claudia drew a deep breath. It was wonderful to have her understand what Dr. Geiger could never understand. She knew again the attachment and dependence she had once transferred to Miss Carey's broad and competent shoulders. Everybody needed somebody at one time or another. Surely, it must be all right to lean, for just a little, provided you knew you were leaning. " If only I didn't feel disloyal to David," she said in a stricken voice. " After all, a lot of people never go home. So I needn't have made anything of it."

" That's one way of doing it," said Miss Carey. " And as for being disloyal, you didn't open your mouth. I simply told you you looked like hell. . . . Here come the children back again."

" Fifteen minutes isn't very long," said Claudia.

" Oh, I don't know," said Miss Carey. " I'm getting to the point where time doesn't count as much as it used to. Fifteen minutes can be as long as you want it to be."

"I see what you mean," said Claudia.

There was no cab in the street, and they had to walk back to the village to get one. "Did you like Marian?" Claudia asked casually.

"She's all right," said Bobby, looking very self-conscious. "She only wears a size five shoe, and my new ones are eight and a half already."

Claudia restrained a smile. "Girls' and boys' sizes run differently," she explained.

"Oh," said Bobby. After a pause, he said, "I showed her my pen. She thought it was nifty."

"Did you tell her how you got it?"

"No," he said. "I just said you bought it."

"That was right. Never muddy the people you love."

"What does 'muddy' mean?"

"It means what you didn't do to Matthew." And what I tried not to do, when I talked to Dr. Geiger, she amended silently. She knew that the only way that she could make herself feel clean again was to tell David about her visit, and tell him also that Miss Carey had helped her to remember the ugly taste of fear.

"Could I buy my marbles while we're in the village?" Bobby asked.

"If we pass a shop, yes."

Bobby bought his marbles, and she bought a newspaper for David. She had an impulse to send Marian the same kind of pen, but it was extravagant, and a little quixotic, even though it was so pitifully little a gesture out of her own abundant riches. "How about sending Marian some paper dolls?" she said instead, "and maybe a book?"

He looked pleased.

"Sure, that's all right. What'll we buy for Matthew?"

"Tangerines," said Claudia.

It was almost one o'clock when they got home. David was still on the porch, with Jerry's book on the table beside him. "You finished it," Claudia exclaimed eagerly. "How was it, did you like it?"

"I haven't begun it yet," he said.

It was on the tip of her tongue to ask him why on earth he hadn't, but one look at his face told her the reason. He had no interest in Jerry's book. He had withdrawn to a world of his own, isolated and unreal. "Run and wash up for lunch," she told Bobby.

"I want to show Dad my shoes."

"Very sporty," said David, scarcely looking at them.

Claudia picked up the book. "It's too bad we're not the kind of people who read aloud to each other," she said. "I must say I like the feel of it, I bet it'll be a great success."

David didn't ask her why she bet it would be a great success. "I notice that skinny little books," she volunteered, "or great big fat books, stand a much better chance with the critics."

She was rewarded by the faintest flicker of amusement in his eyes. She bent to kiss him. "Hello," she said.

"Hello. . . . Oh, by the way, Lydia Trent telephoned to say that she'll count on us for Tuesday, she has a couple of houses lined up for us to see. And Phil will be down at two to pick us up."

"Fine," said Claudia.

"I hope I'll be able to go," he said. "This throat's still bothering me."

"I think it's just because you slept out in the damp air last night."

"That's ridiculous. I've slept out in all kinds of weather."

She had no answer for that.

On Tuesday morning, she beat him to it. "How's your temperature?" she asked, as he came into the bedroom.

"Normal. What's the matter, don't you say good morning any more?"

"Good morning. How's the throat?"

"It's all right."

"You must be sick to be so healthy."

" Are you pulling my leg ? "

" I'll give you three guesses."

Bobby came in.   " Congratulate your father, my lad, he woke up with nary a disease."

" You have a very fresh mother, my lad," said David.

It was a poor imitation of themselves, but Claudia could see how Bobby reacted to the echo of old times. He threw his arms around Bluff, who had ambled in after him, and kissed him noisily.   " What's a new current event ? " he demanded.   " I have to have one for Assembly this morning."

" United Nations."

" I used that last week."

" Russia," said Claudia.

" Russia's old.   I had it."

" Have it again, it's always good," David advised.

" Hey," Bobby protested, getting the idea that they weren't very serious about his current event, " I have to have one."

" I'll give you one," said Claudia, " that really is an event. We're going to Lake Placid this afternoon, and we won't be here when you get home from school."

" When will you be back ? "

" Probably in time for supper."

" Gosh," said Bobby.

" Gosh what ? " asked Claudia.

He looked blank.

" Mr. Goshwhat," said David.

" You're both silly," Bobby commented contentedly.   " I guess I'll go and have my breakfast. We have to have prunes on account of Matthew, the dope."

David was affronted.   " Matthew should damn well have his own prunes."

" That's what I say," said Bobby.

" Go out and raise the roof for orange juice," David exhorted him.

" Listen, you two, we're out of oranges, and a prune won't kill you for once."

" I strike," said David.

" So do I," said Bobby.

" Very well, while you two are striking, I'm going to make hay with the bathroom."

" Oh no, you don't ! " David grabbed his towel and bolted. Bobby looked after him. " Dad's feeling pretty spiffy this morning, isn't he ! "

Claudia nodded. " It's nice, isn't it," she said softly.

Bobby didn't answer, but suddenly, of his own accord, he kissed her, instead of Bluff. It could have been that he was happy because everything was spiffy, or it could have been that he was telling her good-bye because she wouldn't be there when he got home that afternoon.

It was a little before twelve when they sat down to lunch, so that David could rest for an hour or so before starting off. They were still at the table when the telephone bell rang. Claudia jumped up to answer it. " It's probably Phil, reminding us that he'll be here at two."

It wasn't Phil. It was a woman's voice, and at first Claudia thought that it was Lydia, with a bad connection. She jiggled the receiver to clear the line. " I can't quite hear you," she said. " Please speak louder. Yes, this is Mrs. Naughton."

The voice went on—and on—and then there was a little click, and the voice stopped—but it kept going on and on, in Claudia's brain.

" Who was it ? " David asked, at her side.

She got the receiver back on its hook. Mercifully, the hall was dim. She clung to the wall to stop the hideous shaking of her limbs. Her tongue and her lips felt swollen and parched and she had to keep moving them before the words came out. " It was the school," she said.

" The school ? What for ? "

She tried again. " Miss Grigsby. She wants me to come right away."

" So. Matthew's in a scrape again—" He seemed less alarmed than angry. She could not tell him that it was

Bobby. "David, call a taxi for me. Please. Tell him to hurry." Someone else must have been saying the words for her, through her swollen lips. Strength like this, to keep from screaming out her agony, could not be hers.

She felt his hand on her arm.

"Now don't be so upset," he said. "You didn't think he was going to turn into an angel, did you?"

He wanted to placate her, argue with her. She turned back to the phone and called the taxi herself, and somehow, through the throbbing emptiness of her brain, the number came. "Hurry! Please! As fast as you can—"

David lost his patience. "Look here, Claudia, this is too much of a good thing. Calm yourself enough to tell me what he's done this time, and let's sit down and talk it over."

A merciful lie helped her. "I have to hurry, we have to leave for Placid at two."

"Then go down and see Miss Grigsby tomorrow. It can wait."

She pulled away from him and ran out of the room. He let her go. Bertha came to the door, and found her sitting on the edge of the bed. "What is wrong?" Bertha whispered. "Your face is so white—"

Bertha's face was pale, too. Poor Bertha. She'd gone through so much in her life. It wasn't fair to tell her what Miss Grigsby had said—not yet—because it might be some horrible mistake, some horrible nightmare that wasn't true—

"Get me my coat, Bertha. And my pocket-book—some-where—in my drawer—" *Thirty-five cents for marbles . . . it's a deal . . . Shakespeare isn't dead, he's still alive . . .* Miss Grigsby was crying, that was why Claudia hadn't been able to understand her at first. She said something about a cat—running out into the street, to follow a large yellow cat—Oh God, maybe it was true, maybe it wasn't a nightmare after all—She pressed the back of her hand against her mouth to keep from screaming. Her teeth gnawed into the flesh—"Child, child—" Bertha moaned. "Be brave—"

She had to be brave. The taxi was late. She thought it would never come. She waited on the porch. David was reading Jerry's book at last, as an example of control. He was a little angry with her for letting Matthew upset her again. It was just as well to let him keep on thinking it was Matthew. " The taxi's here," he said, " and this time I'll handle that young man when he gets home."

She was in the cab before it came fully to a stop. The driver was new, and courteous to a degree. " Sorry, Miss, to be so late, but there was quite a traffic jam in the village, couldn't get through—terrible accident, a little boy was run over in front of the school and killed."

" Claudia ! " David suddenly called to her from the porch, " Wait !   I'll go down and see Miss Grigsby with you ! "

She looked back at him. He had got up from his chair, and he was standing by the rail. The sun was on his hair.

She shook her head. " No, darling, let me go alone." He couldn't have heard her, because she made no sound.

" Where to, miss ? "

" The school," said Claudia.

ELEVEN

THERE WAS A FEELING she always remembered. It had
come to her only once, and that was after Bobby was born
and the long agony of childbirth was over with. She
remembered that it had been as if she were lying in the
lap of a great, quiet pain, and as if the pain were clearing
her out so that the Universe could come within her and
make her one with it. It was not something she had ever
been able to talk about, even to David, for the feeling
had transcended itself into the sheerness of an experience
that had become part of the essence of her being. The
feeling hadn't come back to her when Matthew and Michael
were born, but perhaps that was because it was not given
lightly to open up the flood-gates of one's heart, and become
in unison with God, or Life, or Eternity, or whatever name
best fitted this sense of oneness.

It had been very different, too, with the baby who hadn't
lived beyond its first weak salute to earth. A new kind
of pain had ripped her to pieces, and because she hadn't
understood it and made friends with it, the sweet healing
of sorrow had not set in, and pain had become her enemy
and had destroyed her wholeness and her sanity. For endless months she lived in the dark with it. She fought back
at it in blind panic, so that she was too lost to know when
pain had gone, leaving confusion and fear to fill its place.
Those were black months that she had all but forgotten,
yet having lived them, they also had become a part of her,
and the experience lay deep within the fabric of her soul.

That was why she knew the pain, now that it had come
again, murdering her sanity and blasting happiness from
her universe. Once more she fought back at it, stifling
screams of agony and disbelief. The taxi driver said, with
his face in profile, " You hadn't ought to be alone, miss.
You should have let your husband come with you."

" I'm all right." She added, in defence of David, " My husband's been ill."

" I guessed as much, Miss. But still, this is no job for a woman by herself." After a few moments, the taxi driver went on, in blundering sympathy, " Maybe it isn't your little boy after all, miss. Maybe it's another little boy."

How strange that his words should bring her neither hope nor comfort. One little boy lay dead, and he became all children, and she became all mothers, and her pain grew big enough to fill eternity. The same feeling that she had known when Bobby was born came flooding back to her across the years, and agony ceased to split her wide apart, and she was cradled once again in the lap of a pain so quiet, and so great, that it was akin to exaltation. She noticed suddenly that there was sun on the mountain tops, changing them into peaks of gold, and wild roses had opened up along the roadside, filling the air with fragrance. All this she noticed, and as suddenly, Bobby was sitting beside her, and they were driving down to the village together, and he was whistling. It had happened that way a few short days ago, and it was happening now, and it would always happen. This was that moment of time, suspended in space, perfect and complete. It was hers for ever, and death could not take it from her. The taxi driver could not know that. She felt sorry for him, for his face, turned in profile, was so full of pity.

The cab drew up in front of the school. A baseball game must have stopped suddenly in the middle, for bats and gloves lay as they were thrown, on the courtyard grounds. There weren't any children around, but crowds of villagers stood on the pavement, as if waiting for something. They hardly talked. They just stood there, patient and waiting.

The taxi driver held on to her arm. He wouldn't take any money for the fare, and that was the only reason that people guessed who she was. A woman wept, loudly, and pity, like the pity of the taxi driver, swept through the crowd. It descended upon Claudia in a heavy mist, black-ing out the sunlight on the mountain tops. Miss Grigsby came through the mist to meet her, her thin hands fluttering with grief. "Oh, my dear," she whispered brokenly. "What can I say—What can I say—"

"Don't say anything—" Claudia whispered back, holding desperately to the thought of Bobby and the sun on the mountain tops. "Please don't . . ."

"God will help you," Miss Grigsby said, but she wouldn't let Claudia walk alone. She led her up the stone path to the wide doors that stood ajar against an empty, frightened corridor. "We called classes at once," she explained in an unsteady voice. "Matthew's in class, too. We haven't told him anything except that his brother's been badly hurt." She paused outside the closed door of the Principal's office, and even though it was her own office, she knocked lightly, hesitantly. The door opened, and Dr. Geiger came out. When he saw Claudia, he shut the door behind him very quickly, but not quite quickly enough. There was a white sheet covering something on the leather sofa, something so little and so still. Dr. Geiger put his arm around her. Claudia tried to keep Bobby with her but the thing on the sofa came between them.

Dr. Geiger wanted to take her home, pretending that it was for David's sake. "I'm not certain what effect a shock like this will have," he said. "I think I ought to be there when he hears about it."

Claudia shook her head. "I'd rather go alone, if you don't mind." She was thinking of David, too. It would only be an additional shock if he saw Dr. Geiger bringing her back. Her spirit swooned from the task, but it would be better to tell him in her own way.

She took Matthew with her. He was too young to realise death, and he was less upset than gratified about being let out of school ahead of time. "Is Bobby hurt very bad ?" he asked her in punctilious concern.

"He hasn't any pain at all," said Claudia.

" That's good," said Matthew, and felt free to enlarge upon his private version of the accident. " Bobby's such a dope," he said. " A boy told me another boy told him that a big yellow cat ran across the street, and Bobby ran right out after him without looking. I guess he thought it was Shakespeare, but I bet anything he's dead, don't you, Mother ? "

She could not speak. He looked at her in quick apprehension. " Are you crying ? "

" No, darling."

" Then why have you got tears running down your cheeks ? "

Still, she could not bring the words to her lips. " I guess because Bobby's hurt," he concluded. After a pause he asked her, in a fairly grown-up way, " Didn't you want to stay with him, Mother, instead of going home ? "

" Yes."

" Why didn't you, then ? "

" Dad needs me."

" How long will Bobby be in the hospital ? "

" Not long."

" Then he'll be able to go back to New York with us, won't he ? "

" He'll always be with us."

" He sure is going to hate to leave without Shakespeare. That dope thinks he's going to find Shakespeare some day."

The taxi driver, who had been waiting outside the school for her, turned with an air of taking off his hat. " It sure looks," he said, " as if the little feller found his cat." He blew his nose loudly, keeping one hand on the wheel.

" What did the man mean ? " Matthew asked excitedly. " Was that cat really Shakespeare ? "

It was as sweet a way as any to tell Matthew about death He listened to her, respectful and awed. He tried not to let the tears come into his voice. " Then aren't we going to see Bobby any more ? "

She put the thought away from her. She must hold on to the thought that Bobby was there, like the sun, still

shining on the mountain tops. " We won't see his body,"
she said.

" Why not ? "

" Bobby doesn't need his body any longer, darling."

" That's funny. Is it like the snake on the farm once,
that came out of its skin ? "

" A little."

Matthew pondered it. " But won't he be lonesome all
by himself with nobody to take care of him ? "

" He won't be by himself. He'll have many people to
love him and take care of him—"

" He will ? Who ? "

" My mother will be so happy to see him."

" Was she your mother like you're my mother ? "

" Yes."

" And who else ? "

" Aunt Elizabeth, Uncle Roger—"

He caught on. " What about Fritz ? " he broke in eagerly.
" Is Bobby going to be with Fritz, too ? "

" Yes. Fritz, too."

" Gosh," Matthew softly said. " The lucky bum."

Claudia almost smiled. Matthew had discovered something rather wonderful about death. . . .

It was a blessed reprieve that David was not on the porch
waiting for her. Bertha was there, nervously dangling the
baby on her knee. Michael was too old to be dangled, he
kept trying to lunge forward out of the circle of her arms,
smacking strange sounds out of his lips.

Bertha didn't rise from her chair when she saw Claudia.
She just sat there, as if paralysed, with the strength all
gone from her solid limbs. Matthew took over, bursting
with the importance of his news. " Bobby's with Fritz ! "
he announced.

Bertha put the baby down, slowly and carefully, so that
he could hold himself erect against the lower rail of the
porch. He bobbed around on his fat legs with the seat
of his rompers inflating like a balloon in the breeze, until
all of a sudden his weight pulled him down on his fat

backside, and he screeched with indignation. Automatically, Bertha bent to pick him up. Claudia was glad that Bertha had Michael to take care of.

In the bedroom, she could see David through the window, putting on a white shirt. She went to him. Bluff looked up from where he lay on the floor beside the bureau. He rolled his great, blood-shot eyes, and gave a heavy sigh.

"Bluff's got troubles," David commented. "I see you brought the young master home with you, what's he done this time?"

An ocean roared in Claudia's ears. "Hey now, wait a minute," David protested from a vast distance like a voice under water, "you're in a fine state—"

She struggled out of the black emptiness that had engulfed her as she'd walked into the room. Maybe it was seeing Bluff . . .

"Sit down," said David, "you're shaking all over. I'll attend to Matthew from here on." He strode to the window. "Matthew! Come in, I want to see you!" he called sternly.

She reached for breath against the pounding of her heart. "I have to tell you something first—"

"Let Matthew tell me."

Matthew came running in. "Bertha's crying," he said in a frightened voice. His world was in chaos, and suddenly he was crying too. "I want Bobby!" he sobbed. "I don't want him to go away!"

Tears drenched Claudia's lips in salt. She tried to silence him. "Matthew darling, stay with Bertha, please let me be alone with Daddy—"

"Just a moment," David interposed. "What's this all about?" He knelt with his big hands on Matthew's scanty little shoulders. "I can't understand what you're saying, son, if you cry like that. Now tell me, slowly and quietly, what's happened—"

"I want Bobby!" Matthew kept on sobbing. "I don't want him never to come back any more, I don't want him to be killed!"

Claudia saw the knuckles come out white on David's hands. She couldn't bear to look at his face, it was torture beyond bearing to see his hands. She knew enough to leave them together, to share the special, private grief of men. She could help neither of them at this moment, as much as they could help each other.

After a little while, David found her sitting on Bobby's bed. He took her in his arms.

It was odd that the hours should move on as if their world hadn't crashed to nothingness. Philip Dexter came to call for them at two o'clock. " ' Tuesday at two,' " said Claudia, when his car drove up. " When Mamma died you told me that the only security in life was insecurity. I never wanted to believe that it was true. Now I have to believe it."

" If you know it's that way," said David, " you stop fighting against the way it is."

They were still sitting, with their arms around each other, on Bobby's bed. " I like to be in here," Claudia had said. " He seems closer, as if he were going to dash in from school any minute and throw his books down and ask if there wasn't any cake to go with his milk—milk was a great bore to him without something to go with it. I can't seem to make myself realise that it's never going to be again."

" The realisation will come, darling. Don't force it."

" Do you realise ? " she asked him wonderingly.

" You're not supposed to realise a whole lifetime in a few short moments," he said. " Our minds and our hearts aren't built to take it."

" A whole lifetime. A whole lifetime of less than eleven years." She beat against the soft pillow in violent abnegation. " David, why ! Why, why ! "

" God ! " said David. " I don't know. If I could answer that, I'd know the answer to a lot of things."

They could hear Phil's hearty shout of greeting as he came up on the porch. " Hi, there, are you ready ? " Then Bertha hurried out to meet him, and there was a quick, deep silence. " Bertha's told him," Claudia said.

Phil attended to everything. The mechanics of death were as urgent as the mechanics of birth. You called the doctor and the hospital and packed a suitcase, and notified friends and relatives . . .

"Please, you and Mr. Naughton go now into the living-room," Bertha coaxed them.

"Yes, come dear," David said.

Claudia shook her head. "I know what Bertha wants. I'd rather do it." She rose from the bed and opened the door of Bobby's closet and took his blue suit from the hanger. "And the polka-dot tie that Candy sent him last week, he loved it." Poor Candy, what a shock it would be. "David, isn't there any way we could keep it from her until after the baby comes?"

"You mustn't want to spare people," said David. "Phil's called John, he'll use his discretion about telling her."

"Has he called Hartley, too?"

"Yes, but he wasn't at his office."

"Mr. John said to tell you he will get in touch with Mr. Hartley," Bertha explained. "And now if you will keep an ear open for the baby, he is in his crib, and Matthew is doing his homework, and I am going out with Mr. Dexter for a while."

Claudia didn't have to ask where they were going. David said, "You stay here with Mrs. Naughton, Bertha. Those are things that I should be doing."

"No, Mr. Naughton," said Bertha, "you are wrong, please forgive me. With Fritz it was the same. There were others to do the things I could not do. It is right that it should be like that."

"It's strange to think," Claudia said, after Bertha and Phil had left, "that both of them have been through the same thing, and still they go on living as if part of them hadn't died. When Phil used to talk about his son, I never really understood what it meant. I thought, 'How terrible to lose a child'—but I didn't know." Her voice fell away. "I didn't know. Even when Lisa died, I didn't really know how Bertha felt . . ."

David lifted her hand against his cheek in answer.

"Do you remember little Joey Cootz at the farm?"

"Yes," said David.

"I never forgot the way Mrs. Cootz looked when I drove past her house a few days afterwards. She was picking vegetables, and no one could tell how she felt—or what was going on inside of her. I know now, though. Every time something happens to you, it brings you close to others that the same thing has happened to. Until Mamma died, I didn't realise how many people lost their mothers. And the same with the miscarriage, and the war, and your having to be up here—I'm talking a lot. I can hear myself and I can't stop. Why don't you stop me?"

"Because they're all things that have to be said," David told her gently. "Talk it out, darling, it's good to talk things out."

Matthew came to the door, his eyes still red with crying. "Michael's sucking his thumb," he said, as an excuse for joining them.

"That's all right," said David. "Have you finished your homework yet?"

"Yes, and now I haven't anything else to do." Desolation gave his voice a new note, like the sad little sound of a bird at twilight. Claudia wanted to tell him that he could play his radio, but she knew that she wouldn't be able to stand the impact of it. Something told her that Matthew wouldn't be able to stand it, either. Matthew would remember this day for as long as he lived. Years hence he would look back on it as the beginning of his soul's loneliness, and the beginning of his growing-up. She drew him down to her so that she could brush the hair out of his eyes. "Go in the kitchen and pour yourself a glass of milk, darling, you didn't have anything to eat all afternoon."

"I don't want anything," he said, and then as an after-thought, he asked, "Is there any cake?"

She felt the quick clasp of David's hand. "I'm sorry,

not a speck," she answered steadily. "Bertha intended to bake this afternoon."

The telephone bell rang. "I'll answer," said Matthew.

"No, I will," said David. "You stay here with Mother."

When he came back, Matthew had ensconced himself over a chair, with his head on the floor, and his legs in the air. "That's no way to sit, let Bluff out," said David.

"He doesn't have to, he did," said Matthew.

Claudia could see that David wanted him out of the room.

"There's bread and jelly," she suggested. "That's just as good with milk as cake."

"No, it isn't," said Matthew, as a simple matter of fact.

"Don't argue," David commanded. "March."

Matthew reassorted his extremities by slow degrees, and gradually got himself out of the room. Claudia looked after him. "I'm glad it wasn't Matthew," she said. "If it was Matthew, I couldn't bear the remorse. All the times we've told him to march."

"And all the times he hasn't," said David.

"We have to be more patient with him. This'll make a change in him. He feels it, but he doesn't want to show how much."

"That's true," said David. "You're right." He sat down beside her again. He had something to tell her and it wasn't easy. "Darling, that was Hartley on the phone——"

"I thought it probably was."

He cleared his throat. "He thinks we ought to bring Bobby home."

"To New York?"

"Yes, dear."

"With the children?"

"No, that would be too much excitement, we could leave them here with Bertha, and go on the eleven-fifteen train tonight. We'd be back by the end of the week."

It made good sense, but it was a hard thing to decide. Dr. Geiger had mentioned the chapel in the village, but Claudia had recoiled from the idea. It had gone through her mind, "He's too little to be away from us."

" Could Bobby be on the same train with us ? " she asked after a pause.

" Yes, dear."

" Then I think I'd like that. It would be wiser—than here—in the cottage—on account of Matthew."

" I'm sure of it. I know where to reach Phil. Shall I call him so that he can pick up our reservations ? "

She nodded, numb with the effort of making up her mind.

" Daddy's phoning a lot."

She looked up. Matthew stood in the doorway, his need for companionship greater than her need for solitude. She held out her hand to him. He came to her, and hung his arm loosely around her, leaning heavily, and for once at a loss for questions. It was a relief when a car stopped in front of the door. " Go see who it is," she said.

He departed reluctantly but when he came running back, his spirits had revived. " Somebody brought a big ham and a cherry pie," he announced with enthusiasm.

" Who ? "

" I don't know. She says her name is Mrs. Jenkins. Who's Mrs. Jenkins ? She's fat."

" She ran the boarding-house we stayed at."

" Before we moved here ? "

" Yes." Claudia dragged herself from the bed. " Is she waiting ? "

" She's in the parlour. She says maybe you want to see her."

" I don't, but I will."

" Why did she bring us a ham and a cherry pie ? "

" To be kind."

" I'd rather have chocolate."

" I hope you didn't say so. Tell Dad when he finishes telephoning not to go in the living-room."

She wanted to spare him Mrs. Jenkins' voluminous sympathy, at least the first overwhelming rush of it : " You poor, poor precious dear," she began at once, her florid face working with emotion. " What a terrible, terrible blow—"

Claudia girded herself against the devastating effect of Mrs. Jenkins' double adjectives. " It was nice of you to take this long trip up from the village," she murmured, " and bring us such wonderful things to eat."

Mrs. Jenkins appealed to some invisible bystander. " Now just listen to her, will you ? What are friends for, if not at a time like this ? Mr. Barwell wanted to jump right in the car and come along with me, but he isn't at all well, you know, not at all well."

" No, I didn't know. I'm sorry." It would be easier to talk about Mr. Barwell than herself, or David, or Bobby. " I hope it isn't anything too serious."

" Serious enough," said Mrs. Jenkins. " Tom Barwell is the last person to take chances, but no, nothing would do but he had to go home at Easter for his sister's wedding, and of course he overdid, and now he's paying for it. So I said to him, ' Now see here, Tom,' I said, ' you're not to budge off that bed, Mr. and Mrs. Naughton will understand.' "

" Of course we do."

Mrs. Jenkins loosened her coat, with an air of staying. " To tell the truth," she divulged, " I never in this world expected to see you, I just said to myself, ' nobody feels like cooking at a time like this, so I'll just drop by with a little food.' It certainly is a revelation to see you so calm and collected."

" What good does it do to carry on ? " said Claudia.

" None," Mrs. Jenkins admitted devoutly. " None at all. The Lord's will be done. In the twenty-odd years I've run my boarding-house, I've watched too many of them go, young and old alike, not to know that there's something in the Good Lord's Mind other than just the plain suffering of human kind. So I always say you have to accept whatever comes in blind trust. That's the only thing to do, accept it in blind trust."

Blind trust. It made Claudia think of the sheep at the farm. Well, maybe that was the way the Lord wanted it— *The Lord is my Shepherd*. There'd been an Easter Festival at school a few weeks ago, and Bobby had sung the hymn with his class in Assembly, squirming with embarrassment because he didn't like to be caught singing with his mother sitting out front . . . she knew exactly how he'd felt. . . . Once, when they'd taken him to the movies the words of a melody had bobbed across the screen, so that the audience could join in the chorus. The three of them had sat there, tongue-tied and a little uncomfortable in the midst of the lusty chanting all around them. " If Matthew'd been along," David had commented with satisfaction, " he'd have sung his silly little head off."

" I envy him for being able to," Claudia had replied, though she had sensed David's pleasure in being Bobby's father.

Mrs. Jenkins' voice, carefully lowered, called her back to the aching present. " The thing that really worries me, is how your husband is going to take it. Anybody could tell by the little things he'd drop now and again, that Bobby was the apple of his eye. Not that parents are supposed to have favourites," Mrs. Jenkins hastened to inject, " but if they did, I'd certainly have said that Bobby was Mr. Naughton's favourite."

" They were very much alike—" Claudia's throat closed up, and the tears came at last in an overwhelming pity for David. Mrs. Jenkins patted her shoulder. " You poor little thing, it does you good to cry, it's unnatural to sit there like a stone. But then again, you just have to bear up for your husband's sake. I was saying to Mr. Barwell, it's a blessing in a way, I said, that she's got Mr. Naughton's health to worry about."

" His last X-rays couldn't have been better," said Claudia mechanically.

" Still," Mrs. Jenkins continued, " if you want to be smart, you'll make him stay up here for another few months, and give himself a chance to get over this dreadful shock. It'll pay you dividends in the long run, you mark my words."

" We'd planned to anyway," said Claudia. " We were going to look at a place this afternoon."

Mrs. Jenkins beamed. "Well now I declare, you remember what I told you when you first came up?" she exclaimed in triumph. "You remember what I said, I said 'Your husband might hate and despise everything about this place now,' I said, ' but the time will come when he'll not want to leave.'"

Claudia regarded Mrs. Jenkins in abject misery. Yes, she remembered; and she remembered, too, that it had seemed inconceivable that such a right-about-face could happen to David. But it had happened, and up to a few hours ago it had seemed a major tragedy that fear should have invaded his robust mind. Now it was no longer important. What did it matter? What did anything matter. . . .

"Yes sir, I've watched it happen again and again," Mrs. Jenkins enlarged. "Take Dr. Geiger himself. He never expected to settle here. And Mary Brooks. You met Mary Brooks, she works at the bank. And why? Because she knows she'll live a lot longer if she doesn't go back to teaching in Indiana. So I should think, all things considered, that you'd be pretty happy that your husband finally got some sense in that handsome stubborn head of his. My goodness, wasn't he a hard one to manage in the beginning, though," Mrs. Jenkins recalled with zest. "Drink a glass of milk? No. He was too good for milk. Rest from two-to-four? Not him. No."

"Yes, he was difficult," Claudia admitted faintly.

"So I say, there's always something to be grateful for. Always." Mrs. Jenkins dabbed furtively at her eyes and blew her nose loudly so that it would appear to be completely nose and not heart. "You've got two beautiful sons to live for. And you're still young, please God you'll have a little daughter some day, if Mr. Naughton's health permits."

Claudia didn't have the energy or the will to tell her that there could never be any more children, and it had nothing to do with David's health. She was glad to hear his step in the hall. Mrs. Jenkins was almost talked out, and all he got was the tail end of her, and still it was more than he bargained for. " What does she think she is ? " he said, when she finally took off. " A special emissary from the Lord ? "

" Yes," said Claudia wearily.

Later, several patients from the Sanatorium came to call, and toward evening the Trents appeared so that one of them, either Byard or Lydia, could drive Phil's car back. Matthew was greatly impressed with all the company. " Is this a party for Bobby ? " he wanted to know.

" In a way," Claudia told him. It was a strange custom —so many people coming—but perhaps the reason for it was that it kept you from thinking until you were strong enough to think. She knew that that was why Bertha asked the Trents to stay for supper, although she said that it was because somebody had to help eat up Mrs. Jenkins' enormous ham.

It was incredible that anyone could want food, and yet they all sat around the table with an outward air of normalcy, except that Lydia made friends with Bluff and timidly patted his head. " What's the matter, old fellow," Claudia heard her whisper, as she gave him a little meat from her plate.

" That's not allowed," Matthew informed her gravely.

" He didn't eat it anyway," Lydia discovered, " it's still on the floor." She stooped to pick it up. " I thought dogs always gobbled everything, including your fingers."

" He's not hungry, I guess he misses Bobby," said Matthew.

" Bertha, may I have another glass of milk ? " Byard asked a little too abruptly.

" Gladly," said Bertha.

" Don't give it to him, that's your third glass now, really," Lydia protested.

" We have plenty," said Claudia. She didn't say, ' We have a whole quart extra,' but David must have been thinking it, too, for she felt his hand on hers beneath the table.

" Something tells me Byard would like another piece of ham," Phil put in wickedly.

" I certainly would," Byard accepted shamelessly. " It's the best I ever tasted."

" I wish you'd take most of it home with you," said Claudia. " It'd be a charity to Bertha, she'll be living on it while we're gone."

" Ham keeps, I wouldn't dream of it," said Lydia. " You'll be glad to have it when you come back."

" I'll take a few slices for my breakfast," Byard compromised.

They left early because of the long ride back, and because Byard was anxious about driving. " I haven't had my hands on a wheel for two years," he said.

" It's high time you began," said Lydia crisply. " The doctor said you could go ahead six months ago. It's a good thing you're being forced into it."

" Lydia's right," Phil agreed. " You're a lazy so-and-so, the next time I come up, I'm going to yank you off your royal rear and take you fishing with me."

" That's what you think," said Byard complacently.

Their well-meant bickering left a sharp silence in the cottage after they'd gone. Phil saw he needed some cigarettes, and went off to the village to buy some. " I should have remembered, there was an unopened carton in the table drawer," said Claudia.

" Those are stale, they're no good any more," David told her. He put his arm around her shoulders. " Tired ? "

" No. But I wish no more company would come. I think I'll pack, David."

" Bertha said she'd attend to it after she got Matthew to bed."

" It'll give me something to do. I wanted to put Matthew to bed myself, but I couldn't. Not yet. He's so much like Bobby in little ways I never noticed before."

" I know," said David. " You go and pack, darling."

She was in the middle of it, trying to fit too much into a small suitcase, when Miss Carey appeared on the threshold.

7

" Hello," she said, " your husband said to come right
in, I was probably the one person you wouldn't mind
seeing. I was flattered."

" You ought to be—hello."

" Sorry to drop in so late, but I didn't want to leave
Marian until she was settled for the night, a neighbour's
staying with her until I get back. Look, you're making
a great mess of that poor suit the way you're folding it."

" I never was much of a packer," Claudia said.

" Go on, get away, I'll do it." Miss Carey settled her
glasses, and with two competent thumps, inverted the
sleeves of David's jacket and laid it in a neat torso on the
bed. Then she emptied what was already in the suitcase
and began from scratch. Claudia watched her. " Now
why can't I learn to do that? I never can turn the corners
of a bed decently, either."

" I don't think you're very bright," Miss Carey said.
" What about those shoes on the floor? "

" They go."

" You're an optimist."

" And David's bedroom slippers."

" I am no magician. Haven't you got a larger suitcase? "

" Yes, but it's too large to take for only a couple of days."

" Oh. Is that all you're going to stay? "

" Yes. I think David dreads the very thought of New
York, although he won't say so. And I don't want to stay
long either on account of leaving Bertha up here alone."

" I wasn't asking you for reasons," Miss Carey said. " I
was merely interested in why, if you intend to be gone so
short a time, you're lugging along such a pile of socks and
underwear. Are you too delicate to do a little rinsing out
at night? "

Claudia dropped into a chair. " I don't know what I'm
doing, I'm just picking things up and putting them down
again in a daze."

" You're doing all right," Miss Carey remarked. " Why
don't you lie down on the other bed and make yourself
comfortable while I work? "

" I think I will."

Her body was grateful for the brief respite, and Miss Carey's brusque presence was like fresh air after the drenching perfume of Mrs. Jenkins' compassion and the calculated avoidance of the Trents. Even when she got around to speaking of Bobby, it was in a matter-of-fact voice that made him alive and near, just as he had been a few short hours before. It seemed so wrong that it should be any other way.

" I stopped in at the chapel before I came," Miss Carey mentioned, as she refolded a bath-robe. " The principal of the school was there, and also one of the teachers, and the wife of the old man who shovelled your snow—and Mr. Dexter."

" Then he didn't go down for cigarettes," said Claudia. " I'm glad Bobby wasn't alone."

" He seemed right pleased about it too," Miss Carey said. " Just as if he were about to smile."

" Bertha told me he looked so nice in his blue suit," Claudia said tremulously. " She slicked his hair back with water the way he always loved it, and he looked wonderful, she said."

" He did. So complete, somehow."

" I couldn't bear it if you'd said ' peaceful.' He was too little and too happy to look peaceful." Claudia's voice broke. " I wish I could believe that he was ready to go, but I can't. I just can't."

" Look, child, the Lord Himself couldn't expect you to see a reason behind all this. Not now, anyway. But as time goes on, I imagine you will."

" What makes you think so," said Claudia bitterly.

" Because I happen to know the stuff you're made of, having nursed you through one miscarriage and one husband going off to war. It was a different kind of pain, but it wasn't a whole lot easier than you're going through now."

" I wouldn't brag about it. I didn't come off with such flying colours."

"We went through all that the other day," said Miss Carey, "and I have no further intention of showering you with compliments. Make yourself out a weakling, if that's the way you want it, but don't expect me to believe it; because your record of performance proves that you're a liar. Fundamentally, you're as strong as an ox."

"I might act as strong as an ox," Claudia's voice rose hysterically, "but how much are you supposed to take without breaking again !"

"As much as you get dished out to you," said Miss Carey. "At least that's the way I figure it. And if you can't take it—" Miss Carey shrugged, "then that's your tough luck. Now let's have those bedroom slippers."

Claudia rose from the bed. Miss Carey said, "Don't be such a fusser. Can't you tell me where they are ?"

"No, I'll get them."

She found the slippers in a chest. Miss Carey wedged them, skilful as a mason, next to David's leather travelling kit, the same one that had gone with him to New Guinea and back.

"So," she said, "that does it. Anything else ?"

"Just this," said Claudia. She opened the top drawer of the bureau, and drew out a cardboard box. In it there was everything that Bertha had brought home that afternoon, everything that had been crammed into the pockets of Bobby's old brown tweed—marbles galore, and a rubber-band ball, and a broken harmonica, and the pen that wrote in two colours. Claudia gave the pen to Miss Carey. "He said Marian thought it was ' nifty.' Take it home to her."

"I will," Miss Carey said. She put it in her pocket-book. "I told her I was coming tonight because Bobby was going home. She sent her love to him. I'll give her the pen. With his love."

"I wish you would," said Claudia. She smiled faintly— it was such a little pen to have gone so long a way.

Miss Carey cleared her throat. "Before I forget, Marian

got the paper dolls and the book. She started a letter to you, but it was uphill work, poor baby."

"Poor baby," Claudia repeated slowly. "That's what I felt last Saturday, when I sent them to her. She was so ill, and Bobby was so full of life and health . . ."

Miss Carey took off her glasses and wiped them carefully, "Isn't it the damnedest thing," she said.

It was her way of saying, "Thy will be done."

TWELVE

AT LAST it was time to leave. They sat in the small, ugly living-room, waiting for the taxi. They looked like strangers in their city clothes. Claudia remembered going away with her mother one summer to a hotel in Maine, and whenever guests went back to town, they too looked like strangers, in dark colours and hats and gloves.

" What are you thinking of, darling ? "

" Just of when I was a little girl . . ."

He pressed her hand. " That's a sure sign of getting old."

" I suppose so. Where's Phil ? "

" Telephoning."

" Who to now ? "

" Oh—attending to things in general."

" There's a lot to attend to, isn't there ? "

" Yes, dear."

" I'm glad Matthew's asleep."

" So am I."

" I hate leaving Bertha up here alone."

" I do, too. But it's the best way, dear."

" I think so too. Is that taxi late ? "

" No, we've another ten minutes—"

" How many times we've waited for taxis in the last nine months. And it was always something important—your first visit to Dr. Geiger—Candy and John going away—this afternoon—David, was it only this afternoon ? "

" Half-past-twelve. I happened to look at my watch as you drove off. I'll never forgive myself for not going with you. You should have told me. It was my right to be with you."

She shook her head. " It wouldn't have done any good."

" Darling, don't grow too strong," he said. " Give me a chance to catch up with you again."

" I'm sorry," she said humbly. She didn't have to ask him what he meant, for wisdom came to sit with grief. In every crisis of their marriage, from the children's sniffles to her mother's death, he had been a source of strength to her, until gradually through the years he had challenged her maturity with his own. But now, in the past months, something had happened to that fine balance of relationship. She knew what David meant. She had let pity take the place of passion, and tolerance usurp respect. There was work to be done on both sides to regain what they had lost.

She was aware that Bertha had come into the room, with a pitcher of milk on a tray. " While you are waiting," she beguiled them. " Come. You did not eat very much, either of you, all day."

David said, " No thanks, Bertha, I had plenty."

" I couldn't either," said Claudia.

Bertha poured. " Try. If you will, Mr. David will."

To humour her, each of them drank a little. Then Phil came back from telephoning, and she made him drink what was left in the pitcher. She needed to take care of somebody.

At last the taxi drove up. David put his arms around Bertha and kissed her. " That was from Bobby," he said, " to thank you for what you've been to us."

As the taxi turned into the road, Claudia looked back. Bertha was standing in the lighted doorway, a lonely figure in the night.

They were surprised to find Dr. Geiger at the station to see them off. He said, " I take off my hat to you two. I've seen some people yell, and I've seen others take it like gentlemen. On the whole, the ones who yell have an easier time of it." He took a small envelope from his pocket. " Here's a couple of sleeping-pills, they're always a good thing to have along."

" I'm glad you thought of it," said David. " Claudia needs a night's rest."

" Don't you worry about Claudia, she's doing fine,"

said Dr. Geiger. " You're the one that can do with a little watching now."

" I'm all right."

" Exactly. And see that you stay that way. Take care of yourself and don't let all these months of hard curing go for nothing. And be careful, no lifting heavy luggage."

" That's why I'm going with them," said Phil, " to see that he behaves himself."

It was good to have Phil along, although they'd both begged him not to upset his plans. " Please," he'd asked them simply. " I promise not to be in your way."

" As if you could," said Claudia. She was ashamed of being so grateful for his being there.

He sat with them in their compartment for a while, talking about a new tobacco, and fishing, and Jerry's book, just as if it were an ordinary trip that they were taking together. " Only someone who's lived through it could have done that," David said, after Phil had gone to his berth in the car ahead.

" Yes," said Claudia.

The porter came to make up their beds. " I'll sleep in the upper," Claudia said. " I like an upper better than a lower."

David caught her gown as she started to climb the ladder, and pulled her in beside him. " Darling," he whispered, " thank you for having given me this year with Bobby."

His words were like a healing hand upon a ragged wound. How had he glimpsed the torment in her. She clung to him in the narrow space. " But if I'd left the children in New York with Candy," she sobbed, " it would never have happened. . . ."

" Come now, be a grown-up girl," he chided her gently. " Don't go back on yourself. Be glad that something bigger than either of us made you do what you did. These months together have been like an extra gift to us."

" You mean it was his time to go——"

" I'm trying to believe it, darling, with all the faith that's in me."

"Well, I don't believe it! There isn't any God, and if there is, I hate Him!"

"I don't think He minds your hating Him," said David. "Because if there is a God, and suddenly I think there is, He must be a very patient, understanding God. So go ahead, darling. Cry it out. You need to cry."

She had not known such agony could be. She writhed in it, as if birth were tearing her apart from limb to limb. "Don't let me," she gasped, "Don't let me!"

"It's good, darling. It's good," he said. "Let it come out, don't keep it all locked up." She felt him close, and closer, his body strong against the trembling that shattered her to pieces. She had not felt his strength for a long while, and she had thought that it would never be given her again to call upon it. Thankfulness came, unbidden, and made less room for hate. "David, what would I do without you—I love you so . . ."

His voice was a breath against her cheek. "I love you too, my darling. So much. So much."

After a time, he said, "What about that sleeping-tablet?"

"I'd rather not. Tonight belongs to Bobby and to us."

"I'm glad you feel like that," said David. "I'm glad you're not afraid of suffering."

Toward dawn sleep came to both of them, lightly, without fully destroying consciousness. They were awake long before the porter knocked at their door. "Bridgeport!" he called out.

Bridgeport brought back memories of the farm. "I'm happy Bobby had the farm," Claudia said aloud.

"And he had the mountains," David said.

"But he never knew the sea. We'd planned last summer to take him sailing with us this year, do you remember?"

"I remember."

"So much has happened in a year."

David made no reply. He said, "I could use a cup of strong black coffee."

It was hard to face the casual bustle of the diner and the smell of food. Phil was there ahead of them. He had

reserved a table; he leaped up when he saw them. " I
was hoping you'd come," he said. The diner was full.
There was an empty place next to David, and a man came
in and sat down in it. He was short and stocky, with
pock-marks on his face. His neck bulged over the back of
his collar as if his frame had put on more pounds than it
could carry. He ordered orange-juice, and milk and bacon
and eggs, and as an afterthought, cold cereal. " Bring
me a side portion of fried potatoes, too," he told the waiter.
He winked broadly at Claudia. " I'm not afraid of my
girlish figure," he said. " Nothing like keeping your
weight up."

Claudia didn't say anything.

He made another try. " I saw you folks at the station
last night. We all got on together."

Phil murmured a polite rejoinder.

The man put a slab of butter on a piece of bread
and spread it lumpily. " Going back for a visit or for
good ? "

It was David's turn to answer. " A visit," he said
briefly.

" Me too." He winked again at Claudia, as he folded
the bread into his mouth. " They can have New York and
welcome. That grime and dust's no good for anybody's
lungs."

The waiter brought his breakfast. His heavy square
hands encircled the plate and reminded her of Bluff. " Pass
the salt and pepper, please."

Claudia passed them. He sprinkled the bacon and eggs
and potatoes lavishly before he tasted them. It always
puzzled her when anyone did that. How could you know
there wasn't enough salt—or too much salt—to start
with ?

His thick voice broke through the protective curtain of
her thoughts. " Did you see they brought a little kid on
last night ? You could tell it was a kid by the size of the
box. Lousy break when it hits 'em young."

" Yes," said Claudia, thinking of Marian.

David pushed his chair back. "We're almost there." He'd scarcely touched his coffee. "Lout," he muttered under his breath.

"We don't know what's behind his face any more than he knows what's behind ours," Claudia apologised for the man.

"Food chiefly," said Phil shortly. "Poor devil, he's dead and doesn't know it. And brother," he added with emphasis, "that's death for sure."

Claudia wondered whether he was thinking of Byard Trent.

The first person she saw when they got off the train was John—without Candy. She waved to him, and he waved back, diffidently, as if surprised that she could wave. "How's Candy?" she asked at once.

He tried to borrow her composure, not knowing how near she was to breaking. "No sign, yet. She'll be waiting for us at Hartley's." He kissed her awkwardly, shyly, with his whole heart in his thin, strong face. He couldn't seem to bring any more words to his lips. He gripped David's shoulder hard, and then let go and said, with monumental effort, "Hartley's in the car. He has a bad leg and has to keep off it."

"He didn't mention it," said David.

"He hasn't wanted to bother you about it. He was fairly miserable for a time, but he's much better now." He looked enquiringly at Phil, and Claudia saw that Hartley's leg was a cover for marking time.

"Go on ahead," Phil answered. "I'll meet you at the house."

"I don't know what we should have done without Phil," said Claudia.

"If he hadn't happened to be there, I'd have come," John told her. "This is no time to be alone."

"A lot of people are," said David. Claudia knew he was thinking of Jerry and Elizabeth, all by themselves in a foreign land. Jerry had written about it, so simply, in his book.

They edged their way toward the exit. The station was getting filled with early commuters. "This is a little different from the mountains," said John, making conversation.

Watkins hurried toward them, his hand extended for the suitcase. "Sorry, sir, that I couldn't leave the car, I'd have got a parking ticket." He looked at them, and like John, he found it hard to speak. "It's a terrible tragedy, the little feller certainly didn't deserve it, God rest his soul." He turned away.

Claudia blessed Hartley for not saying anything. He made room for them beside him, the portly contour of his cheeks squared off into a pallid mask. After a moment or two, he said, "I'm glad you came home, children."

"I'm afraid you couldn't have made it with your bad leg if we hadn't," said David.

"I'd have made it, doctors or no doctors."

"What seems to be the trouble?"

"Never mind me, boy." He peered at David anxiously. "The point is, are you all right?"

"I'm all right," said David.

"I never pictured this kind of a home-coming. Julia and I planned on having the red carpet rolled out for you when you got back."

"Where is Julia?" Claudia quickly asked.

"On her way home. I telephoned her yesterday. With good flying weather, she ought to be back in time."

"I know what that trip is," said David. "You shouldn't have asked it of her."

"I didn't have to ask." A note of sternness came into Hartley's voice. "When a thing like this happens, a family should be together."

The car turned up Fifth Avenue, John cleared his throat. "Well, David, how does the old town look to you?"

"Just the same," said David. "Except that there seems to be quite some excavating."

"There is. A lot of new apartment houses and office buildings are going up."

"I hope it doesn't rain," said Claudia. "It looks so dark and muggy."

"It won't rain." John smiled. "You forget this is just New York's heat and grime. Besides, it's early yet. The paper said sun. Today and tomorrow."

Sun. Sun that turned the mountain-tops to gold. Bobby belonged in the sun, the sun would bring him back to her out of the grey mist of despair and loss. It was a secret thing inside of her, a source of strength and comfort, to share with no one, not even David.

Candy was waiting for them at the door. It was startling to see her, swollen into womanhood, with her little girl's face smudged with weeping. She tried to smile and keep her voice from shaking, but she wasn't very successful at it. John saved her from an ignominious gulp of tears. "Don't you think she looks remarkable?" he asked them gravely. "Could you ever tell that she was pregnant?"

Candy swallowed the lump in her throat. "John can tease me, but really I don't think I show very much."

"Neither do I," said Claudia solemnly. "You were much bigger the first month than you are now."

David laughed. "Look who's talking. You weren't any different with Bobby."

A stunned silence fell upon them, as if it were hard to hear Bobby's name, spoken easily and sweetly. The pity of it, that they had already banished him to the solitude of death. "You mustn't do it to him!" Claudia cried out fiercely from within herself. "You mustn't do it to David and to me!" Suddenly the tears began to roll down Candy's cheeks. "Oh, damn me! Why do I have to be such a blubbering sissy—"

Hartley gave her his handkerchief. "I'm a sissy, too, Candy, and I haven't got the excuse of having a baby."

Suddenly, as they stood there, the shadow of a long black car drove up in front of the door. Hartley pushed them off toward the lift. He seemed in a hurry to get them out of the hall. "The whole top floor is yours, children. Get bathed and rested," he said.

David pressed the button. " Bobby would have loved this lift," Claudia said.

" Maybe he is loving it," said David, who had never believed that there was anything after death.

Something that she'd joked about a long time ago came back to her. " We're so satisfied with just being alone with each other," she said to David, " that when I die—" (she never minded playing fast and loose with her own funeral) " —we won't have had enough people to dinner to send me flowers, and I'll be mortified."

" I'll send you some," David promised.

" No, don't, one single wreath would look too skimpy. Just pretend I left it in my will not to have any at all, I wanted the money to be sent to some hospital or charity. Which I do, come to think of it. Flowers are a sinful waste. . . ."

She didn't feel that way about it now. She welcomed every flower that came for Bobby, and they kept on coming and coming, until Hartley's lofty walnut library was transformed into a garden. " How beautiful," she said to David, as they stood there, together. " How soft and beautiful."

" It is," said David, deeply moved. " Where did they all come from ? "

" People I never dreamed of—Helen Drew, and Jim Varney, and Julia's aunts. And David, look at those lovely roses, from the Ferrises, away out in Los Angeles."

" We haven't seen or heard from them in years," said David. " That's pretty nice of them."

" Even our old laundry man sent red carnations ; Candy showed me the card. And think how little he could afford it."

Nancy Riddle, who could have afforded a whole florist shop, came to call on Friday morning, looking more than ever like a comic Valentine in the self-same purple hat she'd worn for as long as Claudia could remember. She brought her usual box of crystallised fruits—Claudia was certain that she had a whole attic-full of the stuff stored

away—and said that she'd sent a cheque of fifty dollars
to an orphan asylum in Bobby's name. "The way I look
at it," she plunged in with her bull-in-the-china-shop
approach, "is that we should take care of the living,
flowers don't do any good to the departed."

"They do good," thought Claudia. "I didn't realise it
before, but they do."

Nancy loosened her scarf, and fanned her handkerchief
in front of her face. "My, but it's warm, or maybe it's
just me. I don't believe in big funerals, either. That's
why I didn't come yesterday. Who was there?"

It was incredible, but that was Nancy all over. "Just
family," Claudia murmured. "And Jerry, of course."

"I heard from somebody who saw them, that his book
got wonderful reviews in last Sunday's papers."

"It deserves them," said Claudia.

"I also hear," Nancy continued, "that he sailed for Italy
this morning. You'd think he'd have waited around for all
the excitement that comes with a best-seller."

"He doesn't care."

"He's crazy," said Nancy. "Did Julia get back in time
for yesterday?"

"No, the plane was held up by bad weather, she's due
this afternoon."

"She's a devil," Nancy affably observed. "Not so
much as a penny post card from her all these months.
Julia's changed this past year. I only hope she doesn't
make a hash of her life. Did she ever go to that medium
of hers?"

"No," said Claudia.

Nancy's voice, if not her eyes, gave a slow wink. "Very
attractive man. Julia would have a fit if anyone told her
she was in love with him."

"She isn't," Claudia denied indignantly.

"Don't misunderstand me, I'm not saying she knows it,"
Nancy explained. "It is the same sort of thing as falling in
love with your psychoanalyst, mostly sub-conscious. Only
this man happens to be an out-and-out fake."

" How do you know ? " Claudia asked with difficulty.

" My dear, because I went to a few séances. He's not only a fake, but he was rude into the bargain. At least his control was rude, that old Indian or Egyptian, or whatever he is, simply didn't care what he said to me."

Claudia wished that she felt like smiling at Nancy. One thing was certain, though, Julia's medium didn't sound like such a fake after all. . . . Her head was aching . . . if only Nancy would go. " David will be so sorry to have missed you," she threw out as a gentle hint.

It was, unhappily, the very opening that Nancy was waiting for. She leaned forward with a fresh burst of interest and lowered her voice to a discreet undertone. " Tell me, how is he ? "

" Fine," said Claudia.

It was not the answer that Nancy expected. " I mean has this dreadful shock had any ill effect on him ? " she pursued. " On his condition, I mean—temperature and all that sort of thing ? "

" He seems all right," said Claudia. (He hadn't taken his temperature since Tuesday, it occurred to her with a small shock.)

" Well, now really, that's wonderful ! " Nancy exclaimed. " When I didn't see him around when I came in, I was literally afraid to ask. I thought, ' my goodness, is he up in bed or what ? ' "

" No, he went down to the office this morning with John. He hasn't come home yet."

" I'm glad to hear it even though I'm sorry not to see him," Nancy granted generously. " It's a blessing he has the office to take his mind off things. I thank my lucky stars I've got cows. You ought to have something to fall back on, too. Have you thought of taking up acting again ? I know it's a little soon, but now's the time you need to fill your life, or you just go into a slump."

Claudia shook her head. " I'm not a child any more, Nancy. I'm over thirty."

"That's nothing, I'd hate to tell you all the actresses I know for a fact are over fifty."

"They're actresses. I'm not. I never wanted to be. Except for a few foolish weeks, and everyone's entitled to one stage-struck fling."

"But my dear, with you it was more than a fling. You were actually good at it, Jim Varney told me that personally, and he knows his theatre upside-down. He said you could really go places."

"I've been places," said Claudia.

Nancy laughed. "Heavens, I'm not trying to force you to anything, I'm just saying you have to have something to fill your life, or you might end up another Edith Dexter. Although, of course, Edith didn't have any other children to live for, and Phil was never the apple of her eye that David is of yours."

"It doesn't help," Claudia cried out silently. "It's hard either way . . ."

"Where are the boys, by the way?" Nancy remembered to ask.

"We left them with Bertha."

"Have you still got that wonderful woman? My God. She must be pretty well on in years now, isn't she?"

Claudia winced at the implication. "Bertha's not young, any more."

"Well, enjoy your luck while it lasts," Nancy advised. "People don't live for ever at her age. At any age, for that matter. Do you and David have to go back to pack up or can she bring the children down alone?"

"We're going back. We're spending the summer at Lake Placid, I think."

This was a piece of news that Nancy had missed. Her voice fell another octave. "Hartley told me you were coming home for good this spring. What's the matter, David not as good as he lets on? You can tell me the truth, I'm an old hand at T.B. Never have any more trouble, and haven't had for over fifteen years, but it's an experience you don't forget in a hurry. I remember I ran ninety-nine something for months and months, and they wouldn't let me budge out of bed. Is David still running a few symptoms?"

"No, I told you he was fine. We just feel it's better not to come back until the autumn."

"Oh." Nancy gave a one-shouldered shrug of disbelief. "Well, a lot of people stay on even if they don't have to, but I never dreamed David was the kind that would." She rose and pulled her skirt away from her in all directions. "Sticky day."

"Yes," said Claudia, hoping that Nancy would not sit down again.

Nancy dropped her scarf, and bent to pick it up. "I must say," she commented, "that you two young things have had your share of troubles, and I, for one, hope that this is the last of them. Although you never can tell," she elaborated cheerfully. "A friend of mine lost her husband last year and her daughter this year. Talking of daughters, that's what you ought to do, adopt a little girl."

Claudia wondered how Nancy knew that she could never have another child. Nancy literally got things out of the air, and what she didn't know for a fact, she pieced together out of odds and ends, and with her combination of shrewdness and stupidity, she often came pretty close to hitting the nail on the head. Claudia didn't feel like having any more nails hit at the moment, and she wished that Nancy would go instead of standing around on one large flat, hand-blocked shoe. And what on earth was she going to do with that huge box of crystallised fruit? It wasn't worth dragging all the way back to the mountains, because Matthew wasn't going to be fooled by the gold paper any more than Bobby ever was. "These are prunes," Bobby would discover in disgust, calling a spade a spade, even though it might really have been a fig or an apricot.

The last box that Nancy had sent them for Christmas

had taken weeks to get rid of. It was as if Bobby and Matthew, together, had formed a conspiracy against the stuff. . . . How nearly alike their voices had sounded over the telephone last night. It wasn't something she imagined, David had noticed it too. " After all, darling, there's only three years difference in their ages," he'd pointed out. " As Matthew grows older, he'll get more like Bobby every day."

But Bobby would never be any different, Claudia had thought. Bobby would remain in their hearts, always the same in a world of change and chaos . . .

She was aware that Nancy was giving her hand limp pumps of farewell. " I have to meet my station wagon at the garage with a new chambermaid—that is, if she didn't change her mind from yesterday about coming. My, how they hate the country. Well, anyway, give my love to David, and keep your chin up. And remember what I said . . ."

Nancy had said so many things. . . . Looking at her now, it was difficult to believe that she had ever been ill. " Half the people you know have had T.B. or somebody in their family's had it, or are going to have it, so don't think it's such a tragedy," she'd told Claudia before they'd gone away. And in the next breath she'd talked about people dying of it.

She sat down to catch her breath from the muddled after-effects of Nancy's visit. How had she phrased it, " Is David still running any symptoms ? " Claudia realised, suddenly, how completely she'd forgotten about David's symptoms, and so had he. Not only had he not thought of taking his temperature since last Tuesday, but he hadn't rested in the afternoons either, nor even so much as drunk a glass of milk. This was the very thing that Dr. Geiger —and Mrs. Jenkins too—had warned her about. And yet, when he'd wanted to drop in at the office this morning, she had envied him the office to go to. Nancy was right in that much. Filling one's life was the one salvation. But Nancy was wrong when she talked about a career.

David was enough of a career, her job was far from finished yet. She was grateful that by tomorrow at this time, he would be back on the little porch, breathing clear mountain air, and building up his strength again. How foolish she had been to pit her ideas against the seasoned judgment of a man like Dr. Geiger, and actually try to convince David that the thing to do was to return to New York, and slowly begin to get back to normal living. She'd called it fancy names like fulfilling a dream, and all that sort of thing. What did it matter? The only thing that mattered was to love and take care of and hold on to those that were left to you. That was enough to fill any woman's life. What had Nancy said? She knew someone who'd lost her daughter and her husband within a year of each other. Yes, such things happened.

She looked at her watch. It was almost noon. What had happened that David had not come home? She was used to having him home with her, so close that she had only to look out of the window to see him, lying in his long chair. Tomorrow at this time it would be that way again.

She rose from the chair, and went to the window, nervously. The library was in the rear of the house, and gave out on a row of yards, well-kept, but barren with a pitiful pretence of potted plants and flowers here and there. She thought of the mountains, with the sun on them, and Bobby—she couldn't find Bobby in this crowded city. She hated it, she wanted to get away. She felt so terribly alone while David was at the office. She missed him, even for the short time he'd been away. Yes, they'd look at whatever houses Lydia Trent had lined up for them to look at, and be grateful to her for her pains. Gradually, David would begin to work a little. Dr. Geiger was right, he didn't have to be so high and mighty about leather bars and rumpus rooms—what difference did it make what you built, as long as you built things? She and her lofty ideas—she should have had her tail kicked. But what was keeping him so long now? He ought to be resting, with a long trip ahead of him this evening. She looked at her watch again. She'd give him ten more minutes, and if he didn't show up by then, she'd call the office. It happened every time—Tom Barwell had gone home for a visit and had landed flat on his back—the man on the train—Byard Trent was smart, he never budged. She pressed her hands to her throbbing temples. Her mind was going around in circles. A dose of Nancy was enough to make anyone crazy.

There was a light knock on the door. " Mr. Naughton is on the phone, Mrs. Naughton."

" Oh, thank you—Annie——" Or Katie, or Lucy, or Fanny or whichever one of Julia's numerous maids it was. " I'll take it in here."

Her hand was shaking as she lifted the receiver. " David——! "

" Hello, darling, how are you ? "

She tried to cover her nervousness, her anxiety, but she couldn't. " I'm all right, but where are you, and why aren't you back yet; is anything wrong ? "

" One question at a time. Are you all alone ? "

" Yes, but please answer my questions first. Where are you ? "

" At the office, dear."

" Still ? "

" Yes—so don't worry."

" That's why I am worried. David, come home ! "

His voice was a caress. " Darling, are you really alone, is no one with you ? "

" Supposing I am. That isn't the reason I'm asking you to come home."

" I thought Candy would be over," he said contritely.

" She will be, as soon as her mother-in-law goes back to Greenwich."

" That meant a pretty lonely morning for you."

" No. Nancy Riddle has just left."

" That's good, I'm glad I missed her. Darling, call Candy and see if she can't have lunch with you."

" Why ? "

" Because I don't want you to be alone."

" You're all the company I need."

" But darling——"

And then it came to her, of course, that he wanted to stay downtown for lunch. " David, you have no right to," she implored him, " you know you haven't ! You ought to eat a decent lunch and not a sandwich, and go to bed for two hours."

" The only thing that's going to bring me home," he said, " is because I feel like a brute leaving you by yourself."

" Well, I'd certainly feel like a silly ass," she retorted with a flash of self-respect, " if I had to have my husband trot home in the middle of the day to keep me company."

" Good girl," he said.

" Good girl, nothing. David, you've got to be sensible ! "

" I'm sensible. Darling, I'm all right, I'm feeling fine, I'll be home later. Call Candy. . . ."

She couldn't call Candy. Candy had her personal obligations, and Hartley was having a treatment for his leg, and everyone—everyone—had his own life to lead. Even David. She felt unutterably weary and alone. Outside in the street, children were playing, and cars were passing, and the world was going on. She knew at last the black emptiness of loss. She was sick with it, like something gnawing deep into her inside. This was death, intense and final. She would never see Bobby again, and nobody and nothing could ever fill his place. He was her son and he was dead. She understood so well why Phil's wife had killed herself.

THIRTEEN

HARTLEY CAME IN a little while later from his treatment. "Why are you sitting here all by yourself?" he asked her in concern. "Where's David?"

"He's staying down town for lunch."

"Splendid," said Hartley, like an ostrich. "That shows he's feeling pretty good, doesn't it?"

"It only shows he's foolish," said Claudia.

Hartley sat down on one chair, and hoisted his bad leg up to another. "We haven't had a chance to talk alone," he said. "I've been worried ever since David wrote me a week or so ago, that he mightn't come home until next fall. What's behind it, Claudia? If anything's gone wrong, I want you to tell me."

"Nothing's gone wrong," Claudia assured him. "Dr. Geiger says David's made tremendous improvement, and he can come home now, if he wants to, but he thinks it's very sensible to take the extra insurance of a summer in the mountains. In fact, Hartley, he said it would be a wise move if we decided to give up New York for good. And I'm beginning to think so too."

Hartley looked shocked. "That's a blow, I had no idea that anything of this sort was in the wind."

"It isn't so dreadful. A lot of people prefer to live up there. The Trents, for example."

"Yes, I know, I know," Hartley interrupted in a white voice. "But David's a different type entirely—David's always been full of hope and ambition, and Trent's a lethargic sort of chap."

"That's why David will live longer in the mountains," said Claudia, quoting Mrs. Jenkins. She wished she had the honesty to admit that suddenly she wanted to take care of him, she needed to take care of him, but Hartley hadn't asked her that question, and after all, it had no real bearing on David's state of mind. " You have no idea how many patients get flare-ups after they leave," she said instead.

" I dare say," said Hartley, still in that white voice. " And yet I got the impression, from the little I've seen of David, that he was ready to come back and start in slowly. I don't think it will be easy for him to go home to the mountains now. Not easy for either of you. Too many memories. . . ."

" It's easier than here," said Claudia, desperately.

" Child, listen to me." Hartley hoisted his leg down to the floor again. " I'm going to call off a business luncheon, and we'll have a bite together, you mustn't be alone like this."

" No, no, please. I'm all right, really I am. I'd rather be alone——"

" Well . . ." He seemed uncertain. In the soft light of the dark-panelled room, he looked a little as David might look some day—handsome and well-groomed and ever so slightly portly. Impulsively, she reached up to kiss him. " Thanks for everything, Hartley. You were right, it's good to be with family at a time like this."

" Then stay a little longer," he begged her. " Perhaps it's an equally wise move for David to try himself out."

" You see how he's trying himself out. Down town since nine o'clock."

" Don't judge by today, child. Today's a hard day. Even for me."

" I know." She turned away quickly so that he could not see her tears. Blindly, she ran all the way up to the top floor. She could not bear the thought of taking the lift. Every moment of living was filled with pain.

It was Watkins who brought her lunch tray. Claudia looked up at him from the bed where she lay huddled beneath a light quilt. " Oh, thank you, but I couldn't eat anything, Watkins."

" You'd ought to have something, ma'am."

" I'll just have the tea then."

He poured it for her. " If you want the car, Mrs.
Naughton, I'm free for the rest of the afternoon to take
you wherever you want to go. Madame wired that the
plane is delayed again, she'll use a taxi from the airport."

" That's nice of you, but I don't want to go anywhere."

He lingered. " And I'd like to say also that if you'd
care for me to drive up and call for the children and bring
them back, I'd be pleased to. I know the place now, and
I could help Bertha close up, and save you and Mr. Naughton the extra trip. Mr. Naughton was discussing it this
morning with me."

Claudia put her cup down. " My Mr. Naughton ? "

" Beg pardon, no. Mr. Hartley."

" But didn't he tell you we weren't going to stay in New
York ? "

Watkins was a poor liar. " Well, yes, he did mention it,
ma'am, but he told me I should make the offer and perhaps you'd change your mind. He said there's plenty of
room in this big house for all of you, and he thought you'd
be quite comfortable, at least until you'd made other plans."

" More than comfortable," Claudia acknowledged gratefully. "This top floor is like a young palace, it's so luxurious.
And it's awfully nice of you to want to call for the children
after what you went through on the drive up."

" Oh, it won't be so bad this time, Mrs. Naughton." He
flushed hotly. " What I meant to say is, the baby's got
older, and so has Matthew."

" You'd still have to stop," said Claudia. " Matthew
likes to stop on general principles. And the baby's walking
now, he'll be a lot more restless in a car."

" I'm sure we could manage him. And the dog's no
trouble. He likes to travel. Slobbers up the windows a
bit, but sits up there on the seat for all the world like a
second chauffeur."

" Yes, Bluff always enjoys motoring. Especially in a
limousine."

" Not the cat, though. I remember how he scrabbled
around in his box, mad as a wet hen."

" Shakespeare's gone."

" Oh, that's too bad, ma'am, he was a handsome cat. Was he stolen, do you think ? "

" No, I think he just went away to die by himself. He was pretty old."

Watkins was astonished " And I thought he was quite a young cat, the way he acted."

She wanted to say, " We got him before Bobby was born." But suddenly she couldn't talk about Bobby. Watkins hadn't mentioned his name, and neither had Hartley. She'd been conscious that they would come right up to it, and veer away.

She gave him the empty tea-cup. " Thank you. And thank you for your offer, but really we have to go back. Mr. Naughton isn't quite ready to live in New York yet."

" I'm sorry, Mrs. Naughton, I didn't know that. I don't believe Mr. Hartley realised it either."

" He didn't, I suppose, when he spoke to you. Oh, and Watkins, if there should be callers, I can't see anyone. And pull the shades down before you go, will you ? "

It might have been minutes, or hours, later that Candy came. " Asleep ? " she whispered from the threshold.

" No, come in."

Candy crept in, and sat on the edge of the bed, as apprehensive as Matthew. " Watkins said nobody could come up," she said, shakily. " But I guess he thinks I'm nobody so he let me."

" I think you're quite a crowd," Claudia returned, with a great effort.

Candy gave a sigh of relief. " Thank goodness. I thought you were just about sunk, and I couldn't bear it."

" No, I didn't have anything else to do, so I lay down a little."

" That was quite intelligent of you. Shall I pull the blinds up ? "

" Oh, leave them down," said Claudia casually, " it cools the room."

" Yes, it does, it's boiling out. And am I wild at not

getting here this morning. My mother-in-law just stayed and stayed and stayed. She said that if she stuck around, I'd take it easy today, she didn't like the way I looked. Honestly, I just frothed at the mouth."

" Frothing at the mouth is very bad for the baby," Claudia remarked.

" Oh, a little frothing can't hurt at this late day. John says I've been an angel all along and a weak-minded fool, too. I'll probably end up spending July and August in Greenwich. Isn't that asking for trouble, though ? "

" Not really, you'll be glad you did, some day."

" That's the way I look at it. I'm so happy that I can afford to make John's mother a little happy, too. Oh, and before I forget, she told me to tell you that there's a darling little place for rent, about a mile away, with a brook; and either for the summer or by the year. Wouldn't it be heavenly ? If you decided to stay, I mean ? Where is David, anyway ? "

" He hasn't come home yet. What time is it ? "

Candy squinted at her watch in the half-dark. " I can't see."

" All right, pull the blinds up."

Candy pulled the blinds up. " Quarter to four."

Claudia sat up in a hurry. " Quarter to four—! I'm frothing at the mouth, too. He ought to have his neck wrung."

" And John should have his neck wrung, too," said Candy. " They'll be caught in the five o'clock rush hour and won't be able to get a taxi."

" I never thought of that. I'm almost tempted to send Watkins down for him in the car."

" Why don't we go along and yank them home ? "

" I think Watkins can do the job alone. I'll phone that he's coming."

" No, don't. Let's go and surprise them. It'll do you good to get out for a bit." Candy didn't wait for an answer. She folded back the quilt. " Tell me what dress and hat you want to wear and I'll lay them out for you."

" Stop rushing me. And get away, I'm not helpless ! "

" Oh, let me fuss over you a little, don't be so damn strong," Candy retorted. She pretended not to notice Claudia's ravaged face. There was no sense in covering up, though.

" I look a pretty sight," Claudia remarked, stopping short in front of the mirror.

" No, you don't," Candy denied too quickly. " Use a little rouge and lipstick, and fluff your hair out. And anyway," she added indignantly, " you have a perfect right to look as bad as you want. You give me an inferiority complex, you're so stoical."

" I'm glad you think so," said Claudia.

" I keep hoping," Candy went on, " that a miracle will happen and you won't go back tonight."

" Miracles don't happen," said Claudia.

" Feeling life is a miracle," said Candy simply. She laid her hand against her stomach. " I haven't, for the last day or so. I miss it."

" It's a good sign that you haven't," said Claudia.

" Either good or bad, my mother-in-law told me. And I'm sure it's good. Oh, what's the matter with me babbling on about myself, when you're suffering torments. I ought to have enough sense to shut up and be quiet."

" No, keep on babbling. I like it. Besides, I'm not suffering now," said Claudia. " I've gone completely dead inside." She was glad that she had. It was the only way that she could face going out.

It turned out to be a completely wasted trip, because when they reached the office, there wasn't a sign of David or John. " They left about an hour ago," the secretary said.

Claudia turned to Candy in dismay. " I wonder what happened, it couldn't have taken David that long to get home ? "

" Oh, they didn't go home," said the secretary.

" Then where did they go ? " Candy demanded.

" They didn't say," said the secretary, with a smile that

implied that even if they did say, she was too well versed in her business to divulge their whereabouts.

" The nerve of them," Candy muttered under her breath. " If they come back, Miss Kelly, tell them we've been here looking for them."

Claudia wanted to ask Miss Kelly if David seemed tired and if he had gone out for a hot lunch, but Miss Kelly didn't look as if she were the kind of girl who would have been concerned with trifles of that sort. " I wish they still had Miss Lewis," said Claudia, as they went down in the lift. Miss Lewis had been middle-aged and very co-operative when it came to matters of skipping lunches.

" So do I," said Candy.

" You told me she was Decayed Aristocracy bravely making its way."

" Who ? "

" Miss Kelly. All I noticed was that she was making her way."

" Oh ! " Candy laughed. " ' Decayed Aristocracy ' left three months ago to get married. Kelly is the best of a succession of bad ones. But at least she can type, and her shape is nothing to write home about. I wonder what my shape is going to be like— Do you think I'll ever go back all the way ? "

" Settle on four-fifths of the way," Claudia advised. " You were just a little too much like a blue-fish."

" You can still count your ribs, can't you ? "

" Not all of them," Claudia confessed, " unless I take a deep breath."

They fell silent for a while. Claudia tried to keep herself from thinking, she tried to hold on to the dead feeling inside of her. Then Candy said suddenly, " Do you mind if Watkins drops me off before he takes you home ? "

" No, of course not, it's on our way up." She gave Candy a swift glance. " You look funny."

Candy laughed shakily. " Don't rub it in."

" That's not what I meant. You haven't even babbled for the last fifteen minutes. Are you feeling all right ? "

" Yes, I'm feeling all right."

" I don't like the way you say it."

" I'm feeling all right," Candy repeated in a deep bellow. " Is that better ? "

" I'll get out with you and see that you get upstairs safely."   Claudia smiled grimly.   " The blind leading the halt."

" I won't let you.   You're as bad as my mother-in-law."

" Don't argue."   She had every intention of getting out until the car drove up in front of the familiar entrance in Beekman Place.   Then, all at once, the deadness within her vanished, like an anaesthetic suddenly wearing off.   She could scarcely breathe with the pain that gripped her.   A little boy went whizzing by on skates, and her heart cried out in anguish.

Hartley came out from the library to greet her.   " I thought you were David," he said.

" Isn't he home yet ?   I went down to call for him and he'd left already."

" That's odd.   I wouldn't worry about him, though, he's a big boy."   Hartley put his arm around her.   " You're the one that needs a little worrying over.   Julia got in about a half an hour ago.   She's getting into some fresh clothes, go up and see her, why don't you ? "

" I will," said Claudia.   If only she didn't have to see anyone now, if only she could crawl into bed again, and pull the covers over her head and go to sleep and never wake up.   " I will," she repeated.

Hartley pushed the lift button.   " No need to walk when you can ride," he said, " even for one flight."

That's all it was.   One flight of senseless agony.   The door slid open with that wonderful obedience of automatic lifts.   Julia's room lay ahead, pale and lovely and remote. There was no outward sign that she had come back to live in it, but in the dressing-room adjoining, a maid was unpacking suitcases and putting clothes away.   " Mrs. Naughton is in the bath," she said.

" Claudia ! " Julia called, " is that you, come in ! "

Claudia went in. Julia was standing by the marble basin, wrapped in a voluminous turkish towel, rubbing cold cream on her face. They couldn't kiss, and that was wonderful. The cold cream stood in the way of their emotion, and made it easier to meet. " You must have had a dreadful trip," said Claudia.

" Awfully bad weather," said Julia. " I'll have this stuff off in a minute—"

There was plenty of room to sit in Julia's opulent bathroom, there was a plastic-covered chair, and a bench to match. It was different from having to perch on the edge of an old-fashioned tub. Claudia wondered whether Julia was remembering too. Julia said, " It's been a long while." The last of the cold cream was gone. Julia's face was pale with exhaustion, but clear and shining. " You look tired," said Claudia, " but you look better."

" I am better, I'm glad to be home. That's being better in itself." She put her thin, fine hand on Claudia's shoulder. " There's nothing I can say. Nothing I want to say." The low husky voice that was the truly lovely thing in Julia, faltered a little. " I can't feel sorry for you. I envy you. You're so rich in all that you had, and have."

It was strange that Claudia should want to put her arms around Julia, as if it were Julia and not herself, who had known bereavement. But Julia had never known this agony of pain that was ripping through her. She was dumb with it, she couldn't speak, or move. Julia was kind. She turned back to the basin and busied herself with a pad of cotton soaked in lotion. " Hartley's told me about your plans," she mentioned after a while. " I'm sorry you're not staying. I was looking forward to it."

Claudia made a gigantic effort. " That's all your eighteenth-century rugs need," she managed to retort. " A Great Dane dog, and a baby who'd rather crawl than walk. And always with a piece of rusk in his hand."

" It'll do the rugs good," said Julia. " They must have

had a lot of that sort of thing in a couple of hundred years. I wish I'd thought of that before, we might have had a dog or two. It's time I stopped treating them like museum pieces, so come along, rusks and all."

"Thanks, Julia. I appreciate your being willing to have us, but David really seems to want to spend the summer in Placid."

"Which amazes me," said Julia. "I had no idea that he'd like the Trents. They're very nice, but somehow, not David's style. Or yours, either."

"We've got to like them," said Claudia. She bent to pick up a lipstick that had rolled off the smooth marble. "Julia——"

Julia reached for the stick. "Thanks. What did you start to say?"

"Nothing. Yes, I did start to say something, but I couldn't bring myself to getting it said. Julia, I don't know what made you stop going to those séances but—they did give you a lot of comfort, and some of the things you told me gave me comfort too——"

"Claudia, don't. Please don't begin with that sort of thing," Julia's voice trembled with earnestness. "I beg of you not to."

Claudia wet her lips. "Was it—really all a fake, do you think?"

"Claudia, I don't know. It's so hard to tell where truth ends and desire begins. And finally you get to the point where you don't want to discriminate, it's like a sweet poison, you keep on taking it because it's so soothing—so promising of fulfilment. And there isn't any fulfilment, Claudia. Nothing comes that easy, nobody's going to do your dirty work for you, not even the spirits."

"But I just want to know that he's somewhere." All the pride in her was gone, her weakness and her longing stood naked. "I'd give my life for one tiny word—one little tiny bit of proof—"

"Then get that proof from within yourself," Julia implored her. "You've earned the dignity of grief, Claudia, so don't diminish it, live up to it." She stopped herself with a small laugh. " Listen to me, holding forth on a lecture platform. As if you needed it. You've always been the one to talk to me like a dutch uncle, not the other way around."

" It's easy to talk like a dutch uncle," said Claudia, " when you don't know what you're talking about. And I'm not strong. I've discovered that. And in a different way, David isn't very strong. I've discovered that, too."

" Nobody's very strong until you're weak," said Julia. " And that's the main thing that I've discovered."

" I said something to Bertha a few months ago, that was almost the same," said Claudia slowly, " but I didn't know what I was saying, it hadn't gone down deep enough inside of me. Look. You want to jump in the tub and take your bath, and here I sit."

" Don't hurry," said Julia. " The bath can wait."

Julia was making strides by leaps and bounds, but she hadn't quite reached the point where she could get undressed in front of anybody. Probably not even in front of Hartley.

It was a case of going from one marble bathroom to another. David was home, scrubbing his nails. " Hello, darling, New York's a filthy city, where've you been ? I'll kiss you in a minute."

" Don't try to disarm me. Where have *you* been ? "

" I asked you first. I've been home for hours."

" Oh, but you lie ! "

" I do ? "

" You do."

How strange that this moment of meeting should hold the flavour of something that had been lost to them for so long. He emanated a wholeness and a robustness that was magic. " I'd like to tell you that you look tired, but you don't," she said grudgingly.

" I feel fine," he said.

" Candy and I went down to the office to call for you."

8

"I didn't know you were coming, or I'd have told you not to."

"That's real nice of you," she said. "Miss Kelly wouldn't say where you'd gone—" A thought hit her suddenly. "David ! Did you go to see Dr. Morrisson ? "

He looked blank. "Dr. Morrisson ? What for ? "

"Because he happens to be the specialist who examined you nine months ago, and sent you away," she returned dryly. "Or don't you remember ? "

"It never occurred to me," he said. "It's like a bad dream that's fading out."

"So I notice. One day back in New York, and you're as bad as ever."

He drew her to him, suddenly serious and intent. "Darling, try to understand. It isn't New York or even getting back to work. It's that something much more important than my body has happened to my soul, and when that happens, I guess you're cured."

She unloosed his arms. "You're never cured. You know that as well as I do."

"All right, Dr. Geiger. But I wasn't thinking of T.B. I was thinking of the fears and the insecurity and the nightmare of panic that's filled me for the past months. You didn't know it, darling, and I could never find the words to tell you. But it was hell. I never knew such hell could be. I lost my grip, I lost everything that was worth living for. If it had kept up, I'd have lost you, too. Your respect. And that's worse than death. Far worse."

The tears flowed down her cheeks. As if she didn't know. But let him think she didn't. . . .

He wiped her tears away. "I'm sorry to have to tell you all this, darling, when you have so much to bear. But you have to know it, so that you can help me to keep what's been given back to me. Suddenly, like a miracle. So don't hold me too close, Claudia. Try to let go. Let me work my way back to health. Health of mind and soul."

"Health of body comes first," she insisted doggedly. "I

can't and I won't let you undo all these months we've been through together. For your sake as well as mine."

"I understand that, dear. You'll have to trust me."

"Trust you," she scoffed, veering back to the safety of the commonplace. "You still haven't told me where you were."

"When ? "

"When I called for you at the office, and you weren't there."

"Oh—I went to a board meeting with John."

"John should have had more sense than to let you go. Neither of you can be trusted. It's a good thing you're going back tonight. You can use eight solid hours of resting, and a couple of quarts of milk. With an egg thrown in," she added darkly.

He made no comment, either for or against it. He rose, and emptied his pockets of keys and wallet, and laid them on the dressing-table. "I think I'll take a shower," he said.

"And then will you lie down and rest before dinner ? "

"Is that an invitation ? "

"It's an order. You've got a long trip ahead of you. I must be crazy sitting here, I have to pack ! "

"You're not very good at packing."

"I'm good enough. Bertha can press everything in the morning."

"Claudia—" He followed her and put his hands on her shoulders. "Don't pack. Let's give ourselves a few days longer. Don't let's hurry back."

"Why ? " she asked starkly.

"First of all, there are some important matters down at the office that I ought to go over with John."

"I thought so. The office." Her lips set grimly. "We're leaving for home tonight."

"It's not our home," he said. "Home is more than a roof, it's wherever we belong, and we don't belong there." He turned and walked into the bathroom, and a moment or two later she heard the rush of water. When he came back, she had begun to pack the suitcase. He took her in

his arms, his body still cool and damp from the shower.
" Poor baby," he said.

She pushed him away. " Don't poor baby me. I don't
know why I'm so good-natured, I should have half-
murdered you for what you've done today."

" What did I done ? " he teased. He lay down on the
bed, and beckoned her to join him.

" No," she said stubbornly, " I have to finish packing."

" Are you coming of your own free will, or do I have
to use brute strength ? "

" I'll have nothing to do with you."

He got up again and came toward her. She felt his arm
creep about her, deliberate and ominous, like a band of
iron. . . . Don't go lifting heavy suitcases. . . . She gave a
cry of terror. " David ! Stop it ! "

" Then stop packing."

" Take your temperature ! " she flung at him.

" All right, I will," he agreed magnanimously. " Where's
the thermometer ? "

" Oh dear, I don't think I took it along."

" There's an extra one in the vest pocket of the grey
suit you just packed. And wretchedly packed, if I may
say so."

She took the suit out, and found the thermometer. He
stuck it in his mouth, and hung the suit across the back
of a chair. " I'll pack it myself," he mumbled, with the
thermometer bobbing between his lips.

" Shut up and keep your tongue on it."

She pushed him down on the bed, and counted his pulse
by the minute hand of her watch. He sat meekly, rolling
his eyes at her.

" How much ? "

" Seventy-two," she admitted reluctantly.

" Now are you satisfied ? "

" I don't put it past you to have slowed yourself up on
purpose. Let's have the thermometer."

He was too quick for her. He warded her off, and looked
at it first. She waited, holding her breath with mingled

emotions. It was too much to expect it to be normal, when the least little excitement this past month had given him ninety-nine or a fraction over.

" What is it ? " she asked, with her heart beating up into her ears.

He presented the glass stick with a deep bow. " Ninety-eight six. On the nose."

She squinted at it. " You didn't have your tongue on it. Take it again."

He took it again, humouring her like a child. It registered to the same hair-line. " There," he said, " that ought to be proof that I'm ready to go back to work."

" It's proof of nothing. It's whistling in the dark."

" We're in the dark anyway," he said, " so we might just as well whistle our way through it."

She wanted to tell him that Bobby had whistled, all the way down in the taxi to the village last Saturday, but she didn't have the courage to bring his dear name to her lips. She, too, had banished him from their midst. She gave herself at last to David's arms, filled with sorrow and confusion. " Oh David, I miss him so much—"

" I know you do," David whispered, holding her close against him. " I know you do, darling."

" I feel as if I'm bleeding to death, inside—as if a piece has been cut out of me—"

" It has, darling."

" Today, there was a little boy on skates—"

" Everywhere I looked today," said David, " there were little boys—" He let her go, and sank to the edge of the bed and covered his face with his hands. It was the first time she had ever seen a strong man sob. It broke her heart to see it, but it was right, and beautiful.

FOURTEEN

FORTUNATELY, Julia and Hartley always dined at eight, and tonight it was even later, so that by the time dinner was over there was very little left of the evening.

It was a sombre dinner, just the four of them in the big formal dining-room. Hartley's leg was still bothering him after the treatment, but he didn't say so. "You should have let me know you were having this trouble," Julia reproached him. "I didn't have to stay away so long. I wouldn't have stayed away so long."

"Why should I have worried you for no reason? I wanted you to have a good time, my dear."

"I didn't have a very good time, Hartley. I'm glad to be home."

"I'm glad to have you home," said Hartley.

It was almost a love-scene, restrained and earnest, and possibly the nearest that Hartley and Julia had been to love in a long while. The word " home," thought Claudia, was merely another word for love. David had said, " Home is where you belong." It was true; and the answer to their homelessness came to her all at once. They belonged where Bobby was, and Bobby was in their hearts, so it didn't much matter where they lived—the farm, or the mountains, or the sea. Bobby could be with them anywhere and everywhere— even on a train or on a boat, and it would still be home.

David reached for her hand beneath the table. "What are you smiling at ? "

"Was I smiling? Remind me to tell you some time."

" David, have a little more ice-cream," Hartley urged. " It's very nourishing."

"No, thanks, I've had enough nourishment," said David, "and very good it was." He glanced at his watch. "Claudia, do you want to run up and get started? We've about half an hour before we leave for the station."

" Yes—if you'll excuse me—"

She pushed back her chair. " No, no, don't stand with your bad leg, Hartley—David, sit down—"

In the hall, she sighed a breath of relief. David must have guessed that, suddenly, it was hard to stay at the table for another instant. It seemed as if you had a moment of hope and vision, and then, just as swiftly, you were drowned in loneliness and despair.

She started up the stairs, and stopped, and went back and pushed the button for the lift. She walked into the little cage and it went up and up and up—and then it came to a stop, and she walked out of it. It was as if she had gone through fire and emerged without the flames destroying her. " This is one thing accomplished," she thought. " I'll never be afraid to go into that lift of my own free will again."

She was gathering the last-minute toilet articles to pack, when David came in. " John just phoned," he said. " He wanted us to know before we left that Candy's begun."

She couldn't help feeling excited, it was always an exciting moment. " It isn't another false alarm, is it ? "

" Apparently not. Dr. Rowland ordered her to the hospital an hour ago."

" I didn't like the way she looked this afternoon. I hope everything will go normally. Do you think I'll have time to dash over and see her ? "

" No, you won't, dear. Especially with traffic the way it is."

She was torn with indecision. " David, I just hate to go before it's over."

" So do I."

" If it began after we'd left, it would be different, we couldn't do anything about it. But this way, it's like walking out on Candy, and Elizabeth, too. I know she'd want me to be with Candy."

" Who are you trying to convince ? " said David.

" Myself."

"I know. You wanted to get me back to that blasted long chair where I'd be under your thumb every minute," he said, half mockingly.

It was more nearly true that she cared to admit. She wouldn't admit it. "You seem to forget that Bertha's stuck up there alone. And what about the tickets? Can we exchange them as late as this?"

David started toward the door. "I'll tell Watkins to drive down, and attend to it right away."

"Tell him to get the same reservations for tomorrow night."

He paused. "Why not leave it open?"

"Because I know you like a book," she returned firmly. "You'll get tied up at the office, and we'll just be putting it off from day to day."

"What's the matter with that? And don't tell me it's the children, Bertha's perfectly capable of managing by herself."

"You are going to keep your health," she informed him, like a well-worn record.

"You mean *you're* going to keep my health," he returned gravely. "Face yourself, darling. That's what it really amounts to, isn't it?"

She nodded miserably. "I'm so filled up with all the stories of people who get flare-ups and land flat on their backs. David, can you blame me?"

He took his time about answering. "No, I don't suppose I can," he said at length. "But why don't you think about the people who don't get flare-ups, and don't land on their backs—like Nancy Riddle."

"I never thought I'd live to see the day that you'd point to Nancy as a good example of anything," she retorted, with an attempt at lightness. "Now go on, or we won't be able to change the tickets."

"It'll be done. Hartley knows the president."

"What president?"

"It makes no difference, he knows all the presidents of everything."

Julia came in. " Are you staying over, children ? "

" Tell Claudia Hartley knows the president," said David.
Julia looked after him. " What did he mean ? "

" Nothing. He was just being silly."

" He's wonderful, really wonderful," said Julia. " That
goes for you, too. You're both wonderful."

" Save all the bouquets for David," said Claudia.
" Believe me, I'm not such a much."

" I think you're such a much," said Julia, with one of
her rare flashes of humour.

The telephone bell rang. They both jumped for it. It
was John. No, the baby hadn't come yet, but Candy
wanted him to let Claudia know before they left for
the train, that everything was going beautifully, not to
worry.

" I'm so glad you phoned," said Claudia. " We're all
waiting on pins and needles." She didn't tell him that she
and David were not leaving for the train—he had enough
on his mind without fretting that he had disrupted their
plans. " Julia's standing right beside me," she said, " and
she says you're to phone the very second the baby gets
here."

Julia nodded emphatically. " No matter what time of
night it is."

" No matter what time of night," Claudia relayed.

" No matter what time of night," a voice boomed in.

" Who's that ? " asked John.

" It's David, on the downstairs extension. David, is
everything settled ? "

" Yes, ma'am."

" Then come on up."

" No, ma'am, I'm smoking a cigar with Hartley."

" A cigar ? " she echoed. " Why, you haven't even
been smoking your pipe for weeks ! "

" I haven't ? What a damn fool I was."

" Say, listen, you two," John got in with a fair imitation
of a laugh, " talk on your own time, this is my penny ! "

" Isn't it strange," Claudia remarked as she hung up,

" how you can laugh when it's the last thing in the world you feel like doing ? "

" I've noticed," said Julia, " that it's a gift that belongs peculiarly to thoroughbreds and imbeciles."

Julia stayed until David came upstairs. " She's a good sort," David commented after she'd said good night.

" From you, that's a rave," said Claudia. " Haven't you finished that cigar yet ?   It smells terrible."

" That shows what you know.   It's one of Hartley's best."

" I'd hate to smell one of Hartley's worst.   It'll keep you from sleeping."

" That's the coffee you're thinking of."

" I'm really thinking of Candy," said Claudia, with sudden bitterness.   " She's going through all that agony. For what ? "

" For plenty," said David.   " Would you give up one day of ten wonderful years we had with Bobby ? "

" I'm glad you've said his name," she answered tremulously.   " I was beginning to be afraid to."

" That's natural, darling.   The strangeness will pass, and he'll be as real and just as close as Michael and Matthew. We can even take him with us to Iceland—or to France. What's the matter ? "

" I was thinking almost that very same thing at the table tonight.   When you asked me why I was smiling.   It's funny, we haven't tuned in to each other like that for the longest time."

" Do you know why ?   Because I've been so damned absorbed in me and myself, that I couldn't tune out of me and myself.   There's nothing like a good kick in the pants to make you get wise to yourself."

" Either that," said Claudia, " or push you over the edge. And you don't seem to be over the edge, you seem to be planning a quite extensive travel tour—Iceland and France, no less."

" Over the years.   Why not ?   Do you think a little to-do in the top of one of my lungs is going to make me sit on my rear for the rest of my life? Life is short and the world is big, and I'd like to see a little of it with you. Do you remember that scene in Jerry's book—the night that he and Elizabeth spent at Amboise?"

"Yes," said Claudia, "it was a lovely chapter, and as they drove south the next morning, I could almost hear the mistral, I could almost see the tall dark cedars bending in the wind."

"I took a bicycle trip through the Burgundy country when I was about twenty," said David.

"You never told me," she reproached him.

"We've had too much else to talk about. Can you bicycle?"

"Certainly."

"I have a feeling we'll go to Iceland before we go to France, though. That deal isn't off by a long shot. John can't pick up and leave with a new baby, but our baby's old and tough by now."

"You make him sound so attractive," said Claudia. "Like a fricassee chicken. Which reminds me that we haven't phoned Bertha yet that we won't be there until Sunday morning."

"I'll do it," said David. He picked up the phone from the night-table. She let him do it. It was like an obstacle race: she'd reached the lift, and she'd talked about the future, and all that it might hold for them, but this was a hurdle she couldn't quite take yet. Matthew would want to talk—he loved to talk over the telephone. "Mother! When are you coming home?" It was what Bobby used to say. The minute he'd come into the house, he'd call, "Mother! Where are you; are you home!"

David must have known she was a coward because he hung up the receiver, without offering it to her. "Bertha says everything's fine, except Mrs. Jenkins' ham, it gets more instead of less," he reported.

"I was hoping it would be gone by the time we got back," said Claudia. "David, I think I'm going to take one of those pills Dr. Geiger gave us. You'd better take one, too."

" Not me."

" Well, I'm not proud, it'll be better than lying awake. I want to close my eyes and not know anything. But it'll leave us with one less for the train tomorrow night."

" You can borrow one from Hartley," said David shortly. " He has a whole medicine chest full of them."

He didn't say it in so many words, but she felt as if she'd lost face a little as she gulped the yellow capsule. " It's just that I'd be tossing around thinking about Candy all night," she apologised.

" Darling," he said contritely, " you take as many as you like."

She eyed him fishily. " Why, thank you."

He grinned a little. Then he said, " Seriously, don't you ever let me catch you getting into the habit of using that stuff."

It was wonderful stuff. It put her out like a light. She'd heard the expression often enough, but she didn't realise how apt it was. She didn't know anything for hours, she simply stopped being. But when she woke up, it wasn't so wonderful. Her mind was open before her eyes, unrested, and heavy with desolation.

" Are you awake ? " David whispered.

She was startled that his voice was so close. " What are you doing in my bed ? "

" That's a nice lady-like question."

" When I went to sleep, you were in your own bed."

" Oh, I wandered over at about four "

" I can't imagine my not hearing you."

" You were dead to the world. Snoring."

She was affronted. " I have never snored in my life."

" How do you know ? "

" Because I know." She studied him anxiously. " David, you didn't close your eyes."

" How could I ? Your snoring kept me awake."

" You worry me, not sleeping."

" Who said I didn't sleep ? "

" People who sleep don't go around visiting in the middle
of the night. Listen to us lying here, and we don't know
whether it's a boy or a girl ! John must have telephoned
and they took the call downstairs so as not to disturb us.
Shall I buzz Hartley and find out ? "

" He'll love you for it. Do you know what time it is ? "

" No. What ? "

" Quarter to five."

" Only quarter to five ! I've been robbed, why didn't
that sleeping tablet make me sleep longer ? Next time
I'll take two."

" Next time you'll take none."

" Do you think we dare telephone the hospital this
early ? "

"You might just happen to find someone up and stirring,"
said David dryly.

Claudia dialled the number. " Maternity floor, please,"
she said. The floor nurse answered. She said that Mrs.
Payne's Special could not leave the patient, and that Mrs.
Payne was doing as well as could be expected.

" But has the baby come," Claudia asked impatiently,
" and is it a boy or a girl ? "

The floor nurse was as bad as Miss Kelly. She couldn't
say, and if she could, she wouldn't. " Is it a relative
calling ? " she enquired cagily.

" Oh, shoot," Claudia muttered under her breath. " Are
we a relative calling ? "

" Tell her we're more than a relative," said David.

" We're more than a relative," said Claudia.

" Oh," said the floor nurse. After pondering it a
moment, she said, " Would you care to talk to Mr.
Payne ? "

" Well, of course ! " cried Claudia.

" Of course what ? " David enquired, leaning up on his
elbow.

" Would I care to talk to Mr. Payne. Why didn't she
say he was there in the first place ? " she frowned. " I

don't like it, if the baby was here and everything was all right, he'd be home asleep."

" You're not," David reminded her mildly.

" Don't be silly."

" Stop borrowing trouble."

When John came to the phone, his voice sounded strained and ineffably weary. " She's having a pretty tough time of it," he said. And then he remembered that they were supposed to have gone back to the mountains the night before. " Where are you calling from, anyway ? "

" We didn't go," said Claudia. " We stayed over."

A note of pleasure crept into his tired voice. " Candy will be so happy, she said a half-dozen times that she wished you were here—"

" I'm coming right over. You should have called me before ! "

" Don't confuse the poor man," David interjected. " He thought you were half-way to the Adirondacks."

" This is no time for logic," said Claudia severely. " John, I'll be there as soon as I can get dressed." She hung up the receiver and swung out of bed in one and the same motion.

" Hold your horses, not so fast, it'll take me a few minutes to shave," said David.

" Oh, I see," said Claudia, " now you want to begin running around at five o'clock in the morning."

" Do you think I'm going to let you go alone ? "

" What's wrong with it, do you think someone's going to kidnap me ? "

" You won't find a taxi at this hour."

" I'll find a taxi. If I don't, I'll walk. It's only a few blocks."

" I don't want you walking along the streets——"

She pulled on her stockings. " David, please don't be an ass. I'm a grown woman."

" I can't go back to sleep anyway."

" Listen to reason," she begged him. " You'll want to

go to the office this morning instead of John, and you've got a long trip ahead of you tonight, and there isn't anything you can do anyway, at the hospital."

" I can be with you."

" I'm not having the baby," she said, a little unsteadily.

" You'll feel as if you were." He took her in his arms. " This isn't going to be easy for you, darling."

" It'll be much easier if I know you're home asleep," she said.

She came back to him after she was out of the door. He had no way of knowing that she was remembering how Bobby had come back to kiss her before he went off to school that last morning. It was something to have learned, always to say good-bye to the people you loved as if you were never going to see them again.

FIFTEEN

IT COULD HAVE BEEN that David's oblique warning that it wasn't going to be easy made her able to face the shock of memory that gripped her as the taxi stopped in front of the hospital. It was the same hospital where Bobby had been born. Like a great many other things, she had known it in her mind, without feeling it in her heart. She stood for a moment on the pavement, in the eerie half-light of dawn, and let it all come back to her. Then she walked up the shallow steps into the quiet entrance-hall.

A young doctor in a white gown passed by and looked at her curiously. Then he stopped and spoke to her. " May I help you ? "

" No—no, thank you. I'm going up to the maternity floor, I know the way."

He seemed taken aback. " But who's your physician ? I'm afraid you just can't go up without going to the reception desk."

" Oh," she hastened to put him right, " I'm just going to see a friend who's in labour."

He smiled. " I'm sorry. That's different." He walked with her to the lift and rang the bell for her. " My sister's the same way," he offered. " She has four of her own, and every time any friend of hers goes through labour, she gets the pains too."

" Oh," said Claudia again. She didn't try to explain that this was a different kind of pain she must have been wearing on her face. She thought, " I'll have to learn to cover up a little better."

The maternity floor looked the same as all the other floors, except for the glassed-in nursery at one end ; and the flowers. There always seemed to be more flowers on the maternity floor than any other floor. They stood banked in great drifts outside the sleeping doors. Claudia thought, " Bobby had many flowers, too, when he came into the world, and when he went out of it."

There was a small bay with wicker chairs, opening up at the end of the corridor. A nurse hurried toward a red light over one of the rooms. Claudia wondered whether it was Candy's room. John was nowhere in sight, and no one else was around to ask. There was nothing to do but sit down and wait. In a little while Dr. Rowland came out of another door, further down the hall, and walked quickly toward the lift, his steps disembodied on the rubber floor. Claudia got to her feet. " Dr. Rowland ? "

He didn't recognize her at once. Then he said, " Claudia ! You're the last person I expected to see, I thought you and David went back to the mountains last night ? "

" We're staying over until this evening on account of Candy. How is she, Dr. Rowland ? "

Dr. Rowland gave one of his professional throat-clearings. " She's not having an easy time of it, but nothing to be alarmed about," he said. " First baby and all that—it's apt to be a bit difficult."

" He's the same old Dr. Rowland," Claudia reflected. He was still a little too handsome for a doctor, although he'd grown respectably old beneath his chin and around his ears. She hoped he wasn't too old to do a good job with Candy. Julia always swore by him. He'd worked on her for years and years until there wasn't any more work to do, which meant that he could bring Bobby and Matthew and Michael at reduced prices, and not lose on the transaction. He hadn't charged anything at all, though, the time Claudia had been so ill. " The war," he'd said : " We don't charge young men who go off to fight a war." He had been tactful enough not to say, " We don't charge for babies that don't live."

She was aware that he was patting her hand. " These must be very hard days for you," he was saying, " but then, you always were a good patient. No, I don't mean that either," he corrected himself with a smile, " you were very difficult to manage at times, very pig-headed. How's your husband ? "

" Difficult to manage," said Claudia, " pig-headed."

" But he's coming along nicely ? " Like Julia, Dr. Rowland's wit could go so far and no further.

" Very," said Claudia.

" Splendid," said Dr. Rowland. " Splendid."

" Is John with Candy ? "

" Yes, he's been with her all night; better see that he gets a cup of coffee." Claudia had a suspicion that Dr. Rowland was on his way to get a cup of coffee too, but John came hurrying down the hall and stopped him. He looked yellow-white, and the smile he gave to Claudia wasn't a smile. " She can't go on like this, Doctor, can't you do something for her ? " he implored.

" We will, my boy. All in good time, you can't hurry these things beyond a certain point. We'll get her up to the delivery room very soon now."

" She's asking to see Claudia."

Dr. Rowland hesitated. " Only for a minute, then. She's quite excitable from the morphine. It has that effect on some patients, unfortunately."

Candy was staring at the door when Claudia walked in. Her eyes looked enormous, because the pupils were so big, and her face was little and peaked, and twisted with the agony that was ripping through her. Her hair told more than anything else—the thick taffy-coloured braids lay in damp, dark cords across the pillow, making her look like another person, and her voice, when it came, was like another person's, high and loud and strange. " Why didn't you go back—I'm so glad you didn't—Claudia, make them do something, don't let them just stand there—why don't they do something—! "

Claudia glanced at the nurse enquiringly. The nurse said, as if Candy weren't there, " It's a dry labour. She's been very good up to a little while ago." She pulled the blanket up over Candy's thrashing arms. " Come now, this isn't helping youself."

Candy's voice trailed off into a moan. "That's all they do, tell me I'm not helping myself—and then they talk to each other about dilatation and they say I haven't got enough—it isn't my fault if I haven't. I don't want to hurt my baby, it isn't my fault, is it Claudia—tell them it isn't—"

"They know it isn't." Claudia pinned one of Candy's cold damp hands between her own. "Try and bear it a little longer, dear. Dr. Rowland just told me outside that you'd be going up to the delivery room very soon—"

"I will?" A proud, pleased look came over Candy's face, like a little girl about to graduate. "The woman in the next room went up and her baby came right away—" Her voice went back to its strange high sing-song. "But they wouldn't take me up, they just let me lie here and suffer and Dr. Rowland went to a party, and I'll never forgive him as long as I live—"

"There wasn't anything he could do," the nurse explained. "I kept him informed—"

"Yes, of course," said Claudia.

"Why did they take the woman next door up! " Candy wept. "And they wouldn't take me up! "

"It's the morphine," the nurse told Claudia in an undertone. "She keeps on saying the same thing."

Claudia said, "Listen to me, Candy. Perhaps the woman next door was ready to go up. There's no use going up until you're ready, dear."

"Yes, and the woman next door helped herself," the nurse chimed in. "She worked every minute—"

"She screamed," said Candy contemptuously. "I heard her. She screamed and screamed. And I won't scream, I won't, I won't! "

Claudia leaned over confidentially. "Go on, have a little scream," she coaxed. "It'll do you good."

"I'd be so ashamed for John," Candy whispered. "Did you scream? "

"I forget," Claudia lied. "But I'm sure I must have."

"I don't believe you. Because you don't forget, nobody could forget—you didn't scream, and I'm not going to scream. I wanted to be different, I wanted to be so brave—and have the baby before John knew anything about it, and now look at me—all my plans just went for nothing."

"They always do," said Claudia. "It never happens the way you want it to—"

Candy's body arched in a spasm of torment. "Why can't I go up; I thought I was going up," she gasped. "Claudia, make them do something! Anything!"

"We're just waiting for the table," the nurse soothed her. "A little more patience, and it'll all be over."

"Even when it's over," Candy moaned, "it won't be over, because there's after-pains, my mother-in-law said so, she said the after-pains were almost as bad as the real pains—"

"You didn't understand her," said Claudia. "You only have after-pains with a second baby, and not always then. You'll love what happens afterwards, Candy, you'll have the most wonderful feeling, so quiet, so beautiful, like you were holding the whole secret of life in your arms."

Candy gave a tired grimace. "You wouldn't fool me, would you?"

"No, I wouldn't fool you," said Claudia softly.

The door opened and another nurse with a white mask over her face wheeled the table in.

"All rightie," said Candy's nurse, in a cheery voice, "now we go bye-bye."

"Listen to the silly old fool," said Candy.

"Dearie me, that's not very nice talk," said the nurse, slipping her arm forgivingly beneath Candy's shoulders. "Now! One, two, three, upsidaisy!"

Claudia tiptoed out.

"Your wife," she reported to John who was waiting outside the door, "is not in a heavenly mood. She's carrying on like a little street urchin."

" Isn't she though?" Claudia was glad to hear him laugh a little. " She gave me a couple of bad minutes in front of the nurse. What she said doesn't bear repeating."

" I can imagine," said Claudia.

They sat down on an unyielding wicker sofa. There was a big clock at the other end of the hall. It ticked away the minutes, and each minute was like an hour. John wiped the palms of his hands with his handkerchief. " God, how do you women stand it and why do we let you in for it—"

" That," said Claudia, " is a cliché if ever I heard one."

" A cliché only gets to be a cliché because it's true," John defended himself. " Was it like this with you ? "

" Pretty bad with Bobby, yes."

He got red. " I'm a damn fool."

" But with Matthew, no," she went on, as if she hadn't heard him. " He was here in no time, though of course part of that was probably Matthew being Matthew, and not wanting to miss a trick."

" It sounds like Matthew." Then he said, in flat wonder, " You've got so strong, Claudia."

" It's bluff," she said.

" It can't be. David told me how you went down to the school the day of the accident—all alone, without telling him."

" That wasn't strength. I had to do it. There was nothing else to do."

" He said he'd never forgive himself for having failed you."

" He mustn't feel that way."

" Do you know something, Claudia ? " said John thoughtfully, " it's a good way for him to feel. I never told you this before, but when Candy and I went up to visit you this winter, I was really worried about him."

A ridiculous apprehension gripped her, even though John was talking about something that had happened months before. " He was getting along beautifully, even then," she said.

"Physically, yes," John acknowledged. "But he was scared, he'd lost his nerve. He was living in his own little private world of fear, he didn't care anything about the office, or whether we came or went. I suppose you didn't notice the change, because you were so close to him."

"I noticed," said Claudia in a low voice. "It happens to so many of them up there. I worried about it too. Terribly."

"Well, you needn't worry any more," John assured her. "Whatever phase he went through, he's over it. Down at the office yesterday, he was just like he used to be. Even better. In spite of everything. God, I was glad."

"He overdid it," said Claudia, with a trace of accusation. "That's not good, either."

"I know it," said John contritely. "But it was a hard day for him to go through. He needed to do what he was doing, so I let him alone. He's pretty smart, though, he'll know how to handle himself from now on. I don't think you have to worry about him any longer, I really don't."

Claudia made no reply. John was trying to be kind. In his awkward, boyish way, he was trying to bring her some degree of comfort. And he was right. David was like he used to be. Even better. In spite of everything David had called it a miracle. But she didn't believe in miracles any longer.

"Do you think it hurt him?" John asked. "I mean, his overdoing it a little?"

"No," Claudia admitted, "he got away with it this once. But he can't afford to take chances. I'm glad we're going back tonight."

"I wish," said John regretfully, "that he didn't have to. I think he'd give his eye-teeth to stay on."

"It'll be a lot safer," said Claudia slowly, "if he keeps his eye-teeth, and goes back and behaves himself for another few months."

"I suppose you're right," said John. "But it's tough on both of you."

Claudia wished she had the honesty to tell him that it was only tough on David, that she was the scared one now. She was no longer strong enough, or big enough, to give him the gift of his own life, or the gift of her maturity. She had thought, before Bobby had been taken from her, that the flame that was David was more important than his body. She didn't feel that way any longer. She had to hold on to what was left, like a frightened, greedy child.

Perhaps John felt that strange things were moving inside of her. He didn't talk again. He just sat there, with his long arms hanging between his knees, staring at the big clock at the end of the hall. "It's almost seven," he said at last, in a tight voice, "she's been up there so long."

"It's not long," said Claudia. "It could take another hour, and there'd be nothing to worry about."

It didn't take another hour. She heard John give a sudden exclamation, and then he was on his feet hurrying to meet Dr. Rowland, who was coming toward them. Dr. Rowland wore a large smile, and his operating mask hung down from one ear. "It's all right," he said, in a loud cheerful voice. "It's a little girl. Nine pounds and one ounce. And your wife is splendid. Splendid. Behaved like a little soldier. She's coming along now."

A whiff of ether hung in the air, as an orderly wheeled the white-sheathed table past them, the nurse walked beside it. She was smiling proudly. Claudia remembered how nurses like big babies, and lots of flowers. A nurse didn't like to nurse nonentities.

John followed the table, like a man following a vision. He followed it into the room. He would be there, thought Claudia, bending over the bed, when Candy opened her eyes. David had been there too, when Claudia opened her eyes after Bobby was born. "It's a boy, darling—" he had whispered. "Thank God you're all right—" Oh God, where are you—what have you done to us . . . Claudia wept in her heart.

Dr. Rowland was talking to her. "You wait here," he said. "I'm going to break a rule and let you see the baby." He was gone before she could call him back. She wanted to tell him not to bother. New-born babies had ceased to be a novelty to her. Michael had been a new-born baby as recently as last year, tiny and red, like all of them, with a shock of black hair that was all front and no back, and didn't mean a thing. But she knew what was in Dr. Rowland's mind, he had only to lay Candy's daughter in her arms, and it would become the little daughter she could never have, and the cycle of life would go on, and the deep and bleeding bruises in her heart would heal. If only it could be that simple.

A woman sat down next to her. She had picked up a magazine from the table, but she just held it in her lap. "I haven't got my glasses," she explained to Claudia, unhappily. "I can see in a movie without them, but I can't see to read. Are you waiting for a baby to come?"

"It's just come," said Claudia.

"Oh, that's nice. My daughter had her baby last night. On the dot of midnight, almost."

"She must have been the one who screamed," thought Claudia.

"She's still asleep, the nurse promised to call me the minute she wakes up." The woman was friendly with nervousness. "Are you married, too?"

"Yes." Claudia didn't want to seem ungracious so she added, "I am."

The woman accepted the encouragement gratefully. "I guess you and your husband are happy together," she said with a deep sigh.

"Why, yes," said Claudia.

"My daughter's separated." She said the word silently, with the wide use of her lips. She looked down at her plump feet, with their give-away bumps in the short-vamped sandals, and crossed and uncrossed them restlessly. "Drink," she added in the same, silent voice.

" That's a pity," said Claudia.

" It's a terrible thing," said the woman. " A wife is entitled to have her child's father at her side at a time like this. Have you any children ? "

" Three," said Claudia, unthinkingly.

" Three ? " the woman echoed in surprise. " I'd have said one, maybe, you look so young. Girls or boys ? "

" Boys. My oldest son is—away——" she faltered.

" Camp ? "

She had to go on with it. " No. He's away on a long trip."

The woman looked disapproving. " He can't be very old to be away on a long trip."

" Not quite eleven." (Oh, God, please make her stop talking.)

" Mercy ! " said the woman, " young women today don't seem to take motherhood very seriously. I don't believe in letting children go away from home, you never know what's going to happen to them, and if anything does, you never forgive yourself."

" I always felt that way too," said Claudia. " But it's different with Bobby. I don't have to worry about him now. He's with my mother, she's looking after him."

" Oh, well then. I guess that does make a difference." The woman gave a small, satisfied laugh. " A girl's mother is her best friend, after all." She eyed Claudia enviously. " You're one of the lucky ones, you've got everything to be thankful for, including a husband to take care of you. I only hope God keeps on being good to you, my dear. I hope it."

" Thank you," said Claudia. She couldn't say, " My husband's been ill for almost a year and my eldest son was killed last Tuesday." Besides, she'd almost sold herself the same bill of goods that she had sold Matthew. She almost believed that Bobby was with her mother and that her mother was looking after him. Perhaps that was the simple, God-given way that faith came into being.

A probationer nurse in a blue uniform with surgical

scissors sticking out of her rear pocket came up to them. " Mrs. Naughton ? Dr. Rowland says you can come to the nursery, now. I'll take you——"

" Nice to have talked to you," said the woman.

" Yes," said Claudia.

She followed the nurse. The nurse said, " It's such a sweet little baby." Claudia's lips smiled. It was like putting a baseball mask in front of her face. Bobby wore one when he was catcher. She could only pick him out from the other boys by knowing the rest of him, the length of his good strong legs, and the way he arched back as he threw the ball. . . .

When she emerged from the nursery, the day nurses were coming on duty and the night nurses were going off. They were talking to each other over their charts. They looked busy and happy. It was wonderful to be busy. Sick people were busy, too. They lived in their own little world, absorbed in getting well, or not getting well. In a way, they were lucky. . . .

The lift was waiting. She hurried towards it. It stopped at every floor, and nurses got on and off, chatting and laughing, and there was an assistant, and a doctor or two. It was too early for visitors.

She got out at the main hall, with all the others. They rushed past her, pushing her a little, and she stood there, alone and lost. She started toward the big, heavy entrance door, and then, suddenly, a wave of dizziness came over her. She had to reach for the arm of a wooden bench that stood against the wall, she had to sit down on the bench because her knees were shaking, and the floor seemed to rise before her very eyes. Everything became strange, and out of focus, like a dream. Wooden bench—stone floor— Thoughts came into her mind and shredded into nothingness before she could catch hold of them to think them out. The present was overlayed with the past, and the old terrifying sense of unreality flooded out her sanity and filled her with sheer terror. John might think that she was strong, and Miss Carey had told her that she was better than new, but it wasn't true. She had lost step with the world again. Her mind was in confusion—and her panic was worse than death. That was what David had said. Worse than death. . . .

There. Suddenly the mist was clearing from her brain. She breathed deeply, reaching timidly for air and afraid for an instant that her lungs could not be satisfied. . . . A wooden bench and a long corridor. . . . Dr. Geiger had led her down a long corridor to a wooden bench. Birth and death, one and inseparable. That was what her brain was trying to tell her. . . .

" Pardon me. Isn't this the lady I'm married to ? "

She looked up, in a daze of giddiness and nausea.

" Don't scold me," David besought her comically. " I had to come."

She couldn't speak to scold him, or to say how glad she was that he was there. He got her out into the air. He didn't ask her any questions and he didn't say, " I told you so." " Let's walk," he said, " it isn't very far."

The city wasn't as awake as the hospital. It was dim, and quiet, and full of a heavy mist. A woman waited for her dog, and a doorman down the street stood on the pavement, trying to hail a taxi. It was early for taxis.

" Girl or boy ? " David asked at last.

" Girl. With a little fuzz of golden hair."

" That's nice," he said. " We always wanted a girl."

They walked a little farther.

" Your hands are getting warmer," he said.

" Maybe I was just hungry."

" Maybe. Shall we stop some place for a cup of coffee ? "

" No, I'd like to get back to the house and phone Bertha."

" What about ? "

" She'll want to hear about Candy, and I have to tell her to begin to pack up. Do you think she can manage to bring the children back alone, if Watkins calls for her ? "

He didn't answer for a long, long moment.   Then he said, merely, " I think so."

They kept on walking.   Suddenly she stopped.   " David, look," she cried, " the sun is coming up."

He couldn't know, that in the sudden, dazzling clarity of her mind, Bobby and the sun were one.   But he smiled, and said, " Yes, darling, it's going to be a nice day after all."